Rosie Archer was born in Gosport, Hampshire, where she still lives. She has had a variety of jobs including waitress, fruit picker, barmaid, shop assistant and market trader selling second-hand books. Rosie has had many short stories published in women's magazines as well as a series of gangster sagas under the name June Hampson.

Also by Rosie Archer

The Munitions Girls
The Canary Girls

The Factory Girls

ROSIE ARCHER

Quercus

First published in Great Britain in 2016 by

Quercus Editions Ltd
Carmelite House
50 Victoria Embankment
London EC4Y 0DZ

An Hachette UK company

A CIP catalogue record for this book is available
from the British Library

PB ISBN 978 1 78429 782 4
EBOOK ISBN 978 1 78429 786 2

10 9 8 7 6 5 4 3 2 1

Typeset by CC Book Production

Printed and bound in Great Britain by Clays Ltd, St Ives plc

For the Pimms ladies; they keep me sane.
They know who they are.

Chapter One

1944

'She said, "I'm your sister!"'

Em Earle stared at her friend Gladys, whose mouth had fallen open in astonishment at her words. Dropping her clipboard, Em made a dash for the door and the lavatory beyond.

Eventually, in the cubicle, Em looked up, relieved that Gladys had followed her. She took a handkerchief from her pocket and wiped her mouth. The wireless playing cheery dance music in the munitions factory didn't make her feel happier, nor did it erase the memory of her encounter last night with Lily Somerton.

Gladys asked, 'Feel better?' She took her own clean hanky from her sleeve and passed it to Em. 'You ain't never had a sister!' Em could see the shock on her friend's face.

She had worried all night, unable to sleep a wink. Now she straightened up, tightened the belt of her navy blue dungarees and tucked away some strands of hair that had worked themselves loose from her white turban, which was standard uniform for the workers at Gosport's Priddy's Hard.

Gladys put her arms around her. 'There must be some terrible mistake, Em. I've known you for years and I'm the nearest to a sister you've ever had. We'll work this out somehow.'

The humming of the machinery suddenly reminded Em that she should be attending to her job of supervising the women on the line. She needed to be on watch at all times as they filled and tamped the dangerous fulminate of mercury into copper shell cases. The light brown powder was very sensitive and highly toxic. One wrong move and they could be blown to kingdom come.

'This Lily's returning tonight with some documents, proof, she says.' She looked pleadingly at her friend. 'Gladys, will you come round to the house?' Em heard doors opening and voices, footsteps coming towards the lavatory. 'We can't talk here,' she said.

Gladys agreed, then shook her head, the bleached blonde curls over her forehead dyed orange from the toluene vapour and acid droplets that discoloured the workers' hair and skin, and made the women sleepy. It also poisoned the air in the workshops. In some cases women lost teeth, but these were known hazards of munitions work. Even the ointments provided for the skin rashes rarely helped. 'Canaries' was the nickname for the girls working in munitions.

'Seven?'

Em nodded.

'You sure you're all right?'

'I am now,' Em replied. She squeezed her friend's hand and took a deep breath as Gladys handed her clipboard back to her. The women in the workshop depended on her.

Priddy's was named after Jane Priddy, who in 1750 originally owned the forty acres of land. It was one of England's main suppliers of armaments, shells, rockets, mines and ammunition. The work was exhausting and dangerous and shifts were twelve hours long, repetitive and mind-numbing. Em needed to be calm and clear-headed should any unexpected incident occur. She smiled at Gladys and they walked back to the workshop arm in arm.

The day whirled by and Em tried not to dwell on the previous evening. But her thoughts returned time and time again to the knock on the door.

Dragging down her daughter Lizzie's blouse from the wooden drying rack suspended from the kitchen ceiling, she'd spread the garment over a folded blanket on the table. Using an iron holder she'd sewn from bits of padded rag, she reached for the flat iron on the gas stove. Em spat on its base, her spit sizzled, and she wiped the iron on an old rag.

She was listening to *Much Binding in the Marsh* on the wireless. Lizzie might need the blouse when she returned from Lyme Regis, where she'd been living for some months. Em received the odd letter from her. Never much news, just a note reassuring her mother that she was well and happy in her bar job. Remembering Lizzie made her think about her other daughter, Doris, and her little boy living with her foster mother, and the letters she regularly sent.

Em was pleased that Lizzie was far away from the bombing but she failed to understand why her daughter had felt the need to leave Gosport and her job at the armament factory so suddenly. She often wondered if it had any bearing on the disappearance of Lizzie's boyfriend, Blackie Bristow, who previously had been her friend Rita Brown's lover. Perhaps memories of the handsome rogue and the love they'd shared, the places they'd visited together in Gosport, had hurt Lizzie too much to stay.

The one thing Em was grateful for was that Sam, her friend and the manager of the Fox public house in Gosport town, had found the job for Lizzie and she knew that he cared too much for Em to put her daughter in danger.

The knock on the door had startled Em.

A blonde woman wearing lots of red lipstick stood on the doorstep. She was attractive in an overblown way. Despite the warm weather she had on a fur coat and Em thought she must be terribly hot.

'Are you Em Earle?'

Em nodded, and the woman had continued. 'You might want to sit down for what I'm about to tell you.'

Fear had overwhelmed Em. 'Is it my daughter? Has something happened to her?'

The woman had leaned forward, putting a hand on Em's arm.

'No,' she said, shaking her head. 'Look, we'd better go inside.' Without waiting for a reply, she'd pushed past Em and strode through into the hall.

Em had followed her into the kitchen, protesting, 'You can't just barge into my house. Who d'you think you are?' She was angry she'd allowed the woman to invade her privacy.

The woman turned towards her.

'I'm Lily Somerton, your sister,' she said.

The words had taken a long time to sink in. Sweat prickled the back of Em's neck.

Finally she blurted out, 'I don't have a sister!' Shaking, she pulled out a kitchen chair and practically collapsed into it, her heart beating wildly.

The woman, who up until then had just been staring at her, began looking around the kitchen. Her eyes alighted on the kettle which she promptly began filling.

'I think you need a cuppa,' she said. Her voice was softer now. Em, her head still reeling, stared at her, watching her quick movements as she set about spooning a miserly amount of tea into the pot without rinsing it. She hated using the leaves over and over until the tea resembled dishwater, but with only two ounces of tea per person a week, what else could she do?

They were of a similar height, and like Em the woman was nicely rounded. Unlike Em, she wore a lot of make-up, with thick, black mascara emphasizing her eyes. Beneath her fur coat, which she was now in the process of removing, she wore a blue dress patterned with small flowers. The sweetheart neckline showed off her ample bosom. Em thought the woman was in her thirties, like her. A thought struck her.

'What's your name?'

'Lily, I told you that. I was married, hence a name change, but the name I grew up with was Symonds, for the couple that adopted me. My birth certificate says I'm Lily May Green. You're Emily Rose Green, or was before you married Jack Earle . . . I think Mum must have loved flower names.'

'You know a lot about me . . .' Em broke in.

'I had to find out everything. Couldn't make a mistake, could I?' She was stirring the pot and had the teacups sitting on a tray on the table, next to the iron that was now cooling on a wire rack.

Em's head was still whirling but she managed to ask, 'I suppose you've got proof of this?'

The woman nodded. 'Plenty. I was given away, and the following year you were born. We've got the same father.' She paused and frowned. 'At least, it looks like it. His name's on both our birth certificates.'

'I'm surprised you've seen a copy of my birth certificate.' Em wasn't used to people prying into her private life. She thought about her mother who, before she died, had begged to be buried with her husband. Em had seen to it that she was. During the fifteen years between their deaths her mother had never so much as looked at another man.

7

If this woman was telling the truth, how had it all come about?

Lily sat down on the kitchen chair next to her. She was wearing a flowery perfume that smelled heady and made Em think of bluebells. She took Em's hand. Em saw her nails were painted with colour the exact shade of her lipstick. Em hadn't been able to buy nail varnish for ages. There wasn't any in the shops.

'Look,' said Lily, 'I know this is a terrible shock to you. But I've been looking for my sister for years. It's taken me until now . . .' She paused, and Em saw that her eyes were blue, just like her mother's had been. 'It's taken me until now to find out what happened and why I was given away.' She gave a huge sigh. 'I used to look at friends at school and envy them their sisters. Now I've found you I want us to be friends.'

Em removed her hand. 'You can't just walk in here, bold as brass and expect me to believe you—'

'No,' broke in Lily, 'that's why I want to come back tomorrow, if that's all right?' She waited for Em to nod in agreement, and then added, 'I'll bring my folder with all the proof in it.'

She rose from the chair and went to her coat, picked it up and put it on. Em didn't speak. It was, she thought, as though she was watching a film and didn't know what was going to happen next. Lily paused and turned to look at her before leaving the kitchen.

Em called out to her, 'You've not had your tea!' Steam was coming from the pot's spout.

She got up to follow the woman, but already Lily had opened the front door and was walking through the gate.

Again she turned and looked at Em. 'I don't want to bother you any more. It's a lot to take in. You need to think about things, to get over the shock.'

And then she was gone, walking down the street with her black handbag and gas mask dangling over her arm and her high heels click-clacking on the pavement. As she reached the Queen's Hotel, with its huge wooden girders holding up one wall where Queen's Road had taken a real thrashing from the German bombers, she stopped, looked back and shouted, 'Tomorrow? At seven.'

Earlier the rain had drenched the gardens, and the June evening was cool now. Her head still reeling, Em closed the front door.

Oh, how she wished Lizzie were still at home. Back in the kitchen she picked up her daughter's photograph that stood on the window sill. The pretty girl with long dark hair smiled back at her.

'Oh, Lizzie,' she said. 'Whatever is this all about?'

Then she looked at the clock on the sideboard. She needed to talk to someone, desperately. Em replaced the photograph. Gladys would be home but by the time she'd walked to Alma Street it would be nearly ten o'clock. It wouldn't be fair to worry her friend, not when they both had to get up early for work tomorrow.

She wondered whether she should go down to the Fox and have a word with Sam. He was a good listener and would do anything for her. She pushed that thought away. The pub wasn't closed yet and she couldn't face waiting for him to shut the bar and clear up before she could get his full attention. Lovely man that he was, it wouldn't be right to involve him in her problems, not when she should be at home getting enough rest to face the possible hazards of her job tomorrow.

In the kitchen she poured herself a cup of tea. Sitting at the table with the iron, blouse and blanket almost forgotten about, she drank the hot liquid. Eventually she went upstairs. It would be a long time before she slept tonight.

It might be nice to have a sister, she thought as she pulled her flannelette nightdress over her head.

Em felt her stomach rebel against the tea and the shock.

Her head was thumping and her body began to shake.
She managed just in time to pull the flowered chamber
pot from beneath the bed before she threw up.

Chapter Two

The old man used both of his gnarled hands to lever himself up from the high-backed chair. Joel Carey could see the difficulty he had grabbing his stick to manoeuvre himself across the room to the bed, where a suitcase lay open. Joel could hear the rasping chords from the man's thin chest as he fought for breath. When he reached the bed, the man collapsed, gasping, on to the yellow candlewick bedspread.

Frederick Cummings had been an officer in the Tank Corps in the Great War. Wounded in France, he had been picked up by field ambulance and brought back to England to Bristol's Beaufort War Hospital. After a slow recovery he was allowed home to his South Downs home to be taken care of by his beloved wife, Madelaine. He was then in his middle thirties.

Madelaine died after a lingering illness in December

1943. Fred had entered the Yew Trees Nursing Home a week ago. Opened only months previously, it was named for the huge yews that sheltered the Georgian building. With up-to-date amenities and the latest in comfortable beds, furniture, furnishings and nursing methods, the owners prided themselves on their modern thinking, calling everyone by their Christian names.

He paid eight pounds a week for the privilege of being well looked after. He had just asked Joel to bring him the small cardboard suitcase from the locker room, which contained a few of his personal belongings, including a photograph of Madelaine.

Joel knew that without Margaret Hill opening her first Care Home for Aged War Victims recently, *he* wouldn't have a job, and Fred, having no relatives, would have had to depend on friends and neighbours to care for him. Not easy, thought Joel when you were as cantankerous as Fred was supposed to be. Joel, unlike the rest of the carers, ignored Fred's quick tongue. The man had given his health for his country, and Joel respected that. But he still gave as good as he got with Fred's barbs and despite being advised not to, had already formed a friendship with him.

Joel stared at Fred's wrongly buttoned shirt that made the unattached collar look as though the studs weren't doing their job properly. He didn't offer any help. It would be more than his life was worth to tell the man he couldn't even button his own clothing. In a moment the collar would be removed anyway, because it was time for bed.

He stood patiently while Fred, his breath restored, searched the case then triumphantly held aloft the silver frame.

'Look at this, young shaver. This is a woman in the prime of her life. Put it over there opposite the bed where I can see it.' The words almost sapped Fred of his strength.

Joel waited until Fred had stopped gazing lovingly at the picture before he took the frame and placed it next to the clock on Fred's bedside table. For one swift moment the sepia photograph made him think of the girl from the Dog and Duck. Maybe it was the way the woman had her dark hair pinned back, from which tendrils escaped to frame her oval face. Mostly, the barmaid wore her dark locks swirling around her shoulders, sometimes in a coil of plaits that crossed over on the top of her head, like that skating star Sonja Henie, who was now a Hollywood film star. Whichever way she chose to style it, the girl's hair didn't detract from her prettiness. Neither did her pregnancy, come to that. He checked the time on the alarm clock that Fred didn't need as the home ran like clockwork but that he insisted be left there, and which his arthritic fingers had difficulty winding nightly. Joel had volunteered to wind the clock but had received a look from the old man that could freeze hell over, and had never repeated the offer.

Joel caught sight of himself in Fred's wall mirror. He ran a hand through his blond hair, which had tumbled down over his forehead. His shoulders were broad and his waist narrow.

He'd done a stint in the army himself, in the Royal Army Medical Corps, until an exploding shell had robbed him of part of his hearing very early on in the war, and ended his career fighting for his country.

His cap badge had stated *In Arduis Fidelis* and 'faithful in adversity' had certainly helped him obtain his job at Yew Trees. Here, inmates could well afford nursing care, their own rooms, full board and all the facilities they might have had at home, including a communal sitting room with a wireless, books, comfortable chairs, daily papers and jigsaw puzzles. On the sitting room wall was a large framed photograph of the manager, his wife, the cook Marie, head carer Pete, and indeed all the care workers and domestic staff. The manager intended to have photographs taken each year and put on display in the long hallway. Joel, having begun work at Yew Trees after the first photograph had been taken, hoped to be in the next one. He'd studied the print and noted four of the staff had already left.

Yew Trees comprised twenty-four rooms of male and female patients, staffed by strong and healthy workers, many with previous medical training. Kindness and a sense of humour were also necessary requirements. Joel sometimes worked a night shift, not minding the long hours. He lived alone and valued his independence, so he didn't live-in like some of the staff.

When the wind sent fresh, salty air across the large, flowering gardens, patients could enjoy the sea breezes from Lyme Regis. Those residents needed to be well enough to either walk or be wheeled to sit outside in the sun. A pergola with seats and cushions gave shade. Fred had been outside this afternoon, reading his beloved Westerns and dipping Nice biscuits into endless cups of tea.

'You want me to give you a bath?' There were showers in the bathrooms down the hall but Fred couldn't be bothered with the newfangled things.

'No, I don't. When I can't bathe myself, I'll be six feet under. And I can run it myself.' He stopped talking to take a few deep breaths.

'Don't let the water rise above five inches.' All the baths had lines marked on the enamel. Because of the war even water had to be rationed.

'I'm not daft. Just old!'

Joel left him to it, taking the suitcase so he could put it back in the locker room later. He could depend on Fred to get to the bathroom, in his own time. Independence was important to Fred. Joel knew he didn't want to be reminded that Yew Trees was the place he'd come to die. All the same, while Fred was in the bathroom, Joel would be waiting outside, keeping an unobtrusive eye on him. He would also remake the old man's bed.

After Joel had placed Fred's clean pyjamas on the bathroom chair and made sure fluffy towels were within reach, he let the old man get on with it.

'Where's your family, lad?' The sound of water running into the bath diluted Fred's words.

'I'm like you, a loner.'

Joel thought of the girl from the pub and wished he wasn't so alone. He thought of Fred's photograph of his wife that meant so much to him. 'Memories keep us sane,' he called back.

'Give us a hand, lad.'

Joel knew the old man had had to summon up courage to admit he couldn't quite make the step into the bath.

He went in, trying not to look at the skinny misshapen body with its genitals wrinkled and hanging like dried tree fruit, and swirled his hand into the wetness, checking cold had softened the effect of the scalding water. Joel stood so the man could use him as a stepping stone into the bath. When Fred was sitting, like a large thin baby, Joel left. He could now change the bedding so Fred could feel refreshed in bed as well as clean.

In room eight he stripped the sheets, ignoring the marks of Fred's incontinence. He wasn't as bad as some of the inmates.

In room twelve the old lady hardly ever left her bed. The resident doctor, Dr Barnaby, saw her twice a day and she was hard work to look after. Her name was Liliah but woe betide any of the nursing staff who tried to befriend her or shorten her name.

In the short time the home had been open, one helper assigned to Liliah had already handed in her notice. Management decreed staff should use their own discretion in the way they approached their charges. Sometimes it was impossible to be on good terms. Sometimes a laugh, a joke, or a sympathetic attitude helped the trust between carer and patient. Joel's army training had been rigorous. Being in the medical corps had undoubtedly helped, but he was by nature a caring man.

With the room tidied, Joel swept up the dirty washing and then left it in the canvas container ready for removal to the washroom. His thoughts were broken by Fred's voice.

'Boy!'

'The name's Joel,' said Joel, back in the bathroom. There were no locks on the doors and once he had Fred standing securely, he handed him the large bath towel. Fred had used soap to wash his hair and it stood to attention.

'I need a hand to get back to bed.'

The striped pyjamas didn't take Fred as long to get into as Joel thought they might; Fred was beginning to trust him. But he made a mental note to obtain a wheelchair – the old man wasn't as sprightly as he thought he was.

Fred saw the tidy room and bed. 'Didn't ask you to do that,' he growled.

'I know,' Joel said, sitting Fred upon the counterpane. 'And if there's anything else you don't want me to do, just ask.' He helped the old man into bed. In a short while the nurse would be round with Fred's medication.

Soon, Joel would be off duty, so he made his way downstairs.

In the large kitchen, Pete was reading, his feet high on a stool and a mug of tea at his elbow. Marie was making sandwiches for staff supper. The delicious smell of beef stew was cooking, more stew than beef. There was, after all, a war on. But tomorrow's dinner was assured. Next to the apple crumble, fragrant and already cooked and left covered on the side, a sponge cake was cooling, waiting for its jam filling. All the residents enjoyed Marie's sponge cakes, which she made when she had the ingredients to bake them.

'All quiet,' said Joel. He pulled out a chair and sat down at the table.

Marie looked up from the Spam she was slicing thinly. Plump and rosy cheeked, her greying hair a bubble of curls, she said, 'Thank Christ for that.'

Pete said 'Liliah's been acting up. Earlier this evening she wouldn't stop crying about people stealing from her. And she was remembering her husband being blown up in the Dominium Theatre disaster. During the Blitz, that was,' Pete said, without looking up. 'That was the start of her turning funny.'

Marie said, 'She was an ambulance driver, apparently. Found her husband amongst the soldiers home on leave there.' She slapped slivers of meat between the slices of bread. 'Only just recognizable, he was, and she had to attend to him.'

'What a dreadful . . .' Joel suddenly realized Liliah

couldn't be as old as he believed she was. 'I thought she was in her sixties?'

'No! An incendiary bomb hit the ambulance, didn't kill her, but it might as well have. She's barely forty, maybe not even that. She never properly recovered from the head wound. No other relatives, no kids. Sometimes she's lucid. It doesn't last. Then she starts imagining stuff, like people taking things from her,' Pete broke in.

'That's so sad,' Joel said. All his training had been about healing people and he hated it when he couldn't be of use to anyone. 'This bloody war,' he said, drumming his fingers on the table top.

Pete didn't have sole charge of Liliah. Although Joel wished more people would apply to work as carers, he knew it took a special type of person willing to clean up after the sick and elderly, especially when those patients rebelled against being looked after.

Joel determined to look in on Liliah more often. He couldn't believe she was such a handful that the original helper assigned to her had left, saying she was too difficult for any one person to care for her. Liliah's memory might be shattered but she was still a human being. Yes, he'd definitely go in for a chat. And not just peek in her room as he had this evening.

He'd already collected his jacket from the hall

coat-stand and now it lay across the back of a kitchen chair. Marie pushed the plate of sandwiches along the table.

'Help yourself,' she said. 'You too, Pete.' She gave them both a broad smile as she nodded towards the brown teapot on its table stand. 'I reckon you both need something inside your stomachs before you get off home.'

Pete put his book down and helped himself to a sandwich. 'You want this after me?' He showed Joel the paper-laminate cover. The book was wartime printing and had no price on the inside flap. 'It's great reading. About the 1942 raid on Tokyo.'

Joel nodded. He fancied reading that. He poured himself a cup of nearly black sugarless tea. 'I'm popping in to the Dog and Duck. You coming, Pete?' He could do with a dose of normality and a pint.

Pete reminded him of a Swan Vesta match. Tall, thin and white-skinned with a head full of bright red hair. He was married and had a couple of small Swan Vesta lookalike boys. He shook his head. 'Need my missus and my bed,' he laughed and snapped the book shut, sliding it across the table to Joel.

The noise of the double doors down the hall announced the arrival of some of the late staff to take over the twenty-four-hour care provided at Yew Trees.

Joel stood up, taking the book and putting it in his coat pocket. 'That's my shift over,' he said, hearing soft laughter from the workers as they fussed with their shoes and coats. 'See you tomorrow.' Marie nodded and began replenishing the plate of sandwiches for the newcomers.

Chapter Three

'Hello, boy. Want a bit of cuttlefish?' Gladys pushed the white bone through the bars of the yellow canary's cage. The bird eyed it suspiciously before chirruping and hopping up and down on its perch, staring at her with its button-bright eyes.

The canary had been a gift from one of her gentlemen friends. Gladys had long ago forgotten which one. Some of the men had been kind, some not so nice, and it had taken her many years and many men to realize that family came first. 'I don't know how long you little birds are supposed to live but you're a bit like me, ain't you, boy, a bleedin' survivor!'

Into the tiny white dish she poured more bird seed. She was alone now, except for the canary. Her wonderful daughter Pixie, Pixie's husband Bob and their daughter Sadie had died in a blast opposite the Criterion picture house. Gladys tried not to think about it when she walked past that bombsite as she did every day to go to work at Priddy's.

Gladys still saw baby George, her grandson, though shortly he would be taken to America by Rita, who had been Pixie's friend and George's legal guardian. Rita was now living in the Midlands to be nearer the man she was marrying, an American serviceman.

Gladys was well aware the little boy would have a much better life in the States than she could ever provide for him in Gosport. She also knew Rita would never let the little boy forget he had an English grandmother. But for now the chirruping of her canary was a welcome sound in her empty house.

Tommy Handley was on the wireless. *ITMA* made her smile. Outside, the wind had risen again. Even the thick blackout curtains didn't keep out the draughts. It was supposed to be summer but the atrocious weather that had held up the D-Day landings had returned with yet another English Channel storm.

Gladys dusted the seed husks off the table's oilcloth covering into her hand and threw them on the fire. Then she set the birdcage back on the sideboard. She put her hands on her hips and looked around her kitchen. A table in the centre of the room, a worn but comfortable armchair beneath the window and a cream and green cabinet that housed her food leaned against the wall. It was a rented house and she paid twelve shillings a week to her landlord, though he would like to get his feet permanently under her table if he could.

Gladys knew she could get away with not paying rent. But then she'd be beholden to Siddy and she didn't want to be answerable to any man, ever again. Siddy came in handy to take her away for a weekend or to do those little jobs round the house that she couldn't manage. The house being his, he never minded handling a screwdriver or a hammer and nails. When she was especially lonely she allowed him to stay over, ignoring the street gossips. After all, Gladys was well aware her reputation had been left in tatters long ago.

She thought about Em and her supposed new sister.

Stranger things happened, especially during the war. She thought back to when they were kiddies and she'd practically lived at Em's house. Em's mum had been a nice lady and Em's dad was . . . Well, like all dads, the head of the household. It was obvious now, as a grown-up, looking back, that he had adored Em and her mum. He was always teasing them and making them laugh and he

26

was never too shy to put his arms around Em's mum's waist and kiss the back of her neck. Em's mum made cakes and met Em from school.

Unlike Gladys's mother, who would often be 'entertaining', as she called it. Which usually meant she had a new boyfriend and Gladys had to keep out of the way. As her mother entertained her male friends upstairs, it actually meant that she had to find herself something to eat, keep herself occupied, and get herself ready for bed after she'd made herself scarce in the evenings. Sometimes her mother would come in to kiss her goodnight smelling funny, of drink and stale perfume. Often the men stayed over and sometimes they had come into her bedroom, then Gladys's mum would get angry and throw the men out. Or occasionally she'd blame Gladys for encouraging them. Gladys, older now, knew the men weren't nice people.

She hoped Em wasn't being taken in by Lily. Gladys never trusted anyone, but if this so-called 'sister' really was a sister then she wanted nothing but happiness for Em. But if this woman *was* an imposter why would she want to go to the trouble of pretending to be Em's sister?

Em had had an unhappy marriage, which ended when Jack had died earlier this year. He'd returned from the war broken in mind and body, and money could never make up for the suffering Em had survived at his hands.

By most people's imagination Em was well off. Her husband's insurance money had been paid out to her and a cash sum had been discovered at the back of the old wardrobe, which Em had decided was a payout for Jack's injuries that he had kept secret. Along with the house she owned, which had been her mother's, she was doing all right.

Gladys wriggled her feet into her court shoes, leaving her slippers beneath the kitchen table.

'Bloody bunions!' she moaned at the protuberances near her big toes. Then she walked down the hall and put on her coat, tying the belt tightly around her waist.

In the hall mirror she outlined her lips, filling them in with bright red lipstick. The lipstick case was almost empty. Oh, how she wished she could simply buy another tube! But pretty things like lipstick and make-up were hard to get hold of. She cursed the war and the shortages it had caused.

Tomorrow she'd get in touch with Em's daughter, Lizzie. The girl needed to know what was happening in her mother's life. Lizzie hadn't been home to Gosport for several months, but surely she would have got over

Blackie's disappearance by now? Her mother, thought Gladys, needed her. Finding out she had a sister wasn't something Em should keep from Lizzie.

Her eyes lit on the *Evening News* lying on the floor where the paperboy had pushed it through the letter box. She bent and picked it up, glancing at the front page.

Since the landings in France in early June there had been little news of how the troops were faring. Ten thousand Germans had been injured and at least four thousand of them had died on D-Day. The war had a long way to go, surmised Gladys. She refolded the paper, replaced it on the hall stand, opened the front door and walked out into the drizzle.

At Em's house she pulled the string through the letter box and let herself in. Calling out to Em to let her know she'd arrived, she took off her coat and put it over the balustrade at the bottom of the stairs and then followed the noise of voices to the kitchen.

Em and a blonde woman were poring over letters and bits of paper spread across the table. A flowery perfume greeted her – a change from Em's comforting smell of baking. Em took after her mother and loved to cook when she could get hold of the ingredients.

'Hello, love,' she said to Em. She received a smile from the woman that somehow never reached her eyes.

'That's my sister,' broke in Em. To the woman she said, 'This is my mate, Gladys.'

'Already made up your mind, have you, that you're related?' Gladys addressed Em. Her heart went out to her friend. She could see Em had been crying. She didn't want her hurt.

'I don't have to make up anything,' Em said. She gave a watery smile. Rummaging through the papers on the table, eventually she came up with a handwritten letter. 'I'd know my mum's writing anywhere. In this letter, she's begging the Hampshire authorities to let her have Lily back, but they won't as Mum's not married . . .'

Gladys put her hand over Em's. 'I can see this is upsetting you.' She looked at Lily who hadn't moved from her kitchen chair. 'You, too, can't possibly find this easy. Shall I make a pot of tea?'

She wouldn't look at the letter and Em let it drop back on the pile.

The happy man and woman who had been Em's parents couldn't possibly have anything to do with giving away a child. Besides, Em and her parents and she had spent many merry nights around this same kitchen table making up jigsaws, playing snakes and ladders or even simply sitting watching the flames from the fire and talking about everyday happenings, when they weren't listening to the wireless. Surely during those evenings some word would have been dropped into the conversation about children being taken into care. But Em's parents had never discussed such a topic and how could that have been ignored, hidden even, if they *had* given away a child? A child of their own? One that they could have loved as much as they obviously adored Em?

Gladys had loved the stability of Em's home. It was something she'd never had from her own mother. Tarnishing those special days of her childhood and of two people she had loved must not be allowed to happen by this, this, Lily person. Unless it *was* all true. Even then, she thought, no one could take away the happiness and care that Em's parents had showered on her.

Gladys watched Em wipe her hand across her eyes and the last vestiges of her mascara put on that morning for work smudged across one cheek. 'Good idea,' she said. 'Tea solves all the problems.' Gladys decided Em wouldn't be pleased to know she'd made a mess of her eyes so she looked away.

Lily was speaking to her. 'I'd been sent to live in the country, on a farm. Later Mum sent another letter telling the authorities she was married and expecting a baby,' she looked at Em, 'you. And that she wanted me back now she was settled.'

Gladys rinsed out the teapot. 'What happened?' she asked. She saw the kettle was almost on the boil.

'They still wouldn't let me go to her because, as another letter states,' Lily fumbled amongst the paperwork, 'It was too much of a risk as I was already secure where I was.'

Gladys watched Lily's fingers fumbling amongst the large haphazard pile of letters and papers. 'Have you read all that stuff?'

Lily shook her head. 'No, not all of it, but enough for me to get an idea of what happened.'

Gladys stole a look at Em's glum face. If those letters belonged to me I'd have read every single line, she thought. In fact, there's nothing she'd like better than to settle down and go through everything so she and Em knew exactly what was going on.

Gladys could almost cut the silence with a knife. She went on making the tea, all the while thinking how awful it must have been for all concerned. 'To become pregnant without being married forty years ago would have been a terrible thing. It's bad enough now with everyone talking about it and the shame. Once people know you've had a kiddie out of wedlock they won't give you a job or let you rent a room. But when we were babies, they used to put women in insane asylums when they were led astray. Of course, the bleedin' man always had his fun and got off scot-free!' Gladys opened the tea caddy and spooned tea into the warmed pot. For a while her attention was occupied by pouring in boiling water. She stirred the spoon in the teapot angrily then fitted on the lid and pulled the knitted cosy over it. She knew she was angry because she and Em had been friends for years, and if Lily was introduced into the equation she was worried she might lose Em's friendship. Jealousy was a terrible thing, but it wasn't only that emotion causing her to disbelieve Lily. She turned and faced them both.

They were of the same age and build, but not at all alike.

Something about Lily growing up in the country didn't make sense. She seemed so sure of herself. If the woman hadn't told her otherwise, Gladys would have thought she was a town woman. She was sharp, quick. Quicker even than Em, who had lived in Gosport all her life and had become overseer at Priddy's.

Gladys had been around, done a lot of things, some not very nice, but she'd seen a lot of life. And Gladys could sense that Lily was similar to her. You didn't get to be like that living on a farm with only four-legged creatures and grass around you. If Em wanted to believe this women, then so be it. But Gladys didn't come up the Solent in a bucket! Lily would have to prove she was Em's sister and Gladys wasn't such a pushover as Em.

Em said, 'Dad didn't leave Mum. He didn't have his fun and leave her to bear the consequences.'

Lily answered her. 'No, he didn't. He was with her when she gave me up. Then they made a home together and had you and tried to get me back.' She paused. 'I found that out from this correspondence.'

Gladys thought she might have shed a tear at this point but Lily carried on, 'It's like a huge jigsaw puzzle. There are copies of the authorities' communications to her and the original letters she wrote to them. Did your mum – our mum . . .' Lily coughed at her mistake, 'ever leave anything that would help make sense of all this. A diary?'

Em looked confused and Gladys saw her swallow, which meant fresh tears could fall any minute. Gladys wanted to protect her. She went on the attack. 'What I want to know is why you've decided that now is the time to look for Em?'

She saw the frown cross Lily's forehead. Her question had caused consternation, not only to Lily but also to Em, who put her hand to her mouth. Again there was silence in the kitchen. Gladys added, 'Em's been through a lot this past year with family stuff and it's left her vulnerable. How long have you had these documents?'

Em got up from the chair and went over to the cupboard, getting out cups and saucers. Gladys saw her lips were a thin line. She hoped she wasn't making her friend angry, but there were certain questions that needed to be asked and answered and Em wasn't in any fit state to do it. She was completely stunned by the whole thing.

Lily spoke calmly. 'I've had them from the beginning of the war. I've been searching for a long time before that. My foster parents wouldn't tell me anything, not even when I finally plucked up the courage to ask them after I discovered my birth certificate when I was looking for Christmas presents in Mum's chest of drawers. I found this biscuit tin and inside were medical cards, letters, certificates, and I found out I wasn't related to them.

'After that they told me I came from one of Dr Barnardo's homes. Mum said they would have all my records. For a while I pretended it didn't matter to me, and I didn't need to know who my real mum was. I suppose I felt I couldn't hurt these people who had brought me up. They died in 1941, in that terrible shelling in Coventry.' She paused; Gladys couldn't help but remember the bombing there that was worse than our boys flattening Germany's Dresden. 'I managed to get hold of this stuff. I can't tell you how, but a friend who works with children told me youngsters were still being shipped off to Canada. I knew if *you'd* been in care when you were younger, there was every possibility you could have been sent to another country. I might never see you again, so the search began in earnest.'

Em took a hanky from her sleeve and dabbed at her eyes. 'What do you mean, "shipping children to Canada"?' The mascara was finally, completely wiped away.

'Barnardo's had been sending children to Australia, New Zealand, all over the place, to give them a fresh start in life. Sometimes to get them away from the bad influences of their parents or the horrors they'd had to endure.' She paused. 'I knew I could search for you in England, but not abroad.'

'Hey! My mother and father brought me up well in this very house!' Em flared up, her face creased with anger.

'I didn't know that, or anything else, remember, until I started piecing things together.' Lily was angry as well. 'Some children were taken into care wrongly. But Barnardo's do the best they can. They try to equip children with skills; especially if they can't place kiddies in loving homes.'

'I think the last children went to Canada just before the war,' said Gladys. She was trying to defuse the situation. Both women turned and looked at her.

Everything Lily was saying seemed plausible and was

backed up by the folder of papers. Gladys was hoping Lily would let Em have a good look at them so they could study them together, without interference from Lily.

Gladys set the tray of tea on the table after pushing aside the letters in case anything was spilled on them. She made sure the cups sat in the saucers. There was milk on the table in a bottle and a glass dish of sugar with a clean spoon buried in it. She looked at the fur coat hanging over the back of a kitchen chair. That had to be Lily's. The woman's bottle-blonde hair was perfectly styled, as was her make-up. Not that Gladys had anything against bleached hair, after all, her own hair wasn't the colour she'd been born with, but there was *something* about Lily she couldn't put her finger on . . .

'You need Lizzie here.' Gladys stared at Em. '*She* needs to meet Lily,' she said, nodding towards her friend.

'You're saying I can't make a judgement on my own?'

'No. I'm saying since your girl's been gone you've been on your own and I don't want you clutching at straws.' Gladys began pouring tea into the cups. She knew she was right. Lizzie must be told. 'Now,' she said brightly, 'who wants a cuppa?'

Chapter Four

It was the kind of drizzle that got into every part of you, thought Joel. A cloud of cigarette smoke and the smell of stale alcohol assaulted his senses as he swung open the heavy door to the Dog and Duck.

'Got any beer, mate?' he called to the barman. They'd had only cider for the past few days.

'Mild?' Joel thought that sounded like heaven and hoped he'd heard right.

'Certainly will. A pint of.' A few minutes later he was sitting on a stool watching the other customers. Word must have got round about the beer, as the pub was busier than usual. Old blokes, young blokes and a few foreign sailors, their voices were loud but didn't drown out the wireless music.

Most men were away fighting. An ancient couple wearing cloth caps sat in the corner playing draughts.

The Dog and Duck was what Joel termed a 'comfortable' pub. The blackout curtains were pulled tight against the taped windows. The customers were mostly locals. It was a pub that could rustle up a passable sandwich, where he could relax after being on his feet all day.

His eyes lit on the girl at the end of the bar, a tea towel in her hand, polishing a glass. Something in his heart fluttered.

She began pulling a pint, her brown arm tightening on the pump handle. She must have taken advantage of the sun today before the bad weather set in. It had touched her cheeks and given her a glow from within that radiated out, encompassing everyone about her.

Someone must have said something to her that made her laugh for now she'd thrown back her head and her pale-skinned neck, where the sun hadn't reached, looked vulnerable. Her hair, dark as the night, hung loose over her shoulders.

Joel wondered about her past. She'd shown up a few months ago, already pregnant and with no man in tow. The manager of the Dog and Duck, Joe, and his wife Elsie seemed fond of the girl. He didn't like to ask anyone about her so made up stories about her life in his head.

Perhaps her husband had been a casualty of the war. She wore a wedding ring. Perhaps he was away fighting.

She was near her time and her man, if she had one, should be with her.

She'd be about twenty, he reckoned. He'd read about love at first sight and never believed a word of it, until he'd set eyes on her. Why did he feel like this about a woman he knew nothing about? He took another mouthful of ale and licked his lips.

And now one of the men at the bar was holding the bar flap up. She'd be coming to collect glasses. He moved an empty pint pot nearer so she'd find it easier to pick up.

She was so close he could smell her flowery perfume.

'Evening, Joel,' she said, giving him a smile.

'Hello, Lizzie,' he answered.

Gladys folded her clothes and put them in her locker. She'd already changed into her navy blue overalls and covered her hair with the awful white turban. All around her women were chattering while they took off their outer wear and anything else that might be a hazard in the workplace. Just one spark from a nail in a shoe could cause an explosion, so special footwear was provided, and all outfits were made of cotton, which reduced the risk of a spark from the build-up of static electricity.

Gladys saw Maisie tuck a packet of fags up her sleeve. She looked away. It was against the law to smoke in the factory, and very dangerous. But she wouldn't tell on Maisie, she didn't need to. Maisie would be lucky if she still had a job when the cigarettes were discovered. She had a screw loose if she thought she could get one over on Em.

Gladys didn't smoke any more. She'd given it up long ago when they started selling the Pasha cigarettes so you could then purchase the Woodbines. Pasha cigarettes, she'd thought, tasted like mud. And she couldn't stand the Turf cigarettes that were easier to come by. Men friends, especially the Americans, used to give her cigarettes, but that was then and this is now. Siddy, her landlord and friend of the moment, didn't smoke.

'Such a bother getting in and out of this place,' said Maisie. 'Just think, there's about two and a half thousand women all changing clothes . . .'

'Not all at the same time,' laughed Gladys. 'And don't forget the men working—'

'How could I forget them when they call us names?' Maisie tore off a bit of the match packet and folded it with a few Swan Vestas and began tucking them into her sock. Swan Vestas would light up easier than normal matches. Gladys knew later Maisie would ask the supervisor for permission to go to the lavatory and then she'd have a crafty smoke.

Gladys looked away. 'What did you get called today?'

Maisie was very pretty, with long dark hair that she was now twisting up beneath her turban.

'Canary. "I'd like you singing me to sleep," called out that fat Harry that drives the train. I wouldn't touch him with a bargepole!'

'Don't take no notice,' said Gladys. 'That's nothing compared to some of the things them blokes come out with.' She glanced through the window, looking at the railway line and the train that hauled goods around the site.

The factory was hidden away in woodland. There was sea access and the site wasn't overlooked, even though it was practically in the heart of Gosport. All the roofs were painted green which helped to disguise it from above, making it difficult for the enemy planes to see the red-brick buildings. There were fine views across to the dockyard, where the *Victory*, Nelson's flagship, was moored. This was also where Allied ships and their sailors docked to spend time in the pubs and meet girls. The ferry boats, which looked like squat beetles, could be seen crawling across the expanse of Solent water between Gosport and Portsmouth.

Gladys caught sight of Em. She could tell she'd had hardly any sleep. Her eyes were puffy and her skin looked like putty. Gladys debated whether she should tell Em that on her way to work this morning she'd posted a letter to Lizzie. She'd told Lizzie what had happened the previous evening, and asked her if she could come home for a few days. She added that Em missed her, which she did, but she also told Lizzie that she didn't like or trust Lily, which she didn't. She had offered to pay her train fare home and told her if she didn't want to stay with her mother, she'd find a bed for her at Alma Street. Gladys was able to pour her heart out to the girl because Lizzie had been a close friend of her own daughter, Pixie, and therefore almost like a daughter to her.

Amidst the chattering women Gladys made her way to her place at the bench. Today she was working next to a young girl, Ruby, who looked hardly old enough to be in a factory let alone doing this dangerous job of filling shells. Marlene, too, was working with them.

'Hello,' Marlene said, giving her a wide smile.

Marlene and she had been friends for years, but Marlene had only recently begun working at Priddy's. Before that she'd had a market stall in the town selling gold and antique jewellery. But times had been hard for her. She had been conned out of a great deal of money by a trickster who had also broken her heart. A wage packet from Priddy's was at least regular money.

Gladys smiled back at her, then reached out and tucked a stray strand of Marlene's glorious red-gold hair inside her turban. Marlene's hair grew almost to her waist.

Gladys looked at the conveyor belt and the shell cases. At least she wasn't putting highly toxic azide pellets into shell fuses like Em would be doing today. Em's hands would be boxed in thick glass panels to localize the vapour. It was a severe explosion risk. But she, Marlene and Ruby were among the girls today making pellets that boosted the ignition of weapons. It was a tedious and very hazardous process using tetryl, a yellow powder that gave them rashes. It was also very sensitive, a high-risk chemical often causing explosions and accidents.

Gladys heard a commotion and stared about her, looking for the culprits.

'What the hell?' Marlene said.

Maisie was shouting and stomping down the aisle between the workbenches. Other workers were looking at the floorshow and Em was standing holding the cigarettes and matches. Her voice was loud and firm as she included the whole workshop in what she had to say.

'If anyone else wants to risk their life, do it somewhere else, not where you're likely to risk my life and everyone else's as well!'

The room went silent, just the wireless playing Bing Crosby singing 'Moonlight Becomes You'.

Gladys knew Maisie was on her way to the manager's office. Whether she returned to her workbench was up to Rupert Scrivenor, who was not a boss to be messed with. Her punishment could well be instant dismissal. Em had told her of a similar incident in a munitions factory in Herefordshire, where the offending girl was sent to prison!

'Why risk a good job for a fag?' Marlene shook her head in wonderment.

'People think they can get away with all sorts.' Gladys's thought turned to Lily. What if she really was up to something?

Em paused at the workbench. She was writing something on her clipboard and Gladys could see that the longer she kept her secret from Em, the more difficult it would be to tell her, so she said, 'I wrote to Lizzie.'

'Thought you might.' Em's reply was terse.

'You don't look like you slept after Lily went.' Gladys knew she couldn't say much, not with the other workers around them. She didn't want everyone to know Em's business.

'You're right, Gladys.' Em sighed. 'It's difficult to take in. But I need to know the truth. Lily and I talked long into the night trying to make sense of those letters and stuff. When I found she was stopping at the Black Bear in the town and intended to walk back in the dark, I asked her to stay with me.' She stared at Gladys. 'She's moved in.'

Gladys's heart dropped like a stone from a great height.

Already her fears seemed to be coming true.

Chapter Five

The searchlights roved across the sky, huge beams of light dousing the stars in the inky blackness. Marlene's heart was thumping madly. She clutched at the blackout curtain, fearfully praying that not a chink of light was showing. The V1 rockets were the worst and they terrified her, leaving her jumpy and constantly on the alert. First there was a droning sound, which was when she held her breath, then, if you heard the engine suddenly stop, you knew it was going to fall.

The doodlebugs, as they'd become nicknamed, were the latest offering from Adolf Hitler and the pilotless rockets were soon being sent over in their hundreds.

The war, and Marlene's nerves, had finally reached breaking point with the doodlebugs. They had begun arriving around the time our troops had stormed the Normandy beaches of France. It was as though Hitler was signalling that he was ready for a further onslaught, and Marlene believed he would never give in.

She let the curtain drop back into place and crossed the room. A flask of tea sat next to her torch on the quilt in the Morrison shelter, along with the small case that contained birth certificates, her ration book, identity papers and some photographs of her mother, Beth, and daughter, Jeannie, the daughter of a lad Marlene had gone to the Grammar School with. She had switched off the utilities; if a bomb landed it wouldn't help that she'd left the gas on. She climbed inside the wire contraption and curled up in the blankets and pillows. At the bottom of the bed sat Teddie bear, one of Jeannie's knitted toys that hadn't accompanied her to Littlehampton. Marlene could be stuck here in the Morrison for ages. Already it had been some time since the air-raid siren had sounded.

The air inside the small kitchen now smelled of cordite and burning, and on the blackout curtains she could see the dancing colours of explosions as bombs landed in the streets of Gosport and beyond.

'Owww!' A huge crash caused Marlene to cry out and cover her head with a pillow. A bomb had fallen too close for comfort. Bits of plaster and ceiling were spinning down like snowflakes.

This was the very reason Marlene had finally persuaded

her mother to take Jeannie to her sister's house further along the South Coast.

'I've stuck here all this time. I don't want to go away now,' Beth had shouted.

'Then think of Jeannie!'

Marlene was using her child as a lever, and it worked. She also knew Beth was aware of her financial difficulties and the mess she'd been left in when Samuel Golden, the clever conman, had tricked Marlene out of her savings. Marlene had also foolishly obtained a mortgage on her house from a friend and given Golden that money as well. Paying the rent to her friend and keeping her child and her mother was hard work for Marlene, Beth had known that. The worry had made Beth's weak heart worse. 'I can still do a few cleaning jobs.' Her insistence had been ignored. That was the last thing Marlene wanted, her mother going back out to work.

Beth's sister in Littlehampton ran a small guest house near the sea, and had welcomed Beth and the little one in return for a few light chores. Marlene also sent money from her wages.

To obtain money for Samuel Golden, whom she'd loved at the time with all her heart, she'd borrowed cash left, right and centre and now she had to repay it. Unable any longer to buy stock, she'd given up her beloved market stall selling gold and antique jewellery, and taken work that paid the most money.

It felt like a big step backwards to her, from being her own boss to working amidst the stink and danger of the armament factory. If she could only get enough money for stock she'd be back out again in the fresh air, working all hours amidst the traders with their quick humour.

A tear trickled down her cheek. 'I miss you, Jeannie,' she whispered, fingering the photograph of her little girl. The child had a cheeky grin and her red hair was pulled into two bunches either side of her head. Marlene's mouth set in a thin line before she muttered, 'If ever I set eyes on you again, Samuel Golden, I swear you'll get your comeuppance.'

Dust was still drifting on the air, making it difficult for her to breathe. The droning outside hadn't let up. If only this war would end, she thought. Another crash caused a window to shatter. It didn't sound like one of hers, and for this small thing she was thankful. The thwump-thwump of bombs falling seemed never-ending. Yet, despite the darkness of the kitchen, she knew outside in the street the constant flashes from ack-ack guns returning the firing from ground bases, and the amazing colours of buildings as they burned, was almost turning night to day.

Marlene was aware that the south was high on Hitler's

bombing list. The dockyard at Portsmouth, the submarine base at Gosport, HMS *Dolphin*, and the many aerodromes and factories spread along the coastline were threats to him.

With trembling fingers she managed to pour herself some tea from the flask, careful not to spill it. She was hungry. But until payday she had to live on what there was in the cupboard. It wasn't much. A tin of Spam, some sprouting potatoes and a piece of hard bread that she could toast over the fire and spread with the jam that was left. She vowed that one day, if she made it through the war, she would search and search until she found a packet of Bourbon biscuits and she'd eat one after the other, dipping them in her cup of tea, until the packet was finished, or she was sick!

She was glad she'd sent her mother and child away for safety's sake but she hadn't realized that being alone in her house would make her feel so starved of company. If it wasn't for working at Priddy's, she could go for days without seeing or speaking to anyone. After Samuel had disappeared Marlene's nerves had been torn in shreds. She'd spent her days moping about. And after being in the market with people and traders all around her, she wasn't used to her own company. It gave her time to brood. The police had all the details of the con that Samuel had played on her and they had admitted knowledge of his pulling similar scams on other women. Catching him was a different matter. She sipped her tea, thoughtfully, glad that she was working in the morning and pleased that Gladys and Em made a point of waiting for her at break times so they could sit and chat together. Yes, she thought, she was lucky to have two good friends at the factory, even if she did owe them money.

Her tea finished, she felt her eyes closing. Searchlights and planes were still filling the skies with noise and colour. The bombing could stop any moment and then the all-clear would sound. Alternatively, it could go on for hours. Marlene put down her blue and white enamelled mug. She picked up Teddie and inhaled the scent of her child on the toy. Clutching it to her breast she cuddled up beneath the blankets and slept.

Lizzie wriggled her feet out of her black patent shoes and lowered her toes into the bowl of salted, hot water.

'Ah! That feels better,' she said aloud. There was no one in the room except the manager's white and grey cat, lying peacefully on her bed like a furry doughnut. The cat's ears pricked up at the sound of her voice, but he continued with his business of sleeping. 'I'll have to stop wearing these soon,' she said, looking at her high heels. 'Won't be able to carry a baby in my arms; I might stumble . . .' The cat stretched, jumped off the bed and waltzed out of the room, tail held high. Lizzie laughed.

She knew she'd soon have to think about finding another place to live. She looked around the room, its white stone sink and greasy gas stove and the battered wardrobe set against one wall. Her bed with its faded silk coverlet occupied the corner space.

The room went with the job and soon she'd have to give that up as well. Elsie, the manager's wife had said, 'Give the kiddie up for adoption; can't have a squalling baby on the premises.' Joe, her husband, was emphatic about Lizzie leaving before the birth, even though he wanted her to stay on as long as possible because she was a good, dependable worker.

Lizzie put her hands beneath her bulky stomach. 'I'm not giving you away,' she said softly. 'You're mine and it will be me and you against the world.' As if in answer, the baby moved. Lizzie followed the contours with her fingertips. 'See, I knew you'd agree with me,' she said.

She thought of Blackie and his dark brooding looks and his hands that had trailed across her skin, making her sigh with the knowledge that before long his flesh would be inside her. He'd be making love to her, kissing her in places that caused her to squeal with delight. Loving him had been so easy.

But then he'd disappeared and no one had heard from him since. She'd visited the local police station in Gosport's South Street and finally made them believe that he'd gone and that it was totally out of character. Of course, first she'd been fobbed off with the explanation that a grown man, unmarried and in his prime, had the right to simply up and go. They said people went missing every day, especially in wartime.

The *Evening News*, which was always on the lookout for headlines, had run an article asking readers if they'd seen Blackie Bristow. Nothing had come of that heartfelt plea.

Em, her mother, had advised her to leave Blackie to his own devices. But then Em had no knowledge of Lizzie's pregnancy.

'I can't stay here in Gosport,' Lizzie had wailed. She knew her mother thought that being in the same place where Blackie had walked, laughed and talked was too hard for her. But that was only part of the problem.

She couldn't tell her mother she was going to have a baby. How could she bring more shame to her doorstep? Within the space of a year so much heartache had happened that it was a wonder her mother hadn't gone round the bend! First, Lizzie had been raped by an unknown assailant. Em had pulled Lizzie through the shame, her fear of men, and the wagging tongues. Her mother had calmly got on with her job at the armament factory, thankful that Lizzie's attraction to Blackie had also helped her sanity.

Shell shock had turned Em's husband into a hateful, cruel man who regularly beat her. When he accidentally died, again Em survived the neighbour's taunts. Then she'd lost her young friend Pixie in a bomb blast. Still, somehow, Em had found the strength and courage to go on with her overseer work at Priddy's munitions factory.

But the last year had taken its toll. Em had grown older and an air of sadness surrounded her. Lines on her face told of her struggle to keep going. Lizzie thought the shame of her pregnancy might be the final nail in the coffin, that it might tip Em over the edge. Lizzie, unwed and pregnant, God how the tongues would wag!

And how could they manage when Lizzie had to give up work to look after the baby? She was aware that Em had found her husband's stash of money in the wardrobe and believed there might have been some kind of insurance payout to Em upon her father's death, but there'd been a funeral to pay for, and debts that Jack, her husband, had run up to clear. They all needed to be paid. In any case, this child was Lizzie's. She couldn't expect her mother to keep her.

Lizzie had begged her mother's friend, Sam, to find her a job where she could live in. He, too, thought it was because she hated being in Gosport.

When Lizzie explained her plight to Elsie, the woman still employed her, promising she'd keep secret the fact that Lizzie wasn't married. The customers loved her quick humour. Lizzie wasn't afraid to turn her hand to kitchen work, cooking, or cleaning and she did it all with a smile.

It wasn't long before men began to flit about her like bees around a honeypot. Naturally slim, her body seemed to want to conceal her secret as well. But, as the child grew inside her, though she laughed and joked with the customers, she rejected all male advances. She wanted no more than to think about what her baby would be like and to sew and knit tiny garments, putting as much love into every stitch that she could.

But no one realized how many tears she shed into her pillow, wondering where Blackie was. It was only now, months later, that she was able to think of him without sadness. Finally, she had accepted that Blackie wouldn't return.

She wore a cheap wedding band to stop tongues

wagging. Customers believed she had a husband who was either in the forces abroad, or who had died, leaving her a young widow. Elsie stuck to her promise. No one knew Lizzie was about to become an unmarried mother. Lizzie knew she had a lot to be thankful for.

Men, being men, had now stopped pursuing her. Those that now frequented the Dog and Duck were either in the forces, too young to join up, too old, or put off by her burgeoning waistline. After all, what man wants to take on another man's child?

Lizzie was beginning to miss the company of men, of dancing, of being told she was pretty. She found that being pregnant played havoc with her feelings. Despite chatting and laughing in the bar, she was lonely. She wanted so much to feel her mother's arms around her. But most importantly, she needed a home for herself and Blackie's child.

'Something will turn up, little one,' she whispered, hoping it would become true.

Chapter Six

Liliah stared at herself in the dressing-table mirror in her room at Yew Trees.

'Who are you?' She saw the lips in the mirror moving, but the strange wild-haired old lady didn't answer her. She looked down at her flowered dressing gown.

'Why are you wearing my gown?' She addressed the mirror and then put her hand to her forehead. The woman in the mirror copied her. 'Who are you? Where am I?' She began to cry. Her sobs grew heavier with the tears.

The young man stepped into the room through the door that was always open. Even at night the door was left ajar. Liliah liked that. It made her feel as though she wasn't alone.

The young man took a handkerchief from the drawer by the side of the bed. Oh, so that's where they hid her handkerchiefs, she thought. He came to her and dabbed at her cheeks. *He was drying her tears.* He smelled nice. Of soap. She could feel the softness of the cotton on her skin. Liliah smiled at him. If she could feel the handkerchief, she must be here!

'What's your name?' She had a feeling she might have asked him that question before.

'Joel.'

'That's in the Bible.'

'So it is.'

'Have you got my papers?' She would check in that drawer when he had gone. If they had hidden her handkerchiefs in there, maybe they had put her papers in that drawer too. She must try to remember which drawer.

'What papers, Liliah?'

Liliah stared at the nice young man. He had a bowl. He'd picked it up off the top of the drawers. She could see slices of peach. Was it dinnertime? She didn't remember when she'd eaten last.

'What's your name?' Liliah asked.

'Joel,' he said in a kind voice. 'Don't you want any of these peach slices? I could feed you.'

'I can feed myself, Joel.' She liked the sound of his name on her tongue. 'That's in the Bible. I want you to give me back my papers. They're mine. She's taken them!'

'Who has taken them?'

'That one who pulled my hair when she washed it. She dug her fingers in me.' Liliah began to cry. Without the papers she didn't know who she was. She was nobody.

'That's me! I've won!'

Joel felt pleased. He didn't have to let his opponent win, as this afternoon Fred had thrashed him at draughts and wasn't going to let him forget it any time soon. The old man's body might be breaking down, but his brain was razor sharp.

He needed to stretch his long legs. Sitting at the small table had taken its toll. Joel allowed his gaze to wander round Fred's room. Now he'd settled in properly with his photographs and war keepsakes propped about, the place looked homely.

'Fancy a cuppa?'

Fred leaned forward. 'I'd rather have something stronger.' He licked his lips.

Joel stared at him. 'No can do. Your tablets and alcohol don't mix.'

'Well, I'll have the bloody tea then, but don't forget to put in four spoons of sugar.'

Joel was about to remind him there was a war on and

that sugar was like gold dust when Fred laughed. The old man was teasing him again.

'You old bugger,' laughed Joel. 'Set the board up, I'll be back soon. Then *I'll* thrash *you*!'

On his way from Fred's room down to the kitchen he paused at each room to check on the inhabitants. Some were taking afternoon naps. Some rooms were empty and he guessed these guests were in the communal lounge listening to the wireless, or meeting with their visitors. The smell of disinfectant hung in the air. Joel liked that every surface that could be scrubbed was done so daily. The heat in the home was a different matter. The old people felt the cold even though it was hot and sunny outside, so the home was kept unusually warm. The heat inside enhanced both the aromas of cooking and the smell of weak bladders. Joel smiled to himself. At Liliah's room he paused. He could see that she was asleep under the covers.

Funny old stick, he thought. He didn't find her awkward, like some of the staff insisted. Forgetful, yes, but that had a lot to do with the injuries she'd suffered from the incendiary bomb. Losing the one you loved in such a terrible way would be enough to turn anyone a bit loopy. She'd gone downhill rapidly since the loss of her husband: suffered from her nerves, and refused to get out of bed. Then muscle wastage followed and it didn't help that she cared so little about her appearance she resembled a scarecrow. If it wasn't for the nurses and helpers, Joel was sure she'd will herself to die so she could join her husband.

Liliah had grown up in the country, a lonely child, a quiet woman, leaving farm life to do something more for her country than muck out stables and feed chickens. The man she'd later fallen in love with had meant everything to her.

He was glad she was asleep. There'd been ructions late the other night when, propping herself on her stick, she'd turned out every drawer in her room, tossing clothes and personal items on the floor. She'd woken up other patients with her constant crying about not knowing who she was because her papers had been stolen. Her cries had turned to screams and eventually the doctor had given her a sedative to ease her anguish. When she'd woken in the morning, she'd remembered nothing of the previous night's ruckus.

Joel stood over her. He listened to her rasping, even breathing. Despite his loss of hearing the noise was loud. Her thin grey hair had traces of the blonde it must have been not so long ago. Her slim body and narrow face still held vestiges of beauty. He sighed. She had only lived part of her life when the tragedy happened that had left her a husk of a woman. He left quietly, leaving the door open a little. He knew she liked it that way.

In the kitchen, Marie was peeling onions and they were making her sniff with their sharpness. Every so often she plunged them in cold water in an effort to stop her tears forming. Pete was at the other sink, cleaning vegetables. The home had a large vegetable garden, tended by an elderly gardener and his young grandson. Its contents kept them supplied with potatoes, fruit and vegetables. The gardens and orchard had been well cultivated long before the home existed.

'Did you hear about Dollie?' Marie patted her eyes with the bottom of her apron as she turned to face him.

'No.' Joel put the kettle on the stove after shaking it to make sure there was enough water inside.

'You missed a treat.' Marie's eyes twinkled despite their redness.

Pete waved his knife to demonstrate upstairs. 'Dollie's convinced she's Esther Williams and is refusing to put on her clothes over her new gold swimsuit—'

Marie broke in, 'You know that swimming film star—'

Pete started laughing and stopped her speech with, 'Course he knows who Esther Williams is, he's a man, ain't he?' He shook his head. 'Dollie's been prancing about the lounge doing the breaststroke. It took three of us to get her upstairs again.'

Joel stared at them both, then frowned. There was a moment of silence between them that the sound of big band music from the wireless didn't quite fill.

Pete explained, 'She ain't got no swimsuit, so there she was swanning about in the nuddy, bless her soul!'

Joel knew he shouldn't laugh at the antics the patients got up to, but Dollie was five feet tall and five feet wide. He gave a giggle that turned into a full-blown belly laugh. 'I was hoping to see Esther Williams' new film *Bathing Beauty*, but I shall be imagining our Dollie all the time!'

Joel was still smiling as he stirred in a half spoonful of sugar for Fred.

'Give us a shout if you need a hand,' said Pete. 'I'll soon be finished here.' He put down the knife, wiped his hands on a tea towel then sidled up to Joel. 'I been meaning to say something, mate,' he said. He leaned across and put a couple of Nice biscuits on the tray. Joel again stirred the teas after he'd poured in the milk. Pete said, 'You like that old man, don't you?'

Joel looked at him. 'Fred? He reminds me of an uncle I once had.'

Pete put his hand on Joel's arm. 'You know as well as I do, you shouldn't get involved. He's not going to last long.' Joel shrugged Pete's hand away. 'Don't say stuff like that!' He shut his mouth tightly. They all knew the home's policy on intimacy with the inmates. This place was the end of the line, and sometimes that was sooner than anyone expected. Pete clapped his hand on Joel's shoulder. 'Like I said, mate. If you need a hand . . .' Joel's eyes burned with sudden unshed tears. He nodded at Pete, and then watched his friend turn back to the sink and the peeling of the potatoes for dinner.

On his way back he paused a moment before stepping into Fred's room.

'About time,' said the old man, eyeing the tray. 'Why didn't you bring ginger biscuits?'

'Because you got no teeth,' said Joel.

Fred cackled. Joel saw he had put out the pieces on the draughtboard. They were all in the correct places.

'How come a strapping bloke like you is looking after us old farts?'

Joel wondered how many times he'd been asked that.

'I like wiping shitty bums,' he answered.

Fred laughed and picked up a biscuit, dunked it in his tea and Joel marvelled that he got it into his mouth before it fell to bits.

Joel said, 'They wouldn't take me back in the army, and

now the women are doing all the men's jobs I got to take what work I can.'

'It pays the bills,' Fred said. He motioned towards the second biscuit and Joel nodded and watched as Fred repeated his trick. 'You know I got kids.'

Joel raised his eyebrows. Fred took a slurp of his tea.

'They don't give a shit about me. After Madelaine died, my girl went to America. My boy followed and I don't know where the hell they are now.'

'That's sad.' Joel wasn't going to tell Fred that his tale was like most of the other residents' stories. They'd got old, got forgotten. Even when their offspring lived in the same town they conveniently forgot them once the doors of the home had closed.

Joel put his cup to his lips. He was young, but for all that had already happened in his life, he felt old. He was alone. He knew what it felt like to go home to an empty house night after night. Of course, there were times when a woman shared his bed. A pick-up, a girlfriend who never seemed to want to go the distance. He'd had his fingers burned more than a few times. That's why he didn't mind working unsociable hours.

He'd asked Annie to marry him. She'd said yes. But the lure of the Americans and their silk stockings and chocolate, gum and gifts for her parents had been too much for her to resist. He'd bopped the bugger and knocked one of his brilliant white teeth spinning across the pavement, leaving Annie to her dreams. Before her, Millie had shared his bed for almost two years. He'd wanted to settle down and have children but Millie wasn't the type. It wasn't long before he was alone again.

'You got a family, Joel?' The old man's voice brought him back from the past.

'Sure, I got you!'

Fred laughed so hard he choked, and Joel had to thump him on his bony back.

Chapter Seven

Joel pushed open the door of the Dog and Duck and let some of the sweat and beer stink escape into the night. As usual, his eyes went to the corner where Lizzie normally stood. She wasn't there. His heart dropped.

He'd had a hard day. Dollie had painted her bedroom with faeces. Two of the cleaners had already called in sick, so he'd set to and cleaned the room himself. Then, one of the residents had died unexpectedly in the night. He'd been a friend of Fred's and this morning the old man had gone back to bed as soon as he'd heard the sad news. Obviously, it had made him think of his own mortality. Joel hadn't been able to entice him from his bed.

Now, he didn't know which he preferred: a pint, or to set eyes on Lizzie.

'Pint of mild?' It was always a question on his lips. He

never knew whether they'd have beer or not. The war saw to that. 'Where's Lizzie?'

The barman took his coins. 'Lying down. She's not too grand.'

Joel wanted to go through to the living quarters to make sure she was all right, but Lizzie would wonder what the hell he was doing knocking on her door. After all, they'd hardly even had a proper conversation.

Women got all sorts of ailments when they were pregnant. He hoped it was nothing serious. Not that he'd first-hand information of pregnant women. Not that he'd got anyone pregnant. Well, at least he didn't think so. All his knowledge of women having babies came from the medical corps.

The wireless was playing 'You'll Never Know' and Dick Haymes was singing his heart out. Joel took a slurp of his beer and let his eyes rove around the bar. A couple of girls in the corner with orange juices in front of them were looking his way. Not his type at all. But then he'd had all types and was still alone.

He knew he was attractive to women. Even some of the old dears at the home fluttered what was left of their eyelashes at him. But the older he got, the more he wanted from a woman. He certainly didn't want another unfaithful one, like Annie. But he did so want to settle down and have kiddies. Pete was forever proudly telling everyone what his kids were up to.

Joel'd not had much of a family life growing up. His mother had disappeared when he was four. His dad brought him up. His uncle lived with them and if it hadn't been for him – and the chip shop on the corner – there were times when he would have starved. His dad thought more of the bottle than of his son, and Joel got used to coming home and finding his dad passed out in a chair.

But now his uncle had copped it in the war and his dad was long gone.

A bloke in a flat cap sat down heavily next to Joel and took out a folded newspaper that he spread out flat on the table.

'All right, mate?'

Joel nodded.

'Look at this!' The man was trailing his finger across the newsprint. Joel took a mouthful of beer and set his glass back on the table. Leaning over, he could smell lime on the man's dusty coat, like perhaps he'd been painting walls. He saw his bitten nails. 'This group of soldiers, bastards from the second SS-Panzer Division, surrounded this little village near Limoges. That's France, ennit, mate?'

Joel would have preferred to read the story himself, but it looked like the man wasn't going to let him. He nodded.

'The bastards told the mayor they was there for an identity check. They rounded up all the villagers. The women and kids were made to go to the church, with the German buggers making them sing as they marched 'em down the road. The men was led into barns and when they was all shut away, the fuckin' Germans put a gas bomb in the church. The church! When the bomb didn't kill all them women and kids, they piled on wood and burned them poor buggers, some of them still alive!' He paused and stared at Joel, and Joel saw the horror in the man's eyes. He went back to his newspaper. 'After that they started killing the men, shooting and burning them. Then the soldiers went round the village to finish everyone else off. An old man was burned in his bed. A baby baked in an oven!' Joel saw the paper shake as the man's grip on it tightened, his white knuckles showing his fury. 'Afterwards, it says here, they went to Normandy and joined the rest of the German army what was trying to stop our boys from invading.' He thumped the paper on the table top, making Joel's beer slap against the sides of the glass. He looked at Joel. 'Why?'

Joel, himself stunned, said quietly, 'It's war. No doubt more atrocities will emerge. We take prisoners too, don't forget.' The man looked at him disdainfully.

'But surely, our lot wouldn't do stuff like that? It's worse than animals, they are.'

Joel downed the last of his pint. 'It's war,' he said again and paused. 'And it's not over yet. Let me buy you a drink, help wash away some of the bad taste of that news.' He couldn't tell the bloke that the newspaper story made his stomach crawl.

He got up and made his way to the counter, just as Lizzie stepped from behind the curtain that separated the bar from the back of the pub.

'Hello, Joel.' His heart did a somersault. She looked as if she'd been crying. 'Do you want serving?'

He told her what he wanted and she got the drinks and put them in front of him. His head was full of the awful things he'd just listened to as he paid for the beers. He left his glass on the bar top and took the other one back to the man with the newspaper who was staring into the distance, yet looking at nothing. No doubt, thought Joel, still horrified by what he'd read.

'Cheers, mate,' Joel said. He left the bloke to it and pushed through the crowd, back towards Lizzie. All he could think of now was that they'd barely spoken, yet Lizzie had remembered his name.

'Do you want something else?' Her dark eyes were deep.

He stared at her. He knew he was blushing and hated himself for it.

'Yes, I want you to come out with me,' he said in a rush. Damn, he thought, he was going to look a right idiot when she refused him.

'I'm expecting a baby.' She looked confused, but not unhappy.

'That's all right, the baby can come too.'

Lizzie began to laugh. Her eyes crinkled up at the corners and finally, when she'd finished laughing, her mouth settled to a U shape.

'I'd like that. When?'

'Now.'

Joel knew he was on a roll and decided to take advantage of his new-found confidence, before it popped like a balloon with a pin in it.

'All right.'

He watched her, his heart beating like a drum as she went along the back of the bar and spoke to Joe, who called Elsie over. It looked like it was going to be his lucky night when Elsie looked over at him and smiled.

Lizzie came back and said, 'Meet me by the back gate in five minutes.'

Joel knew the stupid grin on his face was growing wider by the second. He drank back half his pint in one go, left the rest and walked out of the crowded, noisy bar, his heart light.

Lizzie had on a black coat, belted over her bump, and wore high heels. Her dark hair tumbled about her shoulders. It was summer but the nights were cold. Joel thought she was the prettiest thing he'd ever seen.

'Where are we going?' She tucked her arm through his. A familiar gesture, but it made him feel ten feet tall.

'Would you like to eat?'

Her big eyes looked like they could swallow him whole. She nodded.

Further along the road there was a large hotel, the Flamingo, where he knew Americans took their girls to impress them. He decided that might just be the place.

Once seated at a table with menus in front of them, Lizzie said, 'I'd like a pork chop.'

'I'll join you, if they've got any. But maybe it'll be Woolton Pie.'

She smiled at his mention of the war's cheap and cheerful meatless meal.

The restaurant was large and there was a stage backed by dark red curtains. A grand piano stood to one side. Cigarette smoke curled in the air and Joel could make out the American voices of some of the other diners. He sat back and looked about him after ordering, surprised and glad that pork chops were available. He twisted the cloth napkin in his fingers.

There were girls with flowers in their hair, wearing cotton dresses with padded shoulders and pretty necklines. The Americans looked smart in their force's uniforms. A few couples were dancing, no, smooching, to 'God Bless the Child' being played by a small orchestra. A girl in a long glittery dress that looked as if it had been sprayed onto her slim body walked from behind the curtain and stood in front of a microphone. Her voice was sultry as she began singing the Billie Holiday song.

'Would you like to dance?'

Lizzie shook her head. 'I look and feel like a barrage balloon.'

He shook his head. 'Never,' he said.

Looking about him, he realized there were very few English lads there. There were a couple of elderly men with younger girls and a few middle-aged couples were being waited on. But mostly Allies and a few women in uniform graced the floor.

The chops arrived, with vegetables and potatoes. He saw Lizzie smile with satisfaction.

'I never thought I'd be sitting here with you, about to eat this.' She prodded her chop with her fork.

'I never expected you to come out with me,' Joel said, cutting the tender meat.

'You must have guessed I liked you?'

Joel stopped his fork in mid-air. 'Well, no!'

'If I wasn't like this,' she looked down at her bump, 'I might have flirted with you. But it's not right to eye up a man when I'm about to give birth.' She treated him to a smile.

His heart soared. He admired her honesty.

'Where's the father?' The words were out before he could stop them. He put the meat in his mouth and chewed at its sweetness, ashamed of his bluntness. He hadn't failed to notice the green line on her finger caused by the cheap ring. It wasn't a proper wedding ring, but a prop to fool people.

'I don't think I want to lie to you. Let's just say he's not around any more.'

'Fair enough.' He got the two words out before she began to cry. Then tears were rolling silently down her cheeks. He put his hand across the table and clasped her fingers.

'I want this child.' Her voice was small.

'Just as well.' He smiled and watched as she removed her hand and used her serviette to wipe her face. 'Can I help in any way? Something besides the baby is worrying you, isn't it?'

She sniffed. 'I've had a letter from my mum's best friend. There's some funny business going on at home and Gladys, that's my mum's friend, wants me to go back to Gosport. Only thing is, my mum doesn't know I'm having a child. The shock will practically kill her.'

'But surely the baby's father can help?'

'I told you, he's not around. And when his name's mentioned my mum will die of shame. I need, no want, to go home, for her sake and mine, but not like this.' She looked down at herself. Then she looked at her plate. 'Oh, I'm sorry, you've brought me out for this gorgeous meal and I'm letting it go cold.' She took a deep breath and began eating again. He watched her trembling.

Unsure of what to do next, he continued eating. But now the meal seemed almost tasteless. He didn't want Lizzie to be unhappy. If she was needed at home, she should be able to go.

They ate in silence with the blonde now sweetly singing 'All or Nothing at All'.

After a while Lizzie said, 'I like Frank Sinatra singing this.'

Joel gave her a smile. Her plate was practically empty and he felt happier now that she'd eaten.

'Shall we see what they've got for a pudding?' He realized he liked her sitting with him. He didn't want to have to take her back to the pub. He wanted her to talk about herself, and if they spent more time together perhaps she'd open up to him.

She nodded and sniffed. He called over the waiter and asked what they had on the menu.

'Bread and apple pudding, bread and prune pudding and carrot pudding.' The man waited, his pencil poised.

'Bread and apple please,' Lizzie said. The excitement was back in her eyes. Joel thought she looked like a little girl.

'Make that two.' The plates were taken and he thought Lizzie seemed happier, even though the dark rings about her eyes made her look tired.

'I'm not good company, am I?'

'You are to me, and that's all that matters,' Joel said. 'Look, if I can help, will you promise to ask?'

The scrape of her chair against the floor startled him, as she got up and practically ran, as best her bulk would allow, towards the lavatories.

She looked back and nodded. 'Of course,' she sang out. 'Won't be long. The meal's lovely but I need to pee every half hour.'

He began to laugh.

Chapter Eight

Joel steadied Lizzie as she stepped from the bus to the pavement.

She looked at the new prefabs stretching into the distance. Clutching his arm, they walked on the paving stones between the rows of housing specially built to help with the homelessness the relentless bombing had caused.

Wire netting surrounded gardens that were smart, covered in lawn, or already full of broken bedsteads and rubbish. Joel guided her towards the last prefab of the row.

'Normally there are lights, but the blackout makes it difficult to see where we're going. We're here now.' He opened a wooden gate and walked up a short path to the side of the squat building. Joel put the key in the lock and opened the door. 'Wait just a second.' He stepped inside and she heard movements then he came back. 'Mind the step.'

He closed the door behind her before switching on the light. She realized he'd gone in and drawn the blackout curtains before illuminating the kitchen.

She marvelled at the enamelled sink, fridge, wash boiler and the enamelled stove that stood along the interior wall. Everything was built in. A small table with four chairs was set below the large window and there seemed to be cupboards everywhere. A child's high chair stood in one corner. Joel was taking a tea caddy down from a shelf. Even her mother's clean, homely kitchen couldn't possibly compete with this modern room. Everything gleamed and looked brand new.

'This is so lovely,' she said. She wondered about the baby's chair, but didn't like to ask.

Joel nodded. 'Go into the living room and I'll bring in a tray. Sit and make yourself comfortable. The back boiler in the range will have gone out but the room won't be cold, it holds the heat.' He laughed. 'It's supposed to be summer,' he said.

She nodded and pushed open the door, smelling polish. It was a long, large room with a sofa and two chairs, a sideboard and a rag rug in front of the fireplace. Full-length curtains almost hid the large windows.

There were framed photographs on the walls. A family comprising a dark-haired man, a pretty woman and two young children, one about a year old, smiled at her. The same woman laughed from another photograph. A larger one sat on top of a sideboard and in this the couple stood in wedding finery outside a church. She stared hard at the crowd, looking for Joel. Lizzie wondered about the family.

'You've got a lovely home,' she called. Lizzie could hear him clattering about in the kitchen. She sat down on the sofa, almost losing herself in its softness. She felt ashamed for having lost control in the hotel. This man was being kind to her. First the meal, then talking to her and listening, really listening, to her problems.

She so wanted to see her mother. Em would never have asked her to go home to Gosport if it wasn't absolutely necessary. Yet, how could she go like this? She looked down at her distended body. It would really give the neighbours and the women at Priddy's something to gossip about.

She looked down at her ankles, swollen and puffed over the sides of her tight shoes. She knew if she took off her high heels she'd never get them back on again.

The sounds of Joel in the kitchen comforted her. She thought back to when she'd run from the table at the hotel. She'd tried to make her exit give the impression she was cheerful but when she'd reached the hotel's lavatory she'd put her cheek against the white tiled wall of the cubicle and cried. Her baby was due soon and she still had no place to live, nor any means of keeping herself until she could get back to work after the birth.

She'd stayed in the lavatory for so long Joel had come to find her, hammering on the door and threatening to come in. She'd wiped her eyes, put on a smile and agreed to come here, to his home.

'We'll stop by the pub and you can let Elsie know where you are,' Joel had said. Once that was done they'd caught the bus to Alderley.

Joel now shook her out of her reverie by bringing in the tray of tea and putting it down on a small table.

'Give me your coat.' She struggled out of it and he put it over the back of a chair.

'Is this all yours?' Lizzie waved her arm, encompassing the living room. He liked the clarity of her voice. He hated it when people mumbled and he couldn't make out what they were saying.

He laughed. 'No, well, yes, sort of.'

She stared at him as he poured out tea.

'This prefab is rented to George Armstrong, my mate. The place is really modern as you can see and they've only been up a few months. The family was lucky to qualify for one.' He paused. 'They'd got bombed out. But unfortunately, his wife became very ill and wants to be near her mum in Birmingham until she can cope again. They took me in when I got the job at Yew Trees.' His voice went quiet before he spoke again. 'I've sort of sublet the place from George, with the council's blessing, I might add.' She took the cup and saucer he held out to her.

'It's amazing how much life can change in just a short time,' Lizzie said.

'You can say that again,' Joel answered.

She drank the tea; it was hot and welcome. Replacing the cup and saucer on the table, she watched as he got up and went to the sideboard where a brown Bakelite wireless sat. He twiddled the knobs and soon Bing Crosby's rich voice came through, singing 'Sunday, Monday or Always'.

Joel stared at her and smiled then he pulled her up and said, 'This is a wonderful song to dance to. I know you wanted to dance but guessed you felt shy back at the hotel. That's why you said you looked like a barrage balloon, which you don't.'

Lizzie could feel his lithe body fitting around her as he held her close. She couldn't speak, for her emotions were in turmoil. She loved to dance. The last time she had danced it had been with Blackie. But Joel wasn't Blackie.

She expected to feel silly, a huge lump of a woman being held gently in this man's arms as though she was a feather-light young girl. But she didn't. She gave herself up to the music and Bing Crosby's deep voice and allowed herself to enjoy the sensation. This man was making her happy. Very happy.

When the music stopped and the news came on, Lizzie sank back down on the sofa while Joel poured her more tea, kept hot in the pot by the knitted cosy.

She listened as the newsreader announced that the third attempt on Hitler's life had failed. A bomb had exploded at his headquarters in Rastenberg. He had told his people that it was a sign he had been saved so that he might complete his tasks under the protection of a divine power.

Joel turned the wireless off. 'I'm sure we don't want to listen to whatever rubbish he thinks,' he said. 'Anyway, I'd much rather talk to you.' He set down her cup. She liked that he felt at ease with her. That he was able to talk about his job, which he obviously loved, and his feelings about some of the elderly people who lived at the home.

'So you get on well with the owners of Yew Trees?'

'I don't see a great deal of them. They're a married

couple, middle-aged, who employed me, yet didn't seem particularly worried about my previous jobs once they knew I'd served as a medic.' He paused. 'They don't live on the premises. Pete and Marie keep the other employees in line. Pete has the edge though, he's an ex-medic and seems to be the one to go to if anything happens. There's almost a one-to-one ratio of carers to patients. Everyone pulls their weight. If they don't, a phone call to the bosses seems to sort the wheat from the chaff.' He stared at her. 'I think you should tell me a little about yourself,' he said softly.

Lizzie took a deep breath. 'I was already pregnant when I left Gosport. My baby's father disappeared. He didn't know I was going to have his baby. The shame of me being an unmarried mother would kill my mum, she knows nothing. When the baby comes I have to leave the Dog and Duck and . . . and . . .' Putting her problems into words cemented the hopelessness of her plight. She collapsed, crying again, against Joel.

His arms snaked around her. It was such a soothing feeling, Lizzie thought.

'I take it you don't have money to rent anywhere else?'

'No,' she snivelled. 'I used to work in the munitions factory in Gosport, the wages there were good but I spent them as soon as I got them. From the pub I've got a little saved, but nowhere near enough to last until things get back to normal, if they ever do. Oh, what a stupid person I am.'

He lifted her chin and looked into her eyes. 'I'd say you were a perfectly normal person. Working and playing hard like your mates did, no doubt. How were you supposed to know things would change?'

Lizzie sighed and tried a smile. It was easy to talk to Joel. He didn't condemn her like she thought he might have.

She should have made sure Blackie used protection when he made love to her. But she was swept away with emotion whenever he touched her. She'd loved him. She thought he loved her. It never entered her mind that one day he would up and disappear.

She squeezed her eyes tightly shut in an effort to stop herself crying again. Joel would think she was a right misery. All she'd done tonight was cry.

Just then the baby tried a somersault.

Joel, close to her, grinned. 'I felt that.' Then his face grew dark. 'You're not thinking of getting rid of it, are you? I mean . . . giving the child up for adoption?'

'No!' Lizzie shook her head violently. 'I want this child,

I told you that already. How I can keep it I don't know, but I'm not going to be parted from my baby.'

His face relaxed. Lizzie could see his eyelashes were very long and blond. He ran his fingers through his hair.

She picked up her clutch bag from the floor and removed the letter from Gladys. She passed him the single sheet.

After a while he said, 'What are you going to do?'

'My mum needs me. It must be important, else Gladys would never have written to me.'

Joel looked into her eyes then his gaze dropped to the huge mound that was her baby. 'I see.' He gave her back the letter and she folded it and put it back in her bag. 'I understand everything now.'

He bent down, picked up the tea tray and walked towards the kitchen. 'When in doubt, another cup of tea is the answer,' he said.

Lizzie didn't know whether she felt better for unburdening herself to a man she hardly knew, but she did feel better for talking about it. He was a kind man, she thought. Maybe working with old people had made him like that. He was the sort of man who should be married with children of his own. Was there a girlfriend? He hadn't mentioned anyone. She'd never seen him in the Dog and Duck with a woman. Yet he was a good-looking bloke. He could have his pick of women, she thought.

Just then he came back into the living room. After setting down the tray he sat opposite her.

'I've had an idea,' he said.

Chapter Nine

'I don't trust her.' Gladys couldn't help saying what she felt. She watched the bomb case travel along the conveyor belt. The noise of the machinery, along with Tommy Dorsey's 'In the Blue of the Evening' made her strain to hear Em's reply.

'Whether you trust her or not, I do like having her around.'

Gladys tamped down the powdered substance in the shell case in front of her. The stink of the workroom seemed to get into everything. Despite drinking as much milk as they could to help protect their skin and bones, the workers often experienced itchy skin, hair loss and chest complaints. Gladys wanted badly to scratch at her head. The turbans they were made to wear to protect their hair made her scalp itch. She sighed and tried to ignore her discomfort.

'You heard back from my Lizzie?'

Gladys looked at Em. 'Not yet,' she said.

'Well, when you write again, tell her how happy I am.' That was Em's way of telling her that she should keep her nose out of things that didn't concern her. But these things did concern her, because she loved Em and didn't want her to get hurt. She felt tears prick at the back of her eyes and while another shell case trundled along on its journey down the line, she looked around the walls where huge posters advised the workers, 'Hitler will send no warning. Always carry your gas mask'. 'God Help Me if this is a Dud' were the words above a picture of a soldier throwing a grenade. Underneath were the words, 'His Life is in Your Hands'. That one was to remind the girls to do their jobs properly; and of course there was also a poster showing a woman standing in front of a factory saying, 'Women of Britain Come into the Factories'.

Gladys sighed. Em had told her that she liked going home to a meal cooked by her sister. Not only that, but Lily had taken it upon herself to clean the already spot-less house in Kings Road. She wondered if Em had sat down and gone through the folder of papers Lily had brought with her. Em wasn't normally a trusting kind of person, but living on her own had made her more needy of company.

'Have you thought about checking out all her letters and stuff?'

Em let her clipboard fall to the worktop. 'The few I've really looked at seem genuine.'

'How can you say that? With a sheet of headed note-paper and a typewriter, I bet our Lizzie with her office skills could have forged something like that in next to no time!'

'You really don't like her, do you?'

'No,' said Gladys, picking up the clipboard and hand-ing it back to her. Immediately the word had left her mouth she knew she had upset the balance. She wished she could scoop back the word and swallow it.

'That's a pity,' Em took her clipboard, 'because with Maisie out on her ear after the fags incident here, we urgently need someone to take her place. I've just asked Rupert Scrivenor for a job for Lily.'

The banging on the door was loud and insistent. Lily wriggled her backside out of the oven and, using her knees, pulled herself into a standing position. She looked at the used S.O.S wire-wool pad and the bowl of soapy water, discoloured by the burnt fat she'd been scraping off the inside shelves. Em loved baking but she obviously didn't like cleaning the oven. Again came the thumping on the door that almost made the house shudder.

'Wait a minute,' she called, wiping her hands on the wraparound pinny she'd borrowed from Em and hurrying down the hall to the front door. She saw the tin of wax polish on the hallstand and smiled. So that's where she left it! She'd forget her head if it wasn't screwed on.

'Oy!' Lily was pushed back against the wall as the figure entered and kicked the door shut with the heel of his shoe. Pinned with his arm across her throat, her heart was beating fast as she tried ineffectually to free herself.

The man was laughing at her, his face so close she could almost taste his breath. The smell of Brylcreem was oily and as usual hadn't kept his hair from flopping on to his forehead. Behind his dark-rimmed glasses his eyes were large and unsmiling.

'So, Gloria, are you going to tell me why you haven't been in touch?' His educated voice was sharp. He took his arm away and she almost fell against him, gulping in air. 'We had a plan, you and I, didn't we?'

She'd become so used to hearing herself called Lily that the use of her real name startled her.

'Lawrence—' She got no further. His eyes had narrowed. She knew he didn't mean it when he lashed out, but sometimes the bruises took a long time to heal. He was always sorry afterwards. Nevertheless, she flinched as he pushed his face even closer.

He laughed. 'You surely don't think Lawrence Greyson would harm the woman he loves?'

She took a deep breath. Thank goodness his being here wasn't going to end in her getting hurt. 'Em'll be coming home soon. It won't do for her to find you here.'

'She'll be back in about a quarter of an hour and that's plenty of time to remind you you're here to do a job for me, for us both, actually. You do want to be with me permanently, don't you?' He bent down his head and nuzzled her white neck, like a vampire about to strike.

'I'm doing it. But it'll take time. So far she doesn't suspect a thing.' She nervously mumbled the words. He grabbed her hand, squeezing her fingers so hard that she cried out with pain.

'Sorry, my love, I forget sometimes that you're fragile.' He let her go and instead kissed her hard on her mouth. Despite her fear, her heart again softened and she melted against him.

Footsteps sounded on the tiles outside the front door.

'Bugger!' He swore and pushed her away.

She whispered, 'Em mustn't see you. Go through to the kitchen and jump the back fence.'

A key was scraping the lock. He stared at her. The

look seemed to bore deep inside her soul. Then he was gone.

The front door opened just as Lily pulled herself together.

Em, puffing with the exertion of her walk home from Priddy's, stepped into the hall, almost bumping into her. 'Whoops-a-daisy,' she said. 'You going out?'

Lily shook her head and quickly plastered a smile on her face. Thank God Lawrence had got out in time.

'Of course you're not going out, you've got a pinny on.' Em frowned. 'I thought I heard voices.'

'Only me, singing.' Lily bent down and picked up the wax polish. 'I came to get this.' She moved ahead and waited while Em took off her cardigan and put it across the banister at the bottom of the stairs. She was still shaking. Lawrence Greyson needed money. She'd made a promise to him that she now regretted, but he didn't let anyone off the hook that easily.

In the kitchen, Lily went automatically to the kettle and lit the gas beneath it.

Em came up behind her and gave her a hug. 'I've been meaning to clean that oven for ages. And my wonderful sister has done it for me. You're lovely, you really are.'

Lily swallowed back a tear.

*

Joel hung his jacket over the hall coat stand. He'd used his key to enter the nursing home, refreshed after a weekend away from the place.

The doors were never left unlocked, as more than a few of the inmates woke up at night and decided to go for a walk. Sometimes they tried to go out alone during the day. The home wasn't a prison, but there was a train line nearby and within the first few weeks of Yew Trees opening they had lost a gentleman who had walked along the track and frozen when the train came. Since then, doors and windows were kept locked and supervision was necessary at all times, especially when residents sat in the pretty gardens.

Joel was feeling happy. Lizzie and he were getting along fine.

He could hear music coming from the lounge and smelt something good wafting from the kitchen. He wondered what delicacy Marie had conjured up for dinner. The meals consisted of breakfast, elevenses of tea and a biscuit, lunch, a light tea – a drink and slice of cake – and then dinner at six, before the nurse gave out medication. Bedtime was early because residents rose early. It took a long time to wash and bathe elderly residents who couldn't do it for themselves, and to change bedding and clean and polish the home to Marie's satisfaction. Joel knew she ruled the cleaners with a rod of iron.

He bounded up the wide stairs and fairly raced along the hallway to Fred's room.

He had such a lot to tell him after his days off. He wanted to share with him his feelings about Lizzie. After all, Fred had loved Madelaine . . .

The door was wide open. Laundered blankets and sheets were piled neatly on the freshly cleaned mattress. A cardboard box was in the corner. On the top of it, face up, was the photograph of Madelaine.

Joel entered the room. The late evening sun streamed through, making patterns on the cleaned carpet. He suddenly became aware of the smell of disinfectant.

Joel sat down on the end of the bed and put his head in his hands.

An empty room meant only one thing.

A hand steadied his heaving shoulders. Pete's pale, freckled face bent towards him. 'He went Saturday night in his sleep.' He ran a hand through his red hair. 'He wasn't in pain. It was a good way for him to go. Come on down, Marie's made you a strong cup of tea.'

Lawrence Greyson flicked through the small pile of passports, and after selecting one in his current name, he put the rest back inside the brown envelope. Next, he chose an identity card and a ration book also in the name of

Greyson. He pulled out the drawer of the sideboard and wedged the envelope beneath it. Then he replaced the drawer and nodded with satisfaction as he looked about the tidy drawing room.

He should already have been carrying these items of identity about his person, but the woman who'd rented him this garden flat in the very desirable heart of Alverstoke village had been more interested in the money he'd handed over than suspecting he wasn't who he said he was. People were so trusting when they heard his plummy accent and saw his bulging wallet.

He walked out of the large room and opened the French doors to the wooded garden, which led down to a garage and shed that could also be reached by a small slip road at the side of his flat. He enjoyed sitting at the bamboo table on the terrace with a drink at his elbow, doing the *Telegraph* crossword.

He smiled to himself. There was a right kerfuffle going on at the moment concerning the crossword. He didn't know a lot about it but then the whole argument hadn't yet been resolved. Apparently some of the words used as clues and answers were the same as the code words used during the D-Day landings: Gold, Omaha, Utah and others. The crosswords published during May were compiled by a headmaster who vowed that some schoolboys had helped him, and they were still being investigated by MI5. So far there was no solution. The *Telegraph*, due to paper shortages, was a shadow of its former self, but Lawrence, like other readers, loved the complexities of the crossword.

Almost as much as he loved the new venture he'd started up in a flat near the Dive café opposite the bus station at the ferry. He'd opened a knocking shop! Of course, it was illegal but he had no intention of getting his hands dirty.

He'd won the premises in a poker game at a hotel in Southsea. Ben Harries couldn't pay his cash debt to Lawrence, so he'd handed over the lease as payment. Two girls came with the flat that comprised two bedrooms, living room, kitchen and a lavatory out the back.

The first thing Lawrence had insisted was that the girls work part time at other jobs so their earnings at the flat wouldn't be questioned.

He wasn't going to sully himself by being anywhere near the place, so he'd told the younger girl, Ruby, to hire a maid. She could look after the practical side of things by paying bills, taking payments, etc, and be there to help should the girls ever have an awkward client. There was a telephone installed in Harries's name and Lawrence had merely taken over the payments without changing the names. He intended to be a sleeping partner. He laughed at his own joke.

He had no intention of trying out the goods. God, no!

Ruby owed him. He'd picked her up off the streets, looked after her, fed her and bought her pretty clothes. She was head over heels in love with him at that time and did anything he asked. He'd put her to work for Ben Harries and Lawrence trusted her as well as he trusted anyone. Now, she worked for him.

So, as the new owner of the High Street flat which he had the deeds to but hadn't as yet informed the Land Registry of the change of ownership, he had a venture that couldn't be traced to him.

Ruby liked the extra money and she relished the responsibility of finding another mate to work with, someone who could look after her and Carla, answer the phone and be a general dogsbody. Carla was dark and exotic-looking and the two girls got on fine.

He decided Ruby could bring him the cash and the books at frequent intervals so he could check he wasn't being taken for a ride. He thought he had everything worked out to his own advantage.

In the meantime, his funds were running low, the Golf Club had asked him for his subscription, his rent was due and what was the point of having a pretty red MG

TB parked outside his flat if he couldn't afford the black market petrol for it? The sooner this little business took off, the better.

He'd set up a scam involving air-raid warden work which was going from strength to strength, so he could live comfortably, but he wanted more than comfort. He loved the fine dining that could now only be found in high-class hotels. He loved the expensive women he picked up in those fine hotels, sophisticated and pretty upper-class girls who turned into tigers in his bed.

He glanced back to the drawing room with its glass chandelier catching the last rays of the sun. It caused a rainbow effect in the delicately furnished room. He walked to the desk and poured himself a shot of whisky. He thought about Liliah Somerton and her will, handing over everything she had upon her death to her sister Em. Could Gloria pull off the deception?

Gloria had found the folder of letters while working as a carer looking after the dotty woman who'd been trying for years to find her sister. Gloria was then sharing his bed, and a right little goer she'd been, before her tits had started sagging, taking her arse south as well. He'd given her the old marriage bit, promising a ring on her finger the moment he had the money to support her. Or rather, the moment he had Em and Liliah's money.

If Liliah died her estate would go to Em. With Gloria pretending to be Em's sister, Em would be more likely to advance her sister money, knowing she'd get it back – after all, everything Liliah owned was set out in black and white. He smiled to himself. Liliah owned houses in Gosport, handed down to her via her husband's will, and also she had an extremely healthy bank account that paid out monies for her stay in Yew Trees.

There had been several chequebooks in the stolen folder of letters and Liliah's signature was forged well enough to fool the tellers at the bank. As they had never met Liliah, sums of money were easily paid out to Gloria that she promptly passed on to Lawrence. He knew it would be foolhardy to cash a huge cheque that would raise eyebrows. But now he wanted more, of course he did. If Gloria borrowed a really substantial amount from Em, he would be very pleased indeed.

And why shouldn't Em lend her sister money when she had proof that Liliah was, on paper, extremely well off? The house deeds were proof of collateral. But during wartime property-selling was slow. After all, who knew when houses might be razed to the ground? He felt sure Em would willingly hand over money to Liliah if she were asked. Sisters did that sort of thing, didn't they?

Gloria had jumped at the chance to become Liliah,

or Lily. Especially when he'd handed her documentation he'd had forged. A ration book to hand over to her so-called sister, an identity card. Anything could be purchased at a cost. The sooner he had Em's money, the sooner, he said, he would marry her.

Besides, she wasn't getting any younger and he was a catch, with his accent, car and clothes. He'd taken Gloria to places she'd never dreamed about, until the silly bitch was putty in his hands. And he'd done his homework well. Em Earle had a healthy bank account with money she'd earned, as well as money from her late husband's government payout and the insurance policy that had matured upon his death.

He threw back his head, downing the rest of his whisky, and poured another. There was only one thing that worried him. He'd lived in Alverstoke before, in a flat in a wide swathe of Georgian houses, very elegant and very expensive. He'd defrauded a pretty red-haired woman who'd had a stall in the market. He'd noted that she wasn't running the stall any more. Not only had she lost her savings to him, but he'd made sure she'd taken out a mortgage on the house she'd owned and he'd taken that money as well.

He doubted she was in touch with Em Earle. But he had met Em at a wedding when escorting the redhead.

He adjusted his horn-rimmed glasses, a disguise, of course. He hadn't worn spectacles then, and now he'd put on a bit of weight. With his dyed hair he doubted Em Earle would recognize him.

But he'd make sure he kept his eyes open for any of the women who had hung around that red-haired bitch. It wouldn't do for him to be recognized.

As soon as Gloria did the business, the both of them could be away from this place. She didn't know it yet but he'd be ditching her too, just as soon as she'd finished being useful to him.

He smiled to himself. Gosport was a town with a fast-moving population and he'd moved on, leaving the red-haired woman without a pot to piss in. Now he wanted to repeat the experience with Em Earle.

Chapter Ten

'Go home, Joel. We can cover your shift today.'

Joel was trying hard not to cry. He was a man, for Christ's sake, men don't cry. He wasn't even related to the old man! He stared at Pete.

'When's the funeral?' His voice was cracked with pain.

Marie pushed a cup of tea in front of him.

'About ten days' time,' she answered. 'Funerals are piling up. Them new doodlebugs are to blame for that. Bloody Hitler and his killing machines.' She sighed. 'Fred had nobody. The boss wrote to the last addresses the old man had for his daughter and his son, but he doesn't expect a reply.'

'You'd have thought they would have kept in touch, his own flesh and blood. Bloody people—'

'Go home, Joel.' Pete broke in, putting a hand on his shoulder. 'You're not fit to work. Why don't you take a week off? You're due the time.'

Joel tried to smile at Pete. It was his friend's way of helping him. How many times had Pete told him not to get too close? Well, now he knew the reason. Thinking about Fred was killing him. Why, the old bugger hadn't even waited until he was on shift so he could be there for him at the end.

'A week's a long time in this place,' he muttered.

'We wouldn't tell you to take time off if we couldn't cover it. Drink that tea before it gets cold,' Marie commanded.

He put the cup to his lips, swallowing the sweet liquid. A thought struck him.

'OK,' he said. Americanisms were catching on quickly, even in Lyme Regis.

Joel knocked on the side door of the Dog and Duck. Elsie stood before him in an old dress with sweat stains beneath her armpits, her hair uncombed. Without her warpaint, she looked washed out.

'We're not open, yet, Joel,' she stressed and made to close the door again. He steadied it with a hand.

'I want Lizzie,' he said.

She stared at him, before opening the door wide enough for him to enter. 'I think she's still asleep, but stay here and I'll get her for you.'

Standing in the grubby passageway, he gazed around at the boxes and packets stored on the concrete floor and the wooden shelves. The place smelled of damp.

It would have been simpler for him to go up to her room but Elsie wouldn't allow that. He gave a wry smile. The worst had already happened, hadn't it? Yet middle-aged women's values held fast, and no men were allowed in women's bedrooms.

Memories of Fred kept floating through his mind. He tried to push them away, but they returned unbidden. The old man had stolen a bit of his heart. He couldn't hang about at the prefab trying to read, or listening to the wireless, for his thoughts would return time and time again to the old man who'd become his friend. To go back to Yew Trees would make things worse. Fred was everywhere there, and concentrating on his job was impossible.

He was determined to get as far away as possible from Lyme Regis and solve one of Lizzie's problems at the same time as his own. Hopefully he'd be strong enough to face the old man's funeral on their return.

Footsteps sounded on the bare boards of the stairs and Lizzie, her dressing gown tied above her bump, stepped carefully down to greet him. Her long hair was loose about her shoulders, her skin creamy white with the bloom of motherhood. He'd often heard those words, yet never really understood their meaning until he looked at her and saw that special glow about her.

'What are you doing here?' He was pleased she didn't look cross at his arrival. 'Come into the kitchen and I'll make you some tea,' she said.

He followed her and watched while she lit the gas beneath the kettle and bade him sit at the table. He looked around at the dresser filled with blue and white crockery. On one shelf was a box without a lid that appeared to be full of paperwork. A large range stood along one wall and a table was in the middle of the room, surrounded by chairs. It was homely, yet obviously the place where a lot of the paperwork for running the Dog and Duck was stored. Invoices escaped their bundles all over the table. Lizzie put down four white enamelled mugs with blue rims. He guessed that Joe and Elsie might appear at any moment.

'Have you thought over my offer?' He watched her face for signs that she might think his suggestion totally inappropriate.

Lizzie put the brown teapot on the table and began stirring the tea inside it.

'I didn't want to jump at it because I was worried you might change your mind. After all, you know nothing about me except what I've told you.' She stopped stirring, replaced the lid and gave him a shy smile.

His heart lifted. This could solve his problem and hers. He began to feel happier.

'I know all I need to know about you, Lizzie. You've been honest with me about your baby's father and your background – what else matters?'

'I might irritate you to death with my personal habits.' She was looking at him from beneath her ridiculously long eyelashes and he wanted to scoop her into his arms and tell her she could never, ever irritate him. Yet logically, he knew there were always irritating things that couples endured if they cared about one another enough. If they couldn't see past those habits, they didn't really love each other. And he knew he was in love with Lizzie Earle.

Pete had castigated him for caring about Fred. The trouble was, how could he not care about people when it was part of his job, and it had also been part of his previous job in medical work? He was a *care worker*, not only by name, but by nature.

'So how do you feel about moving in with me *today*?'

She stared at him. They'd discussed the possibility of her sharing the prefab. She pushed the mug of tea towards him. He felt hot, the back of his neck sweaty.

Supposing she wasn't ready? But if she said yes, then maybe she'd agree to the second part of his plan.

Without hesitation, she said, 'I'd like that.'

'Do you have much stuff?' She looked perplexed. 'I'm only asking because I need to know whether to borrow a car . . .'

'Oh, no. Just a suitcase of my things and a small box of stuff I've managed to get together for the baby.'

He nodded. She suddenly reached forward and put her hand over his.

'You do realize that if we do this, people will suspect the baby is yours?'

His eyes met hers. 'Actually, that hadn't occurred to me.'

'They won't say it to your face, but they'll tittle-tattle behind your back.'

'If I can't hear gossip it doesn't matter, does it?' He smothered her hand with his, jumping as he heard Elsie's voice.

'Stop that canoodling, it's too early in the morning for that. So it looks like she's bein' shipped out to your prefab, then?'

Elsie came into the kitchen and poured a mug of tea for herself, dripped in milk and took a big slurp.

Joel realized she must have overheard the conversation. He was glad it was all out in the open.

Elsie poured more tea into the remaining mug and stirred in sugar. Joel noted she was now dressed in what he supposed were her working clothes of a frilled blouse and tight skirt. No doubt the full warpaint that he was so used to seeing would be put on just before opening time. 'I know me old man'll be pleased. He said she'll be all right with you.' Then she looked at Lizzie. 'Now you got a place to go you should get in touch with the midwife.' She looked Lizzie up and down. 'I'd say you've not long now. You don't want to be caught on the hop, do you?'

Joel made a mental note that Lizzie might need to do more than just put together a few clothes for her coming baby. Maybe he could get hold of a pram? He'd heard that new ones were like gold dust because of the war shortages but . . . He pulled his thoughts back to the present, just in time to hear Elsie say,

'I'll take this tea up to Joe.' She looked at Lizzie. 'Look, love, I care about you, you know I do, but you can see my hubby's point; a busy pub isn't the best place for a woman giving birth. Newborn babies haven't a clue about night and day and he needs his sleep to run this place. But I'll do whatever I can and you're welcome here anytime.' She smiled at Joel. 'You an' all.' And then she left the kitchen.

Lizzie shook the teapot and then looked enquiringly

at Joel. His refusal seemed to please her and she poured the rest of the tea into her own mug.

'I'll get hold of a car, anyway. You pack up your stuff. It's not good for you to be hopping on and off a bus.' She got up from the chair and came to him, throwing her arms around his neck.

'Thank you,' she said. 'You know it won't be easy. There'll be talk about the pair of us, but we can weather that storm, can't we?'

'We'll think of something,' he said, loving the feel of her arms about him and the smell of warm bed that came from her nightclothes. 'I've had another idea. That letter you've had from Gladys asking you to go home to see your mother—'

'I can't see her like this!' She stepped away and drew her hands down her distended body.

'Actually, you can.'

She frowned. She picked up her mug and hastily swallowed the tea.

'How?'

'If people are going to think I'm the father, let them. I'm not suggesting you tell lies.' He shook his head. 'But we can go down to Gosport together. We can see your mum, find out what's upsetting Gladys.' He stared at her and said quickly, 'You've been worrying because no one down there knows about the baby and it being that Blackie fellow's kiddie, well,' he let out a big sigh and the words tumbled quickly from him, 'how would your mum feel knowing *we* were living together and thinking the child belonged to *me*?'

Lizzie stroked her belly.

He could see her thinking over his words.

'You'd do that for me?'

'Why not?' He shrugged. He saw the tears flood to her eyes, then she shook her head and let out the breath she'd been holding.

'You don't know what my mum and Gladys are like. The first thing they're going to ask, when the shock of looking at me wears off, is, "When are you going to make an honest woman of her?"'

His head began to swim. 'Of course, it's a bit like putting the cart before the horse, isn't it?'

Lizzie put her fingers beneath his chin and tipped his head up towards her. 'So far this is all a wonderful idea. I need to find out what's going on with my mum and Gladys.'

He smiled at her.

Even the touch of her fingers made him tingle. 'One step at a time, then. I'll go off and get a car, you put your stuff together. We'll sort out the prefab,' he laughed, 'and see which neighbour is first to come and borrow something.' Lizzie was laughing too now and nodding her head in agreement. 'Tomorrow, if you're not too tired, we'll go down to Gosport and see your mum.'

Lizzie looked happier than he'd seen her in ages. He got up from the kitchen chair.

'I'll be back early this evening.' He needed some money, so had to go to the post office to take out enough to tide them over the next few days and the trip to Gosport. Pete's brother had an Austin that Joel had driven before. He'd be glad of a couple of quid for a loan of it for a few days, but he was worried about using Pete's brother's petrol ration.

She nodded her head vigorously. 'But what do we tell my mum?'

'I'll think of something,' he said. 'But I'm not going to tell your mother an out and out lie unless it's absolutely necessary. Promise me you'll never tell me lies?'

'I promise,' she said. He had no reason, he thought, to disbelieve her. But he always remembered that old saying, 'You can believe a thief but you can't believe a liar.' He knew he would always tell Lizzie the truth. But he needed to put her mother's mind at rest as to why the baby was being born out of wedlock. How the hell was he going to do that without lying?

Chapter Eleven

Lizzie packed the last of her clothes in the brown cardboard suitcase. It didn't have a key to lock it but that didn't matter, it was just a vessel to hold her clothes until she arrived at the prefab. She lugged it down the stairs and set it beside the back door. Just at that moment, Elsie came from the kitchen.

She gave Lizzie an envelope. 'Call this extra wages,' she said, pressing it into Lizzie's hand. 'I know I gave you a cuddle earlier, but I just want to say goodbye, and you know where I am if you need me. I can't stop, we're busy in the bar.' She winked at her. Without Lizzie having time to answer, the door closed behind her, just as a sharp knock sounded on the outer door.

'All ready?' Joel's eyes were shining.

She returned Joel's smile just before he caught sight of her case and swung it up. 'Cor, what you got in here, the kitchen sink?'

'It's my stuff and baby clothes,' she said worriedly. 'Is it too much?'

He laughed. 'I'm only teasing you.' Lizzie felt happier. She took the door key to the back door of the pub from her purse and put it on the table with a note she quickly scribbled, thanking Elsie for the unexpected money and Ted for his kindness. It was a sad thing to be leaving the bustling pub, but she was looking forward to the sparkling modern prefab.

And then Joel was pushing her suitcase onto the back seat of the Austin Seven.

'Whose car is this?'

Joel opened the front passenger door. 'Belongs to a mate of mine's brother from work,' he said. 'He's charged me for petrol, which God knows how he's got hold of. There should be enough to get us down to Gosport tomorrow. There's a couple of full petrol cans in the back as well.'

Lizzie sat on the leather seat and Joel shut the door. 'I can give you some money towards—'

She got no further for Joel glared at her and said, 'If I need money from you, which I certainly don't, I'll ask!'

Lizzie decided to shut up and let him drive. She looked back at the pub as they drove off. She was sad to leave, but excited about the start of her new life. And even more excited about seeing her mother tomorrow. She sat close to Joel, thinking what a good man he was.

As they drove near The Cobb, the town's harbour wall that provided a breakwater to protect the town from storms, Lizzie strained her neck to look along the beach to the sea. The tide was far out. It was calm and clear today, and she wondered how many people were searching for fossils.

'Have you ever hunted for fossils on the foreshore?' As though reading her mind, Joel asked the question.

'No,' Lizzie replied. 'But I do know loads of reptile remains have been found. People come from far and near to hunt.' She looked at Joel. 'It's not something I'm interested in, really. To tell the truth I've hardly been near the beach since I arrived here, I've been too busy working.'

'Didn't you take time off?'

'Yes, but after being on my feet all the time in a smoky bar all I ever wanted to do on a day off was read and sleep.'

'I know exactly what you mean,' Joel said, 'but The Cobb hosts celebrations all the time, like bonfire night with its torchlight procession and huge bonfire on the beach. Though I believe the war and blackout halted that; at least, I didn't hear anything about last November's do.'

'The war's put paid to a lot of things,' Lizzie said. 'I just wish it would soon end.'

Deep in thought about the beauty of Lyme Regis and how different it was to Gosport, she wondered how Joel would feel about the place where she was born and had grown up.

'We're nearly there,' Joel said, as the prefabricated houses came into view.

'We've got prefabs in Gosport now as well,' Lizzie said. 'Me mum wrote and told me some had been built at Clayhall and some at Elson.' She paused. 'It's not quiet, like here, Joel. We get a lot of bombing.'

He turned and smiled at her. 'It'll be fine,' he said. Lizzie's heart soared as Joel parked in a lay-by right next to her new home.

'I'm excited,' she said, as he opened the car's door for her and helped her out. She saw the front garden was laid to lawn, with flower borders.

At the front door he put down her case and said, 'I think we should do this in style and give the neighbours something to talk about.' He turned the key and as the door swung open he lifted her in his arms and swept through into the little house.

Lizzie was giggling. 'Put me down,' she squealed. Then,

'You only carry a woman over the threshold when you're married! You daft thing!'

Joel smiled before he set her down and went back outside for her case. He sent Lizzie into both the bedrooms to choose which one she wanted. He'd already explained that he'd been sleeping at the back, but if she preferred him to move, he would. Both rooms had double beds.

'The front one,' she exclaimed. That was the bedroom where he had set up a cot, so he moved her case in and left her to it while he went and made tea. He could hear her rattling cupboards and wardrobe doors. He decided it was comforting to have someone else in the place.

Joel had fallen head over heels in love with her.

He also knew he wouldn't do a thing about it, certainly not before the birth of her child.

Her baby was due within the next few weeks and Lizzie needed calm surroundings, good food and peace of mind. He intended to make sure she had all three. That included him taking a back seat in whatever affections she had for him, if any.

Just as he was putting the teacups on the tray, Lizzie found her way to the kitchen. Her smile went from ear to ear as she came towards him and gave him a brief hug. 'Thank you for the bed for the baby.'

'I picked it up from Marie's sister. Put a bit of white paint on it,' he said. He was glad she liked it. He'd wondered if she would mind it being second-hand. 'It's too big for a newborn, but Marie suggested putting the little one in a large drawer inside the cot, which'll help the kiddie get used to sleeping in the bigger space when the time comes.'

'That's a good idea,' Lizzie said. 'Now, how much do I owe you for it?'

He frowned at her. 'I told you I'd ask for money if I needed it. That's a gift.' She turned away from him. He could feel a sudden chill in the air. 'Lizzie.' She swung round to face him again. 'You needn't think I'm giving you stuff that you have to pay for in any way. You know what I mean, don't you?'

She nodded. He pushed a cup of tea towards her. The kitchen felt warm and comfortable and the smell of toast still hung in the air from breakfast that morning. 'This is your home now,' he said. 'You aren't fit to work and my wages will easily keep us both. There are times when I have to work nights, but I'll try to make sure my boss gives me as many day shifts as possible, so I can be with you when the baby decides to come. But we'll get you sorted with the midwife and a neighbour to keep an eye on you. All right?'

Lizzie nodded. Joel didn't want her to feel he was telling her what to do, but he hated the thought of her going into labour alone. He noticed the ring on the third finger of her left hand was cutting into her flesh where her hands were swollen. She was still smiling at him as she dug in her pocket and then handed him her ration book.

'You'd better hang on to this. Keep it with yours.'

'All right, I'll do the shopping. I don't want you carrying heavy bags in your condition,' Joel said. 'I'll put the ration books on the mantelpiece. And you should take that ring off before it does you some damage,' he said.

She began to twist the band. 'I might need some soap to ease it off. I'll feel funny without it, like announcing to everyone that I'm not married.'

He nodded. 'Let people think what they like. But if it worries you that much, after the baby's born we'll get another ring. One that doesn't cut into your finger or make it discoloured.' He grinned at her then remembered he had something to tell her. 'At the home Marie sometimes cooks food that for some reason or other gets left. So don't be surprised if I bring home a few treats now and then. Some of the old dears won't eat this and that. They get fussy and forget that Marie has a tough time trying for a balanced diet for them while there's shortages in the shops.' He often wondered how Marie came up with all the delicacies she managed to cook.

Lizzie looked confused.

'It's proper leftovers, not food off plates,' he hastened to explain. She looked relieved.

Joel thought about the vegetables that were freshly picked every day. The garden was a godsend, especially with the fruit that grew on trees and bushes

Thinking about the fruit reminded Joel of Fred and his love of apple crumble. His heart grew heavy. Why did people have to grow old and die? So far he'd kept his feelings about Fred to himself. Lizzie had enough on her plate without him dragging her down with his unhappiness over a man she never knew.

Lizzie was staring out of the window. 'Would you mind if I helped you in this garden?'

He'd made a lawn each side of the path that led to the front door and the flowers were still in bloom. He liked to keep the garden neat. Marigolds, Livingstone daisies and marguerites were in flower, amidst a few rose bushes.

'Not at all,' he said. He was happy they had something in common. 'I started digging over the back to plant vegetables, but because I work odd hours there never seems to be much time . . .'

'The exercise will do me good.' She turned and smiled at him. 'Do you have any food?'

He opened a long cupboard and showed her the few tins he had stored there. Lizzie leaned in and searched, taking out a tin of corned beef. 'I could rustle up corned beef hash,' she said. She put the tin on the table top along with a tin of peas.

Joel liked the idea of that. 'I'll peel the potatoes,' he said. 'Then, if you want, I'll help you finish sorting out your bedroom. After we've eaten we could go to the pictures. Unless you're too tired . . .'

She fixed her brown eyes on him. 'Actually, I'm really whacked out, what with worrying and leaving the pub. If we have to get up early tomorrow, I'd much rather go to bed.'

'Oh, Lizzie, I'm sorry. Let's get an early night.' He looked at the teapot and nodded towards it, as though enquiring whether she wanted any more tea. She shook her head and said, 'Maybe later after we've eaten. I'll sort out my suitcase, OK?'

She left him and returned to the bedroom. He could have kicked himself for forgetting she needed as much sleep as she could get in her condition.

He stood at the sink peeling the potatoes. Thin peelings fell into the bowl. Once upon a time people wasted food, now there wasn't enough to go round. It was nice listening to the sounds of Lizzie in the prefab. He was pouring water into the saucepan when he heard her call.

Joel wiped his hands on the kitchen towel and went through the living room into her bedroom. She looked like a waif sitting on the mattress amidst her clothes. She got up.

'Could you help me move the wardrobe? I'd prefer it opposite the window so the mirror on the door gets the light.' It took him but a few minutes to walk the wardrobe across the rose-patterned lino. He stood waiting for her next request. The double bed with the brass bedstead was moved against the wall. He smiled. Their beds were separated only by the thin dividing wall.

'If you need me, bang on the wall,' he said. Lizzie put her hands over her taut belly. 'I hope it's not too soon,' she said. 'Did you think I'd choose this room?'

He laughed and nodded. 'This used to be my mate and his wife's room. The kids had my room and I slept on the sofa in the living room.'

'Was it comfortable?'

'I've slept worse,' he said. 'And luckily, due to my sub-standard hearing the children never kept me awake. I'll get fresh bedding.' He went into his room, previously tidied, and took down a pair of clean sheets, blankets, two pillows and a rose-covered quilt from the built-in cupboards.

'These are clean,' he said, going back into Lizzie's room. 'Been put away.' He sniffed them. They smelled of a lavender bag. 'We'll need to get some more sheets, naturally the best stuff was taken by my mate.' He saw she was watching him with a smile on her face.

'Can you turn the mattress?'

He put the bedding on a chair and quickly flipped the mattress over, standing back to admire his handiwork.

'Mr Atlas!'

He picked up a pillow and threw it at her. 'Work for your living and help me make up your bed.' He saw the suitcase was on the floor, open, with camiknickers and camisole tops spilling from it, amidst knitted baby clothes. 'But I'm not putting that stuff away.'

Again she laughed. When she laughed it made him feel happy.

They made the bed together and when it was done, she said, 'It looks so inviting.'

Joel thought about lying next to her on the rose-patterned quilt, then was disgusted with himself for his thoughts. 'I'm going to put the dinner on,' he said gruffly. 'And no, I can manage. I'll call you when it's ready. The bathroom is just outside this room and the lavatory is next to it.'

He left her without looking at her. Already the front bedroom looked lived in.

Back in the kitchen he clattered about preparing the meal and all the time thinking how he could explain that Lizzie was pregnant with his child, yet despite being single he wasn't able to marry her. He hated having to lie, but the main thing was that her mother should be able to hold her head high and ignore the gossips that could ruin people's lives. Lizzie's reputation had, somehow, to appear unsullied. Slowly, his thoughts began to form a plan.

Half an hour later, table laid, the meal ready, he went back to get her.

She was fast asleep on top of the bed, fully clothed. His heart went out to her as he stood watching her from the doorway. One arm lay protectively across her huge belly. A small dribble had slid from the corner of her mouth to the white pillowcase. He smiled at her vulnerability and gently closed her bedroom door.

Chapter Twelve

Gladys rushed to the front door, her heart thumping inside her breast. The bombs terrified her, but the V1 rockets were worse. When the engine cut out you knew the rocket was going to drop. When would it all end? she wondered. Queen's Road had taken a bad bombing recently and the yawning gaps between the houses looked like teeth that had been pulled.

'Hang on! I'm coming!' Surely they'd heard the siren cutting through the night? Who would be out in this?

Her feet were killing her after standing all day at Priddy's.

'I can't take much more of this,' she mumbled to herself, as a loud thwump sounded, indicating that a bomb had landed close by. The house seemed to rock on its foundations. A picture fell off the wall in the hallway and she heard the glass shatter. More frantic knocking came, along with a man's voice shouting out, 'Gladys! Are you in there?' She didn't recognize the voice, but a flash lit up the glass fanlight above the door just as she opened it.

'Lizzie!' Gladys cried out. 'You can't go wandering around Gosport when a rocket attack's going on!' She looked at the tall man with his arm around Lizzie's shoulder. 'Come on in.' The stench of cordite followed them.

She bundled them along the hall, shouting, 'Look where you're treading, a picture fell off the wall, don't want no cut feet.' Then through to the kitchen, begging them to be careful as she'd turned off the utilities and it was dark in the small house.

'Perhaps this is a one-off, something to do with our boys testing stuff and nothing to do with Hitler?' said the man.

'If that's the case, then why did the bleedin' siren go off? Where you been? Living in the country?'

'Sort of,' said Lizzie, taking off her coat.

'Blimey, girl, you been eating a lot of bread pudding!' Lizzie didn't laugh and Gladys looked at the tall young man. 'S'pose that's your fault?' Neither of them answered her, so Gladys threw her arms around Lizzie. 'You don't know how glad I am to see you.'

The droning noise made Gladys hold her breath. The

canary in its cage on the sideboard jumped, screeching, hopping from its bell to its perch.

'What's that?' Lizzie looked terrified.

'Me canary! Surely you ain't forgotten the little bugger!'

'No, that droning noise.' Lizzie was clutching Joel as the V1 rocket zoomed overhead. 'We heard that funny noise earlier.'

'Hitler's latest offerings.' Gladys helped the scared woman into the Morrison shelter. 'Get down in there.' She was petrified the engine of the doodlebug would cut out.

"I'll be all right out here—'

'No, you won't, man,' yelled Gladys. 'Squeeze up in there!'

She didn't get inside the metal contraption until the other two looked comfortable enough, then got on all fours and squeezed herself inside along with them.

'Them bloody pilotless rockets are coming over the south in their hundreds,' Gladys moaned. She let out a huge sigh then stared at Lizzie. 'You going to introduce me?' she asked, looking at Joel.

'Meet Joel Carey. We . . .' Lizzie paused. Gladys could see the girl was shy about speaking of her relationship with the young man.

'Live together,' said Joel. He leaned across and took

one of Lizzie's hands in his. 'I've got one of the new prefabs.'

Gladys nodded. It was obvious they were a couple. Em knew nothing of Lizzie's pregnancy, so it wasn't up to Gladys to ask questions, even if she was dying to know. Lizzie would tell her mother and if Em wanted, she'd confide in Gladys.

The young man looked kind and she could see he cared about Lizzie. That's what mattered, she thought. She gave a quick glance at Lizzie's hand. No ring.

'Joel's a carer, looking after elderly people.'

'In them new-fangled homes?'

'That's right,' said Joel.

Gladys sniffed. 'You're not in the forces, then?'

'Royal Army Medical Corps, until they got my hearing. I was invalided out,' Joel said. Gladys was mistrustful of any man of fighting age who wasn't in the forces.

She gave Joel a satisfied nod then said, 'Oh, I nearly forgot, Joel, behind you there's a flask of tea. We'll have to share the flask top. I'm not getting out of here until the all-clear goes.' She looked at Lizzie. 'You look ready to drop, girl. When's it due?'

'A few weeks yet,' Lizzie said.

'If I'm not mistaken you won't go that far,' Gladys said. She did the sums in her head. Lizzie must have met this young man almost immediately after she'd left Gosport. Some modern men wore wedding rings, but Joel's hands were ringless too, so Lizzie definitely wasn't wed to him. If this baby was his, why weren't these two married? No doubt she'd discover the reason soon enough. Em would certainly want to know the answer to that.

Overhead, another V1 screamed. Gladys grabbed hold of Joel. God, she hated the bloody things.

Lizzie was pouring out the steaming tea, 'Careful,' she cried, 'this is hot.' She passed the first cup to Gladys, who despite the steam coming from it, drank it back quickly.

As she passed the cup back to Lizzie she said, 'How long can you stay?' She was relieved the doodlebug seemed to have fallen further away. But now it was the turn of the planes, roaring above them like screaming banshees, the falling bombs shaking the earth as they hit and flattened all in their path. Across the kitchen the blackout curtains were pulled tight across the window, but through the cloth colours flashed from the burning fires and the searchlights as they hunted down the enemy.

'Joel has almost a week off,' Lizzie said.

'You're welcome to stay as long as you like,' Gladys said. 'I got a double bed going spare in the back bedroom. I don't see the point of making you,' she poked

Joel who almost lost his grip on the mug of tea, 'sleep on two armchairs pushed together down here.'

She saw the look that passed between them. Looking again at Lizzie's big belly Gladys thought she'd made the right decision. Many would have said it wasn't the done thing to let a couple sleep together if they weren't married, but the damage had already been done, hadn't it. And by the look of Lizzie, she needed someone with her all hours of the day and night in case that baby decided to make an appearance. Lizzie was in no fit state to go straight to her own mother and face the interrogation about the baby and Joel.

Lizzie said, 'Thanks for the offer of the bed. You need to tell me what's going on with Mum and why you're so worried about her.'

Despite the noise of the fighter planes overhead, the smell of burning seeping through the house, the dark of the small shelter, and the fear she felt, Gladys told them all she knew about Lily.

'Leave her asleep,' said Joel. He looked fondly at Lizzie sleeping, dead to the world, a quilt wrapped around her.

'Even the all-clear hasn't woken her,' said Gladys, standing up and stretching her arms. Joel watched as she then went down the hallway and switched the electric light on. 'I'd better sweep up that glass.' He heard her picking up the larger pieces. She came into the kitchen and put a picture of poppies in a cornfield on the table. 'I liked that picture,' she said, going into the scullery. He heard the back door open and the dustbin receive the glass. 'If you want to make a pot of tea, I'll go upstairs and get the back bedroom ready,' Gladys called. He stared at the small blonde woman as she came back in and bustled about with a dustpan and brush in her hands. 'C'mon, make yourself at home. If you're going to be staying here for a few days I'm not waiting on you hand and foot.'

He gave her a grin. He liked her plain-spoken ways.

Gladys stomped off upstairs and he made sure there was water enough in the kettle, then lit the gas beneath it. He looked around at the stone sink, the copper in the corner and the line strung across the small, whitewashed room with washing drying. It was very clean and smelled of bleach. The kitchen was comfortable enough. Gladys wasn't house-proud but she seemed proud of her home. He discovered where she kept the mugs and cups and saucers and began looking for the tea caddy. He was rinsing the teapot when Gladys returned.

'I reckon we've got to get hold of those papers that Lily says prove she's Em's sister.' Gladys stared at him as she spoke.

'Do you really think Em's so lonely she's clutching at straws?' He poured boiling water into the teapot.

'I do.' Gladys sighed. 'I've known her all my life and there's never been no mention of no sister.'

'Does Em have money?' He was trying to think of a reason why anyone would turn up pretending to be someone else. Perhaps the woman wanted Em's savings? He took the tray into the kitchen and put it on the table.

'She's got a bit put by, insurance payout mostly. And she deserves every penny! She's had a rotten life.'

Gladys's voice had risen. Joel checked that Lizzie hadn't woken. Her eyes flickered open. As if on cue, the canary made a squawking noise.

'Likes to be the centre of attention, does that bird,' said Lizzie.

'I'm sorry, love. We never meant to wake you. How d'you feel?'

Joel thought Lizzie looked wonderful, her eyes all sleepy and her long hair tousled. He thought about the drive down. She couldn't have been very comfortable scrunched up in the front passenger seat but she hadn't moaned, not once. They'd turned off the main road a couple of times to get a cup of tea and something to eat, but the day had been warm and the inside of the car stifling, even with the windows wound down as far as they would go.

'I'm fine,' Lizzie said. 'Could do with a cuppa.'

'There's another thing,' Gladys said. 'Wouldn't you think a long-lost sister would want to see her mother's grave?' She poured out the tea and left a cup on the table for Lizzie, who had crawled out from the shelter and was now on her way down to the bottom of the garden to the lavatory.

'Too right,' said Joel. He tried to imagine how he would feel if he hadn't known his family. Not that his father had cared much about him, but at least he knew where he'd come from. Gladys was right. He'd be begging to see other members of his new-found family, and yes, certainly he'd want to take flowers to the cemetery. 'So you're saying she's only interested in Em?'

Gladys nodded, her bleached blonde curls bounced on her forehead.

'That's very strange,' he said, his forehead creased into furrows. He heard the back door sneck lift and Lizzie came back inside.

'The sky is alight with burning fires.' She shivered. 'It might have been a warm day but there's a nip in the air now,' she said. 'The back of this house seems intact, but there's a few windows out further down.' She looked at Joel. 'The war's at its worst down here, isn't it? All along the south coast there's stuff Hitler wants rid of, like the dockyard, the submarine base, the shipyard, the air force base at Lee-on-the-Solent, and if the Germans knew about the munitions yard, that would be high on the list for their bombers to have a go at too. In all the time I've been up in Lyme Regis I'm sure we've not had bombing like this.'

'Well, we've survived another night,' said Gladys. She was thoughtful. 'I only hope my Siddy's house is still standing.'

Lizzie said, 'You still stringing your landlord along? Why don't you marry the bloke and put him out of his misery?'

Gladys grinned. 'I'm not sure I want to be tied down. Not like you.' She pointed at Lizzie's bump. 'Perhaps you'll tell me why you ain't tying the knot?'

'And perhaps I won't,' said Lizzie. She changed the subject by saying, 'I'll try not to disturb you, but I'll be needing the lavatory in the night. This little blighter seems to be lying on my bladder.'

'I'm not having you traipsing down the bottom of the garden in the pitch black in your condition. You can take a jerry up and put it under the bed.'

Joel could see Lizzie was embarrassed, so he winked

at her. A blush worked its way over her face and neck.

Gladys went into the scullery. 'I've got some stew, not a lot of meat in it, but it's tasty enough, made today. I'll heat it up. You two must be starving after your trip down.' She paused. 'I hope that car's all right outside in the street. The kids'll be climbing all over it tomorrow. We don't get many with cars in Alma Street.' Her voice rang through into the kitchen. Joel smiled at Lizzie.

'She a right character,' he said. 'Salt of the earth.'

'See what I mean? She loves my mum, doesn't want anyone to hurt her. How d'you feel about this woman who reckons she's my aunt?'

He gave a long sigh and stretched out his legs. The armchair gave a creak at his movements. 'I think we'd better see your mum tomorrow night. She'll be at work during the day but we can always go up there just before she's due home. If Lily's there it will be a good time to meet her on her own.'

'I think that's a good idea. I've got my key, so we can go straight in. Though I expect the key is still on a string through the letterbox.'

He nodded. At least that would prove to Lily that Em's daughter still had a place in her life and her home. A sigh escaped him. 'We need to get hold of those papers belonging to Lily.'

He could hear the rattle of spoons and the smell of stew drifted in from the scullery. He hadn't realized he was so hungry, and Lizzie must be starving with two to feed. He yawned. That set Lizzie off. He realized that although she'd had naps during the day and in the shelter she must be more than ready for bed.

'I'll sleep on the floor,' he whispered low, so Gladys wouldn't hear. He raised his eyes towards the bedroom above.

Lizzie didn't answer. He could see she was mulling things over in her mind.

Gladys bustled in with two dishes full of fragrant food. 'Get up to the table,' she insisted.

Joel looked around for the cutlery.

'In the drawer of the sideboard.' Gladys put the plates down. 'I've got a nice bit of fresh bread to mop it up with.'

It wasn't long before the three of them were hungrily eating. Gladys had switched on the wireless and Joel thought how homely it all was with Dinah Shore singing 'You'd Be So Nice To Come Home To' in her velvety voice.

Lizzie scraped the last of her stew. 'You've been a real friend to Mum for taking us in like this and caring about her,' she said.

Gladys grinned and Joel saw the traces of red lipstick in the creases about her mouth. For a middle-aged woman she was still handsome, with her blonde curls and trim body. She made Joel feel comfortable and able to speak his mind even though they'd met just a few hours ago.

'You, young lady, need to get to bed. Joel can help me clear the table.' She looked at him as Lizzie rose unsteadily from her kitchen chair and pushed back her long hair that had fallen forward over her face. 'There's fresh cold water in the washstand upstairs, Joel can take up the kettle if you want it warming up. There's a clean towel on the rail.'

Gladys piled the dishes inside one another. Joel took them and moved outside to the scullery, rinsing them beneath the tap and leaving them on the wooden draining board. He heard Lizzie's footsteps on the stairs. Gladys came in and took the soiled saucepan off the stove and filled it with water at the sink. 'Leave the washing up,' she said. 'There's not much. I'll sort it in the morning. Why don't you take a look to see if your car's still there and in one piece, then follow Lizzie up? Time enough tomorrow for you to tell me how you two met and when you're thinking about tying the knot!'

His heart banged inside his chest. He didn't answer. How he was going to hate spinning her some sort of lie. It wasn't in his nature to tell lies. Joel bent down and kissed Gladys on the side of her face. A warm feeling stole over him as he saw her blush.

'Goodnight, Glad,' he said.

'Sleep tight,' she said. 'Mind the bedbugs don't bite!'

He smiled at her and went along the passage. A blast of cold air enveloped him as he opened the front door and cast an eye over the car, which was dusty but otherwise safe. He looked down the street and saw a pile of rubble from a fallen chimney stack. A lone ARP man was shining his torch over the bricks. He closed the door again and went back along the hallway and up the wooden stairs to the lighted bedroom.

Lizzie was at the washstand, drying her face and arms with the towel. As he entered, she held the towel in front of her.

'Want me to come back when you've finished?' She nodded nervously.

He went back down the stairs just as Gladys was turning off the light.

'Sorry,' he said. 'Need the lavatory.'

'There's paper on a nail,' she said.

He grinned. 'We have San Izal at the home where I work.'

'Well, I ain't that posh. It's the *Daily Mirror* cut up, on a string! And you lock up after you when you come back.'

He laughed as he unlocked the back door and went down the long path to the lavatory at the bottom of the garden.

Afterwards, he stood looking at the stars. The air smelled of cordite. He wondered if they'd get another bashing tomorrow. He saw a shadow pass by the curtain in the back window and decided that Lizzie was now in bed. All the houses were quiet. Orange colours lit up the sky where the bombs had sought and found their targets. The house secured, he noted the light beneath the door in Gladys's room and went in to join Lizzie. She was in bed, the covers pulled to her neck.

He gave a small smile and took off his shirt. He never wore a vest and was a little shy in front of the woman he cared so much for. Then he poured more of the cold water into the washstand bowl and sluiced himself, drying his upper body with the same towel she had left hanging on the side of the washstand. Joel had already noted that Lizzie had opened his holdall and set out his striped pyjamas on the bottom of the bed.

He looked at her watching him, but she turned away. Neither of them spoke. He knew Gladys would have her ear practically glued against the wall. The air felt taut. Joel could hardly breathe. He turned his back to her, even though she was no longer facing him, and put on his pyjamas.

Joel stood looking at her for a few seconds, then pulled off the quilt and wrapped it around himself. He lay down on the floor by the side of the bed. He realized he'd forgotten to take the pillow. He struggled up to find Lizzie leaning over him.

'What are you doing?' she whispered, looking cross. 'Gladys will go daft! You'll spoil everything.' She threw open the sheets. 'Bloody get in!'

He stood up. 'No woman has ever shouted at me to get into her bed,' he said quietly.

'She can hear a pin drop!' Lizzie said. She tossed back her hair. She smelled of the rose-scented soap Gladys had left on the washstand.

He threw the quilt back over the bed and knocked Lizzie's toothbrush from the bedside table. She raised her eyes heavenwards. He picked it up, catching the smell of peppermint and put it on the washstand, realizing he hadn't brushed his own teeth. His nervousness had got the better of him.

But why? He'd been in enough women's beds before, but not one had him acting like a young lad courting!

He climbed into the sheets. Lizzie bent over him, her hair falling like a scented curtain over his face. She kissed him gently on the lips, pulled away and said, 'And that's as good as it gets!' Then she hauled a pillow free and set it between them. 'Just in case!'

Joel lay there, hardly daring to breathe. She was on her back, her arms out of the covers. Presently he was able to hear Lizzie's deep breathing that told him she was asleep. His hand moved across the quilt until he found her fingers.

Holding her hand, he, too, slept.

Chapter Thirteen

'Mrs Somerton, let me help you back into bed.' Pete caught her hand, which was flailing wildly, and held it still. He'd been taught how to care for patients who were in danger of hurting themselves and as Liliah Somerton was frail, he was scared he might break her fragile bones. She gave up the struggle and melted against him. He was amazed that one weak woman could cause so much havoc.

'Who are you?' Even her voice was frail.

He let her bony body use his strength to lead her towards her bed while he surveyed the mess she'd made of her room. Drawers had been turned out, the cushions from the armchair were lying on the floor and even the rug in the centre of the room had been pulled up and now lay against the bed. On the bed was an empty chocolate box with a picture of kittens playing with a ball of red wool. Photographs were scattered over the yellow counterpane. Most were of a young woman – her, he supposed – and a young man, probably the man she had married. The man had his arms about her and stared at her proprietorially.

'You know who I am, I'm Pete and I got you ready this morning to go out into the garden.' He saw her eyes drift towards the window. She looked at him but the look seemed to travel right through him.

'Where's Joel?'

Pete was astounded. She'd remembered Joel's name and he'd been away now for a few days. Usually Mrs Somerton forgot who had washed her that morning.

'Look in that top drawer, where my hankies are. I think Joel put my papers in there.'

She sat down on the edge of the bed. Pete sat alongside her. She'd uttered two sentences that made perfect sense. But there was a space where the small drawer had been, and it now lay on the carpet, empty.

'It's in the Bible.' She was still looking at him. I want my papers,' she said. 'I don't know who I am any more.' She began to cry.

Pete got up, he felt like crying himself. He moved her bodily back into the bed, tucking the coverlet over her thin limbs.

He saw her eyes move towards the photographs, then she looked back at him.

She asked him, 'Are you my husband?'

Marlene took off the boots provided by Priddy's and flexed her aching feet. It was quieter in the changing room, yet the machinery still rumbled in the workshops. She was one of the last to leave the late shift that ended at eleven o'clock at night. She'd worked a twelve-hour day and was tired. She put her boots in her locker and took out her shoes and her outer wear, then undressed and folded her overalls neatly.

Patsy came and gave her the once-over. The women were searched upon entry and exit. 'You're late tonight.'

'Got nothing to hurry home for,' Marlene said. She undid the scarf turban, threw it into the locker and shook out her long hair. 'That feels better,' she said, having a scratch at her head. She stared at her hair in the mirror. Just as blonde hair turned orange with the chemicals, red-haired women often found their hair sported a green tinge.

'How's your mum?' Patsy knew Marlene lived alone now and that her mother and her little girl were living down the coast.

'She's fine.' Marlene bit back a tear. She didn't want

Patsy to see she was lonely. She tied her gabardine rain-coat around herself – there'd been a shower as she'd left home this morning. Her badge had come undone and Marlene clipped it closed. All workers at Royal Ordnance Factories were handed a small badge to wear on their coats. The words 'ROF, Front Line Duty' meant when they were not at work the wearers should be allowed preferential treatment. Yet, as the factories didn't exist officially, not many people knew about the badges or what they meant. Only a few workers were ever given the special treatment they deserved. After making sure her badge was secured, Marlene said goodnight to Patsy and went out into the darkened yard.

She yawned. She was tired but the need for money was important. That bastard Samuel Golden had well and truly stripped her of all she possessed. No longer did she own her house, no longer had she her own business selling gold in the markets. She'd had to sell the small van she'd bought and all her market gear. If it wasn't for the extra shifts at the bomb factory she wouldn't be able to send her mother money to keep herself and Jeannie. But most of all she was tired and lonely. She couldn't even go down the Fox with the girls for a drink and a laugh when they invited her. There was certainly no money for that. And oh, how she hated working with friends that she owed money to. And as for meeting another feller, she didn't want another man as long as she lived!

Bert, the old chap at the gate, called out goodnight to her. He was a nice man, she thought, as she hurried along the dark expanse of Weevil Lane. She almost wished she'd left with the other girls so at least she wouldn't be walking in the moonlight alone. When clouds obscured the moon, it was as dark as the ace of spades.

The noise made her pause. She could hear the muffled sounds of a woman's voice and a man exerting himself. She paused and slowly parted the brambles where the sounds seemed to be coming from. She knew it was none of her business, whatever was going on in the under-growth, but if someone needed help and she didn't intervene she'd never forgive herself.

The man had his back to her. He was almost blotting out the shape of the small form against the tree. The woman was groaning. He was strangling her! Even in the darkness, she could see his hands at the girl's throat.

'Get off!' she cried. The thick piece of branch she'd spotted and picked up she now wielded as a weapon, beating the man about the back and head.

'What the fuck!' He pulled away from the girl and Marlene could see his trousers fall to his ankles, showing his pale spindly legs. The girl dropped her clothes, too late to hide the fact she wore no knickers. The elderly man, on his knees now in the undergrowth, was rubbing at the back of his head and whimpering.

'Bitch!' he cried. 'Is this some kind of game?'

She stared at the girl who glared defiantly at her.

'Ruby!' Marlene had no idea that this sweet-faced girl working on the line with her had a boyfriend. Then she guessed the man couldn't possibly be her boyfriend, for he was so much older than Ruby. It wasn't hard for Marlene to work out the man and Ruby were having casual sex, or would have done if she hadn't intervened.

'He ain't going to pay me now,' the girl wailed, bending down and trying to see to the man.

'Get the fuck away from me,' he shouted, and holding on to the tree managed to rise. He looked at Marlene. 'You're mad!' he said, before staggering away clutching his trousers with one hand and holding his head with the other.

Marlene let the branch fall to the grass. 'I'm sorry, Ruby. I thought he was hurting you.'

Ruby began straightening her clothes. 'I think you just lost me one of my regulars.'

It took a while for Marlene to realize what the girl meant.

'Regular? You're doing this for money?'

'Well, I ain't giving it away.' The girl laughed and then couldn't stop and a fit of the giggles took over. Marlene watched helplessly until eventually Ruby said, brushing the tears of laughter from her eyes, 'I don't know what the hell he's going to tell his missus! But Jesus, you don't half pack a mighty wallop.'

Marlene had no idea what to say to the girl. Obviously the man was one of the workers from Priddy's. Ruby's words broke into her thoughts.

'Do you want a job?'

Marlene looked at her. Whatever was the girl on about? 'What job?'

'Packing that punch! Giving that bloke a hefty pop made me realize you'd be a good person to have around if any trouble started—'

Marlene grabbed at her arm. 'Hang on, I'm no tart!'

Ruby started laughing again. 'You don't have to sleep with the punters, only take their money and make sure they ain't going to get lairy with us.'

Marlene couldn't believe the girl's words. 'Do you mean you want me to stand around while you does the business, then take their money? I'm not standing outside in all weathers while you drop your knickers . . .' She thought for a moment. 'And who's "us"?'

'Carla. She's my friend; a bit older than me. We got

a flat down the town opposite the ferry. But the bloke that runs us needs another woman, one with her head screwed on right to take care of the money side of the business, pay the bills and generally take care of us.' She paused. 'A sort of maid.' She stared Marlene up and down. 'You could be an asset.'

'I'm not getting involved in prostitution.' The thought horrified her. Whatever would her mother think?

'You won't get copped.' Ruby ran a hand through her hair. 'We got a judge, two high-up coppers . . .' She paused. 'They certainly wouldn't want it known they was coming round to see us. And I know you had a market stall before you worked at Priddy's, so you'd be right handy at the money side of it. And now I know you're strong enough!' She smiled at Marlene. 'The pay would be much more than you're getting at Priddy's.'

Marlene's ears pricked up at the mention of money. 'How much?'

'How long is a piece of string? The bloke needs us to have a part-time job, so no one can say we're taking money for services rendered. So, while you're doing shifts for the war effort all your wages and income tax is legal. But the money we make on the side from men can't be traced, see? It's really good money – we charge high prices. You won't be sorry, I can promise you that.'

By now the two of them were walking down Mumby Road towards the ferry.

Marlene liked the way Ruby chattered on and liked even more the idea that she might be able to pay off some of the debts she owed. How lovely it would be to have her mother and baby Jeannie back in Gosport so she could see more of them. It was good they were away from the direct bombing, but some families had boarded out their kiddies just beyond Wickham, at Shedfield, and that was only a bus ride away. Oh, she did miss Jeannie and her mum.

She could hear big band music coming from the Fox. Through the open doorway American sailors were smooching with a couple of girls Marlene had seen around the factory. One of them waved at Ruby, who waved back.

'Let's go in and have a drink, and I'll tell you all about this job,' Ruby said.

'Here, you're not going to pick up any blokes while I'm with you, are you?' Marlene really didn't want to get involved with Ruby if she was going into the pub looking for customers.

Ruby laughed and grabbed her hand, pulling her through the doorway into the fug of smoke and beer. 'I'm paying.' She opened her purse and took out some money.

'I can't afford to buy you a drink in return . . .'

Marlene got no further, for Sam, the manager of the Fox, stood the other side of the counter and said, 'Behave yourself,' to Ruby. He looked at Marlene. 'All right, love.'

Marlene smiled at the big bluff cheery man. He was Em's man and loved the bones of her. But Em didn't see as much of him as she liked because she couldn't stand the tittle-tattle of workmates and neighbours. Because she and Em were mates, he knew all about Marlene's troubles. She could tell he was also aware of Ruby and didn't want any problems in the bar.

'You love me, really,' winked Ruby. Sam raised his eyes heavenwards. Then he poured two gin and oranges and set them down.

'On the house,' he said. Then, 'Marlene, can I have a word with you?'

She nodded. 'Thanks,' she said, sipping the drink.

The bar was full, and normally the Fox would have been closed by now. Sam must have had a dispensation to keep open. As though reading her thoughts, he called out, 'You got another fifteen minutes and I'm calling time.' To Marlene he said, 'We had a wedding party tonight, one of the local bigwig councillors.' He looked along the bar where his two barmaids were busy serving, then lifted the hatch in the counter and came round to where Marlene and Ruby stood.

'It's about Em.' His face creased as though he was in pain. 'She hasn't been near me for ages, not since that woman went to live in her house. When she told me she had found her long-lost sister, I was pleased as punch for her. It's not been easy, her living on her own, with Lizzie getting on with her own life elsewhere. I'll be honest with you, I asked her to marry me but she turned me down. Said she didn't want to marry again just yet. I can understand that, her Jack wasn't a good man to her. Takes a while to get over a bad marriage.' He sighed and shifted from one foot to the other. 'I could take her not coming down to see me so much because she don't like the gossips, but now I don't see anything of her . . . Is she all right?'

Marlene thought about Em at work, bossy as always and sharp at her job. No change there, she thought. 'Em's fine. What d'you think of her sister?'

'I haven't met her.' He frowned. 'We've not been introduced or nothing.' He tapped his fingers on the bar. 'I'm a bit worried . . .'

Marlene put her hand on his arm. 'She's all right. But come to think of it, I haven't seen her outside work for ages. I could tell her I've spoken to you.'

A smile broke over his kindly face. 'Would you?'

Marlene nodded. She felt Ruby tugging on her arm. She turned to see the girl bagging a couple of chairs that had just been vacated by some soldiers, and, after again promising to talk to Em, she went to join the girl. Looking at her animated face, Marlene said, 'I gather Sam knows you're on the game?'

Ruby's drink was swallowed quickly. 'He told me off about a year ago for sidling up to a sailor in here. You know what Sam's like, strait-laced really. He told me he'd bar me if I ever approached blokes in his pub again.' She paused and then smiled. 'Me and Sam understand one another. Besides, I don't need to solicit. There's always a queue of blokes down the flat.'

'If that's true, why were you with one of Priddy's men in the bushes?'

'Oh, him! It was a favour. His wife's pregnant and won't let him near her. He asked me, he's had me before, you see, down the flat . . .'

Marlene nodded. She had been thinking a lot about the extra money. The sooner she could have her mum and her daughter back, the happier she'd be.

'Where do I find this man?'

Ruby anticipated her words.

'You do it all through me. I hire you. You have nothing

to do with him, he has nothing to do with you. I'm the go-between. He's thought of everything.' Marlene watched as the slight-figured blonde pushed back her chair and got up to go to the bar. Sam had already rung the last orders bell.

Marlene watched as Sam waved to her and again rejected Ruby's money. She vowed to have a good chat with Em. Sam didn't deserve to be ignored by the woman he loved. Marlene'd spotted Lily, her sister, at the munitions yard enquiring about the vacancy left by Maisie. She had noted her closeness to Em. Come to think of it, Gladys, Em's best friend, was looking a bit lost just lately . . .

Her thoughts were broken as Ruby pushed a second gin and orange towards her and took a sip of her own drink.

'Now then, Marlene, what d'you say?' Ruby gave her a big grin.

Chapter Fourteen

Joel rang to catch up on all the news in the home, and chatted to Marie for a while before she told him, 'You shouldn't be phoning us, you should be enjoying yourself. But we have missed you, even your friend Liliah has asked after you – she remembered your name – so that's something.' She paused. 'You got to stop thinking about Fred, Joel. It might be better if you didn't come back for the funeral.'

They said their goodbyes and he put the receiver back in its cradle and pushed open the phone box's door. It was hot in there and smelled of sweat and pee. He was glad to be in the fresh air again. Marie was right. He had to stop thinking about Fred, but the old man had got under his skin. He'd begun treating Joel like he was a son, and Joel had responded by thinking of him as a father figure.

'You all right?'

He looked into Lizzie's pretty face. She'd been patiently waiting while he'd made his call. He nodded and put his arm about her shoulder.

'Come on, let's get down to your mum's place.'

His words were cut short by the sound of a wailing siren. He looked up into the dull sky. Searchlights were already flashing through the dusk. It wasn't late, but there'd been rain and the clouds hung low, dark and ominous. The siren rose in pitch, the dreadful drone of enemy bombers approaching from the south.

'Quick, let's find shelter.' Looking into the distance he could make out Heinkels approaching, so too were more German bombers. Spitfires were close behind, harassing the fighters. All the planes had distinctive and familiar sounds. He wondered if the German aircraft had already dropped their cargoes. If they hadn't, then it was possible the pilots would release their bombs randomly along the south coast, simply to make their getaways faster. He hoped they wouldn't drop them on Gosport.

He looked about, but there didn't seem to be any shelter. He pulled Lizzie inside a tall garden gate. Honeysuckle drooped over the pathway. He clicked up the latch of a shed and thrust her inside. The small wooden space was piled high with garden implements, pots of paint and jars of nails stacked on shelves. Spiders' webs were festooned like party garlands.

'You take me to the most wonderful places,' Lizzie said.

'At least we're not out in the open,' he replied.

'I hope the owner of this place doesn't come out and shout at us for trespassing,' Lizzie muttered. A wide window allowed them to stare out into the night.

She gave a cry as a Spitfire took a hit and smoke and flames began pouring from its tail. Joel looked on helplessly. He searched the sky for signs of a parachute, and watched as the small plane began a nosedive. The thwump that came next filled his heart with fear. Joel prayed that the pilot had lost consciousness before the craft catapulted to the earth.

He pulled Lizzie as close as he dared as another explosion, nearer this time, lit up the sky with myriad colours. Retaliation from the ground sent sparks of fire into the dull sky and the searchlights swayed back and forth trying to keep the German planes in sight. The earth was set on fire by the release of bombs. The smell of burning seeped inside the shed, like the remains of an autumn garden bonfire.

The Heinkels were on their way across the English Channel, the Spitfires buzzing around like irritating mosquitoes. Joel closed his eyes and prayed for the safety of our boys. Some were really hardly more than brave youngsters, with the fate of the country in their hands.

The noise of the fighter planes began to fade and still the Spitfires chased their counterparts. He realized Lizzie was shaking. His arms tightened about her. He bent his head, his lips to her hair. Again, the near silence was shattered, but this time by the all-clear siren.

Next came the clanging of ambulance bells and fire engines.

Joel said, 'Let's get out of here.'

But the ringing noises of the fire engines were coming closer. Joel prayed it wasn't Lizzie's mother's house that had copped it. He locked the gate after they left the shed and still holding her hand, they made their way across the railway lines towards Kings Road, then on to the junction near the Queen's pub. Lizzie gave a sigh of relief to see King's Road empty of vehicles. Above the rooftops an orange glow and thick black smoke tainted the air. A human tide of people suddenly appeared as if from nowhere and began swarming along the street carrying stirrup pumps and shovels.

'Where's the fire, what's been hit?' Lizzie seemed deaf to his pleas to slow down as she tried to keep up.

Then he saw it. Smoke and flames pouring from the

church hall at the bottom of Queen's Road. One of the side walls was nothing but rubble and people were standing about, dazed, crying and covered in blood and dust. A large group of people were watching the shooting flames, dumbstruck.

A woman was screaming, 'My child's in there!'

The firemen were now tackling the blaze. The noise and heat were tremendous. ARP wardens were doing their bit, trying to salvage whatever they could from flames and ashes.

Joel asked a man with a blanket around him, 'What's going on?'

'Kids' party. Youngsters celebrating, little bit of dancing and then pow!'

Lizzie was crying.

'You can't be upsetting yourself, let's get away,' Joel pleaded. Her face was as white as fresh washing. He tried to pull her back but she stood, fascinated, watching the flames shooting into the sky while being dampened down by the firemen's hoses.

A fireman looked their way. His face was sweat-stained and sooty.

Lizzie moved towards him and he seemed know what she was asking. He shook his head. 'No one,' he said. Then sadly, 'Not one kiddie recovered.'

Lizzie turned and threw herself into Joel's arms. 'Is this what happens?' she said. 'We women give birth and then our children die?'

She was now sobbing so hard that he forcibly dragged her away from the heat and the onlookers. The women remained huddled together, moaning and crying as though drawing strength from each other.

Joel pulled her along Queen's Road, threading their way through people who had come to gawp. When they reached Kings Road he said, 'Give me your key.' He searched the doors for numbers and approached a neat front garden with a tiled path leading to the front door.

'You need a cup of tea and a sit down,' he said, inserting the key in the door.

The smell of polish hit him first and then the sound of voices rising above the band music playing on the wireless. He turned to Lizzie, motioning her to be quiet. She'd already told him that her mother would be at work, and her sister might now be at Priddy's with her. Obviously not.

He turned to Lizzie and noted the frown lines above her eyes. The questioning look told him all might not be right. There was a pause in Glenn Miller's music. Joel pushed open the kitchen door, saying loudly, 'Hello, anyone there?'

A man in spectacles stepped away from a blonde-haired woman. The woman looked relieved to see Joel, which didn't make sense to him, as she didn't know him. The man was now in the process of stuffing notes into his wallet, which took but a few moments, then he said, 'And who might you be?'

Lizzie stepped from behind Joel's bulk and asked, 'This is my mother's home. Who the hell are you two?'

The man seemed to deflate, then he took a deep breath and said, 'I'm a friend of . . .' and here he paused, appearing to forget the woman's name. 'Lily.'

He moved closer to Lily and Joel couldn't help but notice how the woman flinched. She said, 'I'm your mum's sister, Lily.'

Lizzie suddenly crumpled before him, holding her stomach. 'Oh.' She looked questioningly at Joel as pain shot across her face.

He propelled her into a large armchair, totally ignoring the man and woman. At that moment, a key rattled against the door. Joel heard the sound of it being drawn up through the letter box on its length of string. He'd forgotten most people left a key hanging on the back of the door. Still, they wouldn't have taken this couple by surprise if Lizzie and himself had entered the house that way. He bent down before Lizzie.

'What's the matter? Is it the baby?'

And at that very moment a voice called out, 'Lily, I'm home.'

Lizzie let her hand fall away from her stomach. 'I'm all right now. Combination of indigestion and sadness, I think.' She smiled up at him before saying loudly, 'Mum, we're in the kitchen.'

Joel got to his feet, turned round and glanced at where the well-dressed man had stood. He was gone! He stepped across the lino and peered through the window, out into the darkness. The back door had been left open, letting a shaft of light strike the wall opposite, but there was no sign of Lily's friend.

'Em doesn't know about Lawrence,' Lily hissed. Joel looked at her through narrowed eyes. Something here wasn't quite right.

Just then, a whirlwind appeared in the kitchen.

'Lizzie!'

Em rushed forward, a huge smile lighting up her pleasant face. She bent down, enveloping her daughter in her arms.

'I'll put the kettle on,' Lily said and disappeared into the scullery.

Joel stared at the woman who had given birth to the girl he loved. They often said women turned into their mothers. He instantly decided he wouldn't mind that at all!

'Oh, my love, why didn't you write and tell me you were coming?'

'We wanted to surprise you.' Joel stepped towards her and held out a hand, hoping she would shake it and accept him. Lizzie was snuggled down in the old armchair and her girth wasn't really visible, but the baby would show the moment she moved or stood up. He so wanted her mother to like him.

Outside in the scullery the hiss of gas told him Lily was putting on the kettle and getting on with the tea.

Em tentatively touched his fingers. A look of suspicion moved across her face. 'Call me Em,' she said. 'And you are?'

'That's Joel, Mum . . .' Lizzie's voice faltered. He began to wish he and Lizzie had worked out some kind of plan. He was going to have to tell Em lies, and he wasn't looking forward to that at all.

Lizzie struggled into a standing position. Joel moved towards her, helping her to her feet.

Em gasped. 'Oh, my God!'

'Yes, I'm pregnant, Mum,' Lizzie said sharply, before Em could utter another word. Joel knew she was trying to pave the way in case her mother started taking it out on him for getting her in that condition. It worked. Lizzie sidled up to Joel and felt for his hand, grasping it tightly. He smiled at her. God, how he wished the baby really was his. 'The baby's due shortly. I want you to be pleased for me.' Again, she smiled at Joel. He felt his heart flip over. 'For us,' Lizzie finished.

Joel could see her mother's eyes wavering towards Lizzie's hands. She would be looking for a wedding band. It was now or never, he thought. He put his arm around Lizzie's shoulder.

'No, we're not wed. It's not possible,' he said. Both women, Em and Lizzie, were looking at him expectantly. 'My wife disappeared during the early days of the war.' He swallowed. If only Lizzie knew how much he hated lying for her. He loved her so much he'd do anything to make her life easier. 'I met Lizzie, we fell in love and I've asked her to marry me. But as you know, until the where-abouts of my wife are known there's nothing we can do.'

Em was holding on the back of a kitchen chair. Her face was white. Joel could see the shock had upset her. He felt awful for causing her grief.

Em said, 'Seven years. You'll have to wait seven years. What a terrible thing to happen to you.'

Joel sighed. He knew he had to embroider the lie, but decided not to make a meal of it. It wouldn't look good if he forgot his own lies, would it? He stared at Lizzie. Then he turned to Em. 'My wife and I hadn't been getting on too well. She'd gone dancing with some of her pals. The hall took a hit. Lots of people died.' He shrugged. 'I don't know whether she's dead or alive.'

'Jesus, I bet you blamed yourself for not going with her.'

He didn't want to answer Em, so simply looked down at the lino.

'Mum, you shouldn't say things like that!'

'Why not? I still blame myself for your dad's death.' He'd heard that Lizzie's dad was a nasty bit of work and had died when his wheelchair overturned. Em had been in another room so hadn't got to him in time to save him.

'If I could, I'd marry her tomorrow.' Well, at least that was the truth, thought Joel.

He saw Em soften towards him. Just then Lily came into the room carrying a tray with teacups piled on saucers and the teapot covered by a knitted cosy. He stared at her. Surely he'd seen Lily somewhere before? No, it wasn't possible, he told himself.

Lizzie was staring at him with a daft look in her eyes. She mouthed a 'thank you' at him. He knew the awkward part of telling her mother about the baby was over. No one would know it was that conman's kiddie now. Em could tell her workmates about her forthcoming grand-child, knowing that Lizzie couldn't marry him until the statutory seven years were up. There were plenty of men and women in a similar predicament because of the war. Husbands in the forces who had gone abroad to serve and who had disappeared without trace, left women waiting for news. In some cases the wives wished to remarry and couldn't. The stigma of simply living together was classed as living in sin. No doubt there would be more couples like them pretending to be married after the war.

Joel got to his feet to help Lily.

'You got a good one, there, Lizzie.' Em smiled at him. 'Not many blokes are as well trained.'

'He does look after me, Mum.'

'Part of my job.' Joel sorted the cups on to the saucers and began pouring in milk from the bottle.

'What's that, then?' Lily began pouring.

'I'm a carer in Lyme Regis at Yew Trees—'

He got no further, for Lily dropped the teapot. The hot tea shot across the tray, down a kitchen chair and onto the floor, where the pot lay shattered.

'Bugger!' Lily cried, and ran out of the kitchen into the scullery. Joel could hear her crying. Em and Joel followed.

'Whatever's the matter?' Em asked. 'It's not such a surprise to you that a man can look after old people just the same as us, is it?' She pulled Lily into her arms and stroked her hair.

'I'm clearing up the mess, don't you worry about that,' said Joel. He was confused. 'Was it the teapot? Was the handle too hot?' He began drawing back the curtain beneath the sink where he thought the cleaning stuff might be kept.

Lily sniffed. 'It burned my hand.' She pulled away from Em. 'Caught it on the side of the pot, I did.'

Joel was now lifting bits of the shattered teapot. The tea cosy had soaked up much of the tea. He began wiping the lino.

Lizzie said, 'Is she all right? Can I do anything?'

He looked over at her, shook his head, and said, 'Can't understand the side of the teapot burning her hand when the cosy was still around it. Still, least said, soonest mended. She'll live.' He squeezed the cloth into the bowl and began the final wipe down. 'I hope your mother's got another teapot.'

'She's got several,' said Lizzie. 'You don't have to worry about missing your cuppa.' He got off his knees and went over to her. 'Sorry I lied to your mum,' he said very softly.

'Thank you.' She gave him a shy smile. 'She'll be able to hold her head high at work and with the neighbours, and she'll be telling everyone about the baby and what a lovely dad the little one will have.' A smile hovered at the corners of her lips. 'Was that a lie about wanting to marry me too?' He never had time to answer, for Em brought in Lily and sat her at the kitchen table. Joel took out the bowl and the dustpan and brush. He threw the rubbish in the dustbin and saw that there was a shining metal teapot on the draining board next to the tea caddy.

He shouted, 'You stay where you are. I'll finish making the tea.' He looked around the scullery. The kettle was gently bubbling over the gas and the whole room sparkled with cleanliness. A line of saucepans stood on a shelf and on the window sill was a packet of Rinso soap flakes.

As soon as the water was on the boil he rinsed out the metal teapot then put in several spoons of tea. A strong cup would do them all good.

He thought about Lily and desperately wanted to talk to her about her childhood. Maybe she'd show them the letters? After all, that was why they were in Gosport, so Lizzie could put Gladys's mind at rest whether Lily was or wasn't her mother's sister.

However, when he set foot in the kitchen and saw Lily's pale face he knew any questions would be quite out of order. The women were already talking about the baby.

'Do you want a boy or girl?' Lily asked him.

Oh, dear, he thought. 'I don't mind as long as Lizzie's all right.' Em looked at him fondly. He reckoned he'd given the right answer. Em poured out the teas and he gratefully took a mouthful.

'So, are you staying here in Gosport so I can be with Lizzie when she needs me?'

He sighed, then told the truth. 'Em, I've a good job waiting for me and my home is in Lyme Regis. I've had time off because a man I grew fond of died. We decided to come and visit . . .' He smiled at Lizzie. 'But if you want to stay here . . .'

'Not without you.' Lizzie blushed.

Em had wound a large bandage loosely around Lily's hand. She sat silently, face chalk-white. He wondered if she was in shock. Then he wondered if she hadn't spoken much because she was hoping he wouldn't say anything about the strange man who'd been in the house when they arrived. What had she called him? Lawrence?

While it was necessary for him to speak to Em about her new sister, it was difficult to bring up the subject while she was sitting there, silent as the grave. Lizzie yawned.

He realized how tired she must be. The fire which had killed the children in the church hall had upset her. They hadn't been able to get their hands on Lily's papers, and now they'd have to walk home to Gladys's house in Alma Street. He wished he'd taken no notice of Lizzie pressuring him to walk instead of using the car.

As though reading his thoughts, Em said, 'Don't bother about going back to Gladys's tonight. I can easily make up beds for you both.'

Lizzie was first to shake her head. 'No, it wouldn't be fair on Gladys.' Em blushed. Joel was surprised that Lily looked relieved.

He looked at the clock. 'We'd better go. You're both at work tomorrow?'

'Lily's working at Priddy's, same hours as me tomorrow.' She pointed to Lily's hand and said, 'As long as her hand's all right, of course.' She paused. 'Will you thank Gladys for putting you both up, from me?'

Joel went over just as she stood up from her chair and gave her a hug. 'She cares a lot about you, does Gladys.' He was thankful he didn't have to go through the business of feeling awkward about sleeping with Em's daughter in her home without the privilege of a wedding certificate. He'd certainly feel easier with Gladys.

'Will you come back tomorrow? I'd take time off if I could, but there's a war on and I'm needed at the factory.'

'We know all about that, Mum.' Lizzie had struggled to her feet again and was now kissing her mum goodbye. Lily stood up and awkwardly shook hands with Joel. He could feel it was an effort for her. She then gave a half-hearted cuddle to Lizzie. Lizzie didn't seem to notice anything was amiss, but Joel couldn't get over how silent the woman was.

Once outside they'd hardly reached the Criterion picture house before it started to rain again. Big fat drops that could mean another summer storm. Neither of them had spoken until then, content in the companionable silence, but now Lizzie said, 'She didn't even mention the news that's been on everyone's lips all day.'

'Neither did we. But perhaps if Hitler had been killed in that explosion in Prussia we'd all be talking about it.'

'That assassination attempt should have killed him, not three of his cronies.' Lizzie's voice was hard.

'See what I mean? Why is she so quiet? Do you think she's like that all the time, even when there's no visitors?' Joel pulled up the collar of his thin jacket.

'Probably not, and she looks more like Gladys with her bleached hair than she does my mum . . .'

'They're both cuddly and have the same colour eyes though. You don't like her, do you?'

'Look, if it was me, I'd have wanted to know more about my sister's child. She hardly spoke to me, yet she's supposed to be my auntie.'

'Perhaps her upbringing has made her like that . . .'

'Well, we won't know unless she talks, will we?'

He stopped outside the picture house and began staring at the photographs in their glass-covered cases. 'Do you like Joan Crawford?' Without waiting for her answer he carried on, 'She looks beautiful but cruel. I think she's very sexy.'

'I don't like Fred MacMurray.'

'*Above Suspicion*, isn't that a spy film? It's all propaganda in the films now. Give me a good musical any time. But if you feel like it, we could go and see it . . .'

He didn't get much further before Lizzie gave a sudden moan and clutched beneath her huge belly. Joel twisted round to her. 'What is it?'

He watched as her gritted teeth relaxed. 'That walk was probably a bit much, thank God it's not much further.'

'Is it the baby?'

She shook her head. 'Just the walking.'

He pulled her towards him. 'I know you were trying to save the petrol because my mate didn't have any more coupons. I should have realized how uncomfortable walking would be for you. Tomorrow we'll use the car.'

'Better not,' Lizzie said. 'We need the petrol to get home again.' He was suddenly happy that she thought of the prefab as home, and smiled at her. 'I wonder why she was giving money – and quite a bit by the looks of it – to that Lawrence bloke?' She was biting her bottom lip and she looked like a young girl, not a mother to be, Joel thought. 'He was a good-looking man, though, what I saw of him before he disappeared.'

'If you like the smarmy type.' Joel wondered why it had upset him that Lizzie had noticed the man's looks.

She laughed. 'So you're not giving up on Mum's so-called sister?'

'Gladys cares about your mum. If someone's taking advantage of Em, we need to nip it in the bud.' He took off his jacket and stood in his shirtsleeves. Beneath the overhang of the Criterion's roof it was dry, but there was still a way to go before they reached Alma Street. He wrapped his jacket around Lizzie's shoulders to keep the worst of the rain off her. He stood for a long time looking into her eyes.

'Come on,' he said, 'let's get you home.'

Chapter Fifteen

Gloria finished washing up the tea things in the scullery sink. She hated being called Lily, because she sometimes forgot it was her new name. Then she got funny looks from people who thought she was ignoring them. In fact, she was fed up with this whole business and wished she'd never agreed to deceive this kind woman, who trusted her.

Not only had Em given her a home, but she'd got her a well-paid job at Priddy's Hard, so she was earning more money than she'd ever seen in her life before. Despite being there only a short time she had managed to put some cash aside. OK, so it was dangerous work. She'd hated filling the small copper shells that started the triggering action on bombs. She was also exposed to fulminate of mercury in her work, which was a brown powdery substance that made her skin itch. She had to be careful not to touch her face or scratch herself because her skin quickly became inflamed.

She loved the easy chatter of the girls, talking about their lives, their men and including her as though they'd known her all their lives. It was all due to Em, this new life Gloria had been given.

She and Em had gone to a few dances at the Connaught Drill Hall. It was lovely being asked to dance by the men in khaki and the Spitfire pilots. They were so young, the boys who flew those planes. She'd been invited to pubs for drinks with the girls and that was a completely new experience, for her to enter a pub for a laugh, not to pick up men for sex.

She told Em she'd grown up on a farm. What a lark! She'd never been on a farm! How would she feel if Em knew she'd grown up in a tidy double-fronted house in a tree-lined road?

With two younger brothers, Gloria was the apple of her dad's eye. He was a respectable banker who made sure his wife didn't want for anything. In August every year they hired a caravan in the New Forest for a week and drove there in the Ford Model A saloon, which he polished to near death at weekends.

A heart attack claimed him when Gloria was a very naive twenty-year-old who watched her mother disintegrate before her eyes upon the realization they weren't as well off as she thought they were. The boys were sent to live with an aunt in Cornwall after her mother hanged herself. Gloria had discovered the body. After the funeral she took a train to London to work in a dress shop owned by a friend of her aunt. From a beloved child to a subservient assistant to elderly, cantankerous, gentlewomen was a sharp awakening.

She could never get the image of her mother out of her head.

It took her ten years, umpteen jobs and various lodging houses, each one more grubby than the last, to show Gloria that the streets of London weren't paved with gold and that with the moving population, friends didn't last long, and men friends – when they discovered she lived alone – tended to expect to share her bed and body. Mark Hemple, after keeping her hanging on for five years, told her he wouldn't be leaving his wife after all. Gloria wasn't surprised, not after discovering Alma Hemple was seven months pregnant while washing her hair during Gloria's latest position as dogsbody in the Cutting Edge hair salon.

Gloria was lonely and poor and every night when her head touched the pillow, she saw her mother.

So she drifted. She knew she wasn't pretty, but she

tried to make the most of her looks. When the feeble jobs didn't allow her to pay her rent she picked up men. One day she answered an advertisement in a newsagent's window for a live-in carer at Bere, a small but pretty hamlet near the sea.

The old man was grumpy, dirty and dribbled when he spoke. She cleaned him up, to the relief of his son, who came to see him once a week and couldn't wait to get away. The bloke was generous as long as she allowed him a flash of cleavage or a hand on her buttocks. When he died, she moved on again, this time to a newly opened care home in Lyme Regis. They seemed pleased she'd had previous experience with elderly people.

One day, while pushing an elderly patient in his wheel-chair along The Cobb, listening to the seagulls screeching and the waves rolling, a man paused to speak to her and her charge.

They all chatted amiably and she liked his upper-class accent, his very white teeth and his manicured hands that showed he did no manual work. He kept staring at her and his eyes told her more than his voice. They talked about the new home for men and women of means, opened only recently, and the expenses involved in living there.

In the hope of seeing the fair-haired man again, she

pushed her charge in his wheelchair along The Cobb the next day. He didn't appear.

She'd been bowled over that such a well-spoken gentleman wanted anything to do with a nobody like her. The next day she left the old gentleman at Yew Trees and walked along the shore alone, hoping for a further encounter. This time, the very attractive man invited her to tea at a hotel. A few days later he wined and dined her and listened as she told him the stories of the men and women being cared for at Yew Trees.

'My wife died last year. I'm not sure if you can imagine how I feel. I'm all right when there are people about me but at nights, alone, the quiet and the memories of all we shared together brings me to tears,' he told her one afternoon in a small tea shop. She could tell by the dampness in his eyes that he meant every word. He went on, 'Money doesn't bring happiness.'

He took to bringing her small gifts when they met. Tiny fossils made into a brooch, a necklace of minute seashells. The gifts made her feel special. She was used to men taking, not giving. And never, ever, did he allow her to pay for the teas or the scones that he plied her with.

Lily pushed away the thoughts that crowded her mind and used the rope and pulley to let down the wooden clothes-dryer hanging in the kitchen. She put the wet tea towels over its slats to dry, then went into the living room and sat down near Em, who was lying down on the sofa with her feet up.

'Tired?' she queried.

Em nodded and asked, 'What do you think of Joel?' The wireless was on and John Snagge was reading the news.

Lily fluffed up the sofa cushion. Her head told her she must stay away from this young man, who might discover she too had worked at Yew Trees. There was no reason why he should, she told herself. She had left before Joel had taken up his post there. She gave a deep sigh, but wasn't this just the way fate worked? She told Em the truth.

'I think he's a thoroughly capable young man.'

'Just what our Lizzie needs. She's got a knack of running around with the wrong 'uns.'

'Oh?'

Em gave a resigned laugh. 'She loved a black-market bugger, a right charmer was Blackie.'

Lily could see that this Blackie had charmed Em as well. Why was it the wrong men, the scoundrels, always made women weak at the knees? She thought of Lawrence and how he had persuaded her to do things she would never have dreamed of doing before she had met him.

'Jesus, will you listen to that!' The news reporter was telling everyone about V2s and the news from Berlin that the bigger and better bombs were ready for use.

'There'll be nothing left of us in a minute,' said Em. 'I've had enough surprises for tonight. Seeing our Lizzie as big as a barrage balloon and unwed into the bargain! I'm off to bed.'

She hauled herself off the sofa and went over to the door. 'You're on the same shift as me tomorrow, so who-ever wakes first makes the tea, all right?'

'I'll tidy up.' Lily spotted Em's sandwich tin and flask left unwashed on the sideboard. 'I might as well do the sandwiches tonight,' she added, and Em smiled, disappearing into the hall. Soon she heard Em's weary footsteps on the stairs.

Back in the scullery, she sliced bread and grated a tiny knob of cheese over the marged slices. A saucer of cress had grown on the window sill and she cut some florets and sprinkled them over the cheese to make it tastier. Thinly sliced Spam went in as well. Pleased with her effort, she opened the drawer of the cabinet looking for some greaseproof paper to wrap them in.

Memories of Lawrence flooded back and she thought how wonderful she'd believed him to be. He'd seemed determined to know all about her job, caring for the elderly. She thought him charming. Then one day, on The Cobb, he broke down and told her one of his businesses was in trouble. He needed a thousand pounds to get himself back on an even keel. 'I shall have to leave this area, sell my flat and my car and all for a measly thousand pounds.'

To not see him any more was unthinkable. Gloria thought his debt was horrendous. However, she began to think of the debt as her own when Lawrence came up with a suggestion.

'The old people, do they have money, jewellery with them?'

She knew exactly what he was getting at. It was true that if it wasn't for the carers some of the old people would never find their wedding rings, expensive watches and jewellery that they took off in the bathrooms and gardens and bedrooms and forgot about. Some wouldn't trust banks so had brought in money, which they kept in little, flimsy-locked boxes. Some had special allowances that were drawn each week by the carers from the bank or post office. Money that mounted up in bedside drawers because there was nothing the elderly needed to pay for.

'If you could borrow the money I could return it within, say, a month? I wouldn't need to move down south where my other businesses are, then.'

Lily had never stolen a thing in her life. Even in the depths of her poverty she had managed without stealing, but if Lawrence left her she would go back to being alone. Images of her mother flew before her eyes. She would become sick, start crying all day again, not wanting to leave her bed. Lawrence made her feel wanted, cherished.

She was like a magpie the way she took and hoarded jewellery and stole money.

Surprisingly, very few of the inmates realized anything had gone missing. There was one time when Marie had her in the office along with two other carers and the kitchen staff and gave them a talk on making sure the patients' trinkets and jewellery were to be put away. In future, expensive items needed to be locked in the safe.

'The old ones won't know if their stuff has been returned if it's in the safe, then?' Lawrence was quite definite about that. Handing over jewellery, cash and watches, she'd breathed a sigh of relief that she still had Lawrence and her job and that she'd been able to help him pay off his debt.

She was happy until he came up with the idea of her going through their lockers.

'I don't want to,' she'd begged him. They were naked, in bed, in his flat. She loved being desired and Lawrence knew how to make her happy. Other men had simply taken her, paid for her services, never caring about her feelings.

That was the day he turned.

'If you don't do as I ask, I'll make sure the owners know about your stealing.' And he produced a gold ring that had belonged to the man in room four.

Lily gasped. One moment Lawrence had been her attentive lover, the next a conniving trickster. 'You wouldn't . . .'

'Oh, yes I would.' He got off the bed and quickly dressed. 'If you don't do as I ask, you'll be out of a job, investigated by the police and then you'll find it extremely difficult to find anyone willing to take you on. No one wants to employ a thief.'

Her heart was beating fast as she stared at him. He continued, 'Those old dears keep papers that mean nothing to anyone else but themselves. Quite a few people distrust banks and prefer to keep their finances near them. On your next shift, you're going to search each room for anything that looks promising. You're on nights for the next week; shouldn't be too difficult when the old dears are asleep, medicated up to the eyeballs. But I don't want you to take anything yet. Simply make a note of what looks promising. Post office savings book, documents, incriminating letters . . .'

She must have looked shocked because he'd laughed and said, 'You'd be surprised by the happenings in their lives and how a little blackmail can work wonders.' He went on, 'A little senility works well too. My old nan kept the deeds to her Stratford-upon-Avon riverside house in her chest of drawers. The land registry and solicitors were absolutely useless at getting stuff done quickly and I happily made a tidy profit from a gullible American before the deal blew up in his face. But of course, I was long gone by then.' He smiled broadly. 'Now, I'm giving you a few days to sort this out.'

She knew then that she loathed him. But Gloria also wanted his approval. She wanted him to love her again. She still wanted his hands on her body, his lips against hers, even though he was playing with her like a cat with a mouse.

His next words proved it. 'I've spent time and money on you and I need a return on my investment.' He was staring at her as she got out of bed and began putting on her clothes. She felt dirty, sick to her stomach that not only did he intend to rob these poor old people, but that he expected her to help.

The patients and staff in the home trusted her.

OK, let him tell the police. It would only incriminate him, she'd make sure of that.

She pulled her dress over her head saying, 'I'm not going to do it.'

The slap knocked her off her feet and onto the bed she'd just stood up from. The punch to her stomach not only winded her, but hurt like hell. She got up from the bed and faced him squarely. His face was like thunder, his eyes the colour of steel as she lurched towards him, hands and nails ready to do damage to him.

'Bastard,' she'd screamed and throwing herself forward, raked his face with her nails. Spots of red bloomed immediately. He was shocked that she'd retaliated and put his hand to his cheek, staring at his fingers as they came away covered in blood.

'Bitch!' He beat at her until she cowered on the floor, her hands above her head for protection. Then he kicked her.

Too exhausted to scream and cry and beg him to stop, she made herself as small as she could, but each of his kicks landed in a fresh spot. Then suddenly, he stopped.

Hardly daring to open her eyes, her body aching with pain, Gloria stayed where she was, hunched near the wardrobe. She could hear him stomping about the bedroom. She could taste the metallic tang of her own blood. She was too frightened to move.

'Get up!' He pulled her by one arm into a standing

position then propelled her across the floor to the kitchen, throwing open the back door. She stumbled out into the darkness and was dimly aware she was being hauled towards his car. Opening the door, he threw her inside and then chucked her handbag and the rest of her clothes, including her shoes, at her. She didn't dare speak. He slammed the door. Rain spattered on the windows. He went to the driver's side, got in and gunned the motor. Gloria was frightened. Where was he taking her? What was he going to do to her? The noise of the engine and the scrape of the windscreen wipers were the only sounds to mingle with the heavy raindrops.

The car screeched to a halt, he got out and opened her door, pulling her and her belongings out into the street. She fell on the kerb and rolled into the gutter, her things spread about her in the rain. She heard the car door close and the window being wound down.

'Thursday you'll give me a list,' was all he said before he drove away, leaving her sobbing pitifully on the pavement in the rain outside Yew Trees.

Since then she hadn't dared refuse him anything.

Still she believed he'd go back to the gentle man he'd been on their first meeting.

Chapter Sixteen

Marlene wiggled the key and when the door opened, stepped inside and began climbing the stairs. She'd give the hallway and stairs a quick clean up before the girls got here, she thought. Once inside the large flat over the fish and chip shop, she went into the kitchen and put the kettle on. A nice cup of tea was just what she wanted after working six hours at Priddy's.

It had been noisy this afternoon at the armament yard. The loudspeakers had been going all day, orders for this, orders for that. Even the wireless had seemed particularly loud.

She'd been working on pellets as one of their girls was off sick; a paintbrush, a jar of paste, and papers with crinkled edges. The papers were about an inch long and she had to paste the paper then wrap a pellet in each one.

Marlene looked at her hands. The paste was sticky,

and had stuck to her hands. No matter how many times she washed them the residue of yellow remained. It was mind-numbing work. She'd been bored stiff all day. Singing along with the girls had eased the boredom. She realized she had no idea where her wrapped pellets went and she didn't care. That was the thing about working at the armament depot – you did your job, but it was only a small part you played, for you never saw the end product of what you were working on.

She poured the boiling water in the teapot, then hung her coat on the back of the door. A drop of tea would hit the spot before she got the flat ready.

Footsteps on the stairs made her turn towards the door.

'I'm just in time for a brew,' laughed Carla, sweeping in with the scent of poppies and throwing her cardigan over the top of Marlene's coat. Marlene had taken to the dark, exotic-looking young woman straight away. She had a ready smile and the longest legs Marlene had ever seen. Marlene thought she looked the dead spit of Dorothy Lamour. 'Had a good day?' Carla asked.

Marlene shrugged and washed up another cup from the draining board full of dirty crockery.

'How's Alice?'

Carla had a little girl, a three-year-old, and a husband

who had sent her a Dear John letter after meeting a girl in France. He said he wasn't coming home after the war. Marlene thought he needed his head examining. Carla wasn't only beautiful, she was kind-hearted and a good mother. She'd been living with her husband's family and his mother had never really liked her, so Carla had left with one suitcase and a holdall full of Alice's stuff.

'I've got to get out from that place,' Carla said. That place was a café in town. Carla lived on the top floor. 'Still, soon I'll have enough for a deposit on a proper flat.' She was popular with the punters. 'That's if I can find someone to take me on with a kiddie and no feller.' It was awful to think that most of the time women still needed a man's signature as surety on a property.

'You got two choices then: either tell the landlord your husband's away fighting – you know how householders feel about women on their own, the Irish and coloured people – or get yourself a bloke!'

Carla glared at her, she knew all about her being taken for a ride by Samuel Golden, and that she was working here to pay back the money she owed. Marlene knew Carla had been hurt so much by her husband's infidelity that another man was the last thing on her mind. Carla's priority was her child; she'd do anything for her little girl.

Marlene poured out the tea then found the tin of biscuits.

'Any Bourbons left?'

'Not when you're about.' Marlene passed her the opened tin and Carla helped herself to two Garibaldi.

After a couple of mouthfuls of tea, Marlene went to the big cupboard in the corner and took out clean sheets.

'I don't know why you bother with that. Clean sheets are the last thing on punters' minds!'

'That's where you're wrong. This might be a knocking shop but it's a clean one. Presentation is everything.'

She thought about the men who came simply to talk to the girls. Many men, even married ones, were lonely. All they wanted was to sit in bed with a pretty girl and chat.

Some punters couldn't manage the sex, but still needed a kiss and cuddle and were quite willing to pay. Some wanted only to dress in the flimsy 'dolling up' clothes that the girls kept in a wardrobe for discerning customers. One large man, bald and a stutterer, paid well to be blindfolded, tied up and locked in Carla's wardrobe while Carla got on with her business in the bedroom. Carla forgot him one evening and it wasn't until the early hours when Marlene was locking up that he was discovered. He paid extra for that!

Leaving her tea to cool, she went into the larger of

the two bedrooms and threw the bedding on the chair, then began stripping the bed. Since she'd started working there'd been no problems with the money she passed over to Ruby to take to 'Mr X', as she'd begun to think of her boss. She sent the washing to the Sunlight laundry in South Street and bought in cleaning materials and groceries such as tea, milk and biscuits, when she could get them. As long as she provided the receipts, including withdrawing her own and the two girls' shares of the takings, Mr X seemed quite happy with both the arrangement and the balance.

'Let's get some air in here,' she mumbled to herself. She opened the window and looked out at the panorama of the ferry area.

Boats were engorged with passengers waiting to disembark onto the wooden jetty, and on the other side of the pontoon more people were waiting to embark.

Across the strip of water she could see Portsmouth and the dockyard with HMS *Victory*, Nelson's flagship. An Isle of Wight ferry stood to attention in the murky water near Portsmouth Harbour's railway station.

In the mud this side, young boys, mudlarks, were digging in the green-grey sludge, black as the ace of spades, for pennies thrown to them by passengers queuing for the boats.

Flowers bloomed in the Ferry Gardens and the cigarette kiosk was busy with people buying papers and fags before they boarded the buses at the Provincial bus station.

Marlene breathed in the salty air, tinged with the smell from the fish and chip shop below. In a while the punters would start opening the street door and running up the stairs. It would be her job to let them in, take their money, then call out for whichever girl the punter wanted. Marlene also took the money for whichever service the men required. She'd painted a menu and stood it on the small counter.

She didn't mind admitting that it worried her that some bright spark might want *her* to hand over the takings to *him*. So she was careful not to let the men see where she kept the bulk of the money, which was in a wall safe out in the kitchen. A cricket bat sat beneath the counter, out of sight, but to hand should it be needed. Twice a week Ruby took the balance of the money and one of the two cashbooks that Marlene kept scrupulously up to date, to Mr X. She kept one set of accounts for herself, just in case. Where Ruby went with the cash, Marlene didn't care, as long as the girl was safe.

There were always regular customers waiting in the office area for the girls' services, so Marlene felt reasonably secure, believing in safety in numbers.

Carla came into the bedroom with Marlene's cup. 'Drink this, it'll get cold otherwise.' Marlene did as she was told. As she handed the cup back, Carla said with a smile, 'I'll give you a hand clearing up. I know you've been on your feet all day, at least I've had time to sit down.'

'Don't know how you have the patience fitting them posh old dears into dresses that are too young for them,' Marlene said.

Carla worked part time in Fleure's, a dress shop in the High Street. Marlene couldn't afford to shop there.

'It's a job,' said Carla, picking up the stained sheets and going towards the door. She looked back at Marlene and started laughing. 'More than this is!' They both began to laugh and were still laughing when Ruby poked her head around the door.

'What's the joke?' Looking at her serious face set Marlene and Carla off laughing again.

'Pfft!' said Ruby and went back out with a look of disgust on her face.

Though Marlene had been with the two girls for only a short time, she'd come to think of them as friends. The work eased her loneliness and allowed her to send more money to her mother. Already her share of the wages had meant the amount in her post office savings book was growing. Paying back people for their past generosity was uppermost in her mind.

Once the cleaning was accomplished, she went out and checked that anything the girls might need was ready to hand. When she'd first begun to work there she was amazed to discover the girls never used protection.

Now the punters had to wear French letters, and she'd made both girls go to the doctor for a check-up. The only thing she left completely to Carla and Ruby were the clothes they wore to do the business in. Some regular customers preferred the girls to dress up.

Ruby said she was worse than Adolf Hitler with her rules but Marlene knew they didn't really mind, because she had their best interests at heart, and since she'd been working there, proceeds had doubled.

'So how did it go then?'

Gladys was waiting up for them with her dressing gown tied tightly around her waist, her scuffed pom-pom slippers on and a headful of metal curlers that made her look quite frightening.

'I hope you don't let Siddy see you like this!'

Gladys rattled the cups and glared at Lizzie. Outside in the scullery, Joel heard the kettle coming up to the boil.

'Lily's very nervy and quiet,' said Lizzie, easing herself down on a kitchen chair.

'She wasn't at first. She was a loud, mouthy woman.' Gladys put her hands on her hips. 'Trying to tell us she was brought up on a farm! Well, I never believed a word of that! That one's been around the block a few times. Did you get the papers?'

Joel sighed. 'Things never went the way we planned.'

It was Gladys's turn to sigh. 'Well, I suppose you done your best.' She went out into the scullery and Joel heard the clatter of teapot and caddy. Then his eyes lit on the floor by the sideboard, where liquid stood in ball-topped bottles. Just as he was staring at it, Gladys came in with the steaming teapot.

'That's petrol,' she said. 'For you.' He stared at her. 'I know you're worried 'bout not having enough fuel to get back home with, and well, Patsy at work has a brother who's a spiv. You know, all his stuff falls off the back of lorries.' She paused. 'It's commercial petrol used for farm workers and such.'

Joel looked at the clear liquid. 'But that stuff's dyed red!'

'Yeah, so was this before her brother strained it through a gas mask.' Gladys picked up a bottle and popped open the top. She allowed Joel to smell it. 'Good stuff, that is, been strained a few times, that has.'

He nodded, the rich smell making his eyes water. 'But it must have cost you the earth!'

'You both came down here, even with her in that condition,' Gladys looked over at Lizzie before popping the ball back in the neck of the bottle, 'to help me save my friend, and her mother.' Again she looked at Lizzie. 'If she needs it,' she added. Then she put down the bottle to join the others. 'It's the least I can do.' She began pouring tea into the cups. 'Besides, Lizzie can't possibly walk about in that condition for much longer and you're going to need your car if anything happens.'

Joel moved over to her and when she put the teapot down, he put his arms around her. 'Anyone ever tell you what a lovely person you are?'

'Get off me, you daft ha'p'orth.' Joel could see the blush rising from her neck to her cheeks. 'There's plenty more where that came from,' she added. 'If the coppers do one of their spot checks on the car to see if you're using the wrong petrol, they won't be able to tell with all the colour leached out of it.'

Joel saw her look at Lizzie, who had her hands over her belly and her eyes closed. Suddenly she opened them and said, 'I don't want any more tea. I think I'll go to bed.' She hauled herself up and went to the bottom of the stairs. 'Good night,' she called. Joel thought she looked tired. He heard her climb the stairs and then the bedroom door open.

'I bet Em's pleased to see Lizzie?' Joel nodded and stared at Gladys. 'I hope she's not put out about you two staying here?' This time he shook his head. The conversation made him think of Lily and the man, and the money that had passed between them.

'I think you're right,' he said. 'There's something going on with Lily. I don't know what, but I'm going to find out.'

She smiled at him and pushed his tea across the table towards him.

'I bet she was surprised about you and the baby.'

Joel knew he was skating on thin ice with the lies he'd told about being the father of Lizzie's child. But he nodded. Then for no reason at all, he said, 'I love Lizzie, and I'd do anything for her, Gladys.'

He chatted with Gladys about Lizzie, the war, and his work while he drank his tea. Gladys busied herself cleaning out the canary and washing its seed and water dishes. The little yellow bird chirruped as it flew backwards and forwards in its cage, with Gladys talking to it.

He was giving Lizzie time to get herself safely beneath

the covers. She was intensely shy about the whole business of having to sleep with him, so he tried to make it as bearable as possible for her.

'Had that bird long?' he asked.

Gladys stopped what she was doing and faced him, hands on her hips.

'Some bloke sent me home from Brighton with this bird. I've forgotten the bloke's name but I love this little feller, keeps me company.' She tucked a piece of cuttlefish between the bars of the cage.

Joel smiled at her. Gladys was so easy to like. He wondered if Lizzie might prefer to stay in Gosport with her own folk. At least there'd be women about to help her with the baby. If Gladys was willing to get more petrol – he'd pay, of course – he could soon come back when Lizzie gave birth.

There were a few days left of his break from Yew Trees and he was worried about leaving Lizzie alone in the prefab while he worked. What if she went into labour when he wasn't there and a nurse or midwife couldn't get to her in time? But he had to earn money and there was no way he could ask for more leave. He still thought constantly of Fred and wished he'd had more time to get to know the old man, but he was ready to go back to work now.

Gladys said, 'I'll just get rid of this rubbish.' She rolled up the newspaper with the bird's sand and droppings on it. Presently he heard the dustbin lid outside in the backyard clatter down, then the rattling of cups and the sound of pouring water.

He helped Gladys wash up and afterwards said goodnight at the top of the stairs as she went into her own bedroom.

Lizzie was a bump in the bed and he smiled fondly at her. Her clothes were hung over the back of a chair, her underwear almost covered by the green and white smock that she insisted was the only thing that fitted her. She wore it over a maternity skirt, a wraparound garment that dipped at the back and rose at the front. He didn't care what she wore. She'd look lovely in a potato sack.

He'd had a quick wash at the sink downstairs so it didn't take him long to undress and put his pyjamas on. When he pulled back the bedclothes he saw the two pillows laid down the centre of the bed, denoting the two separate sides. He got in and immediately felt the heat from her body, which had permeated the whole bed. He wanted to tell her he loved her and would never hurt a hair of her head; instead, he said softly, 'Goodnight, love.'

*

Lily checked the back door was locked. She'd made their lunches and packed them in the Oxo tins. She'd cut two pieces of the carrot cake she'd made that afternoon. It didn't contain as much sugar as it was supposed to, she'd substituted walnuts for some almonds she'd discovered at the back of the cupboard, but the egg powder was a blessing. Extra grated carrots had made it moist. She still hadn't got over the shock of meeting Em's daughter and Joel. Em would think she was going loopy when she found out she'd made a cake and forgotten all about it. Now she swilled water with torn-up pieces of newspaper in the flasks to clean them and after rinsing left them sparkling on the draining board.

Lily would be working on the line tomorrow in what was called the stemming shop. This wasn't as dangerous as some of the work she'd already done at Priddy's. This part of the operation meant filling rubber tubes with powder. There was a container that she had to top up with powder that emptied into a drum, then she turned a handle and the powder dropped into the rubber tubes.

She'd be breathing in the powder that drifted in the air and covered her clothes, though. Already the front of her hair had turned orange, despite the turban she wore. She'd be itching all over by the time she got home again, and even after a wash down the staining wouldn't come off her skin. All the same, she loved the chatter of the girls as they worked and the camaraderie as they sang along to the wireless and its never-ending supply of music.

She also liked the wages. Lily insisted on giving Em money for her keep, but the rest she'd squirrelled away, until today.

Lawrence had insisted she get Em used to her borrowing money.

'Start asking for minor amounts and pay it back immediately; she'll have no inkling you're going to fleece her good and proper.'

When she'd said she didn't want to ask Em for anything, he'd gripped her arm so tightly that his fingerprints stayed on her skin.

He'd wanted twenty pounds.

She couldn't bring herself to lie any more to Em. She gave him five pounds.

'This is the beginning of the scam,' he said. 'I'll give this back to you later in the week so you can return it to her. Next time, ask for ten pounds. Tell her you have an unpaid debt and that you'll soon return the money. Lull her into a false sense of security.'

Lily had taken the cash from the post office where she'd stashed her wages. She couldn't bring herself to ask

Em for money. Using her own was fine, this time. But his expectations would grow, along with requests for bigger sums of money. Her savings didn't amount to much. Lily wasn't sure how she'd cope with larger amounts.

'Em will come into everything you, as her sister, owns. The will states that. And it's a considerable amount. Make sure she sees the documents. Once you've buttered her up she'll be handing over enough cash for us to go away together.' He'd looked into her eyes. 'You want this, don't you?' She'd nodded. He kissed her briefly on her forehead.

But was it really what she wanted? She had friends now, and Em, who treated her like the long-lost sister she purported to be.

She'd never forgotten the pain and indignity of being thrown from his car in the rain.

With the morning's chores sorted for an early getaway to the munitions yard, Lily climbed the stairs. As she closed her bedroom door, Em called out, 'Goodnight, sis.'

As the kind words were softly spoken in the darkness, a tear seeped from beneath Lily's eyelid. She was living a lie and she wanted an end to it.

Chapter Seventeen

Lawrence counted out the white banknotes with a satisfied smile. He looked at the four portions of money and
picked up the second largest.

'Here you are, Colin,' he said to the dark-haired man
sprawled in one of the armchairs with a whisky in his
hand.

'And very welcome it is.' The man rose, leaving his
now empty glass on the mantelpiece. He stepped forward
and took the money. 'Nice little earner this is becoming,'
he said, the money going into his wallet. He picked up
his white helmet with the black lettering that spelled ARP
and put it in a brown carrier bag.

'Don't forget to remove your identification,' Lawrence
said and watched as Colin unclipped his silver lapel badge
of a crown with the letters ARP below it. 'Send the boys
round in the morning, their cut is ready to collect.'

He walked to the door of the flat with the man and let him out.

'Tomorrow?'

'I don't think so.' Lawrence frowned. 'The Luftwaffe appear to be leaving a few days in between the bombings. Mind you, those new V2s don't come in any pattern.'

'Friday?'

Lawrence nodded. The big man disappeared into the darkness and Lawrence closed the door of his ground-floor flat near The Crescent at Alverstoke.

It had all started with the silver badges he had discovered in the roadside ruins of the town hall.

He'd been walking back to his car after standing near the ticket office of the ferry boats' shipping office. Every so often he'd keep a wary eye on his business across the road. He was far enough away from the premises not to be discovered, but he could make out the trail of punters entering and exiting the brothel's stairway. The business was going well. The new woman was making him money despite the chits he found in the books for sundries she'd instigated and he'd paid for. He was well pleased; he laughed to himself. Apart from Ruby he had no idea of the other two women's names, nor did he need to know. He couldn't identify them, and they knew nothing of him.

Ruby was the weakest link. He'd picked her up from the street. She was a right mess then. He'd fed her, clothed her and put her back on the street, but she was aware of the debt she owed him.

He fingered the badge he wore and thought back to the air raid that had forced him into the public shelter near the ferry gardens.

The place stank of sweat and fear but he'd endured it and luckily his stay in there was reasonably short. Cordite hung in the air, along with the smell of burning. People crawled from the shelter happy to be alive, but terrified that when they reached home their houses might no longer be standing.

Walking near the council offices he'd noticed the small cloth bag, lying partly hidden by rubble. Earlier that week the town hall had taken a hit from a V1. No lives lost and surprisingly a great deal of the papers and metal filing cabinets had survived. The fire wardens had been a godsend helping the firemen retrieve whatever they could, but sometimes small items got overlooked and lay in the dust for kids to find. He'd picked up the little canvas bag and inside were half a dozen small badges. They were identification for the wardens who patrolled the streets during the blackouts. He'd kicked about, seeing what else he could discover, but finding nothing walked back to his car.

He'd sat in the Village Home pub nursing a gin and thought about his find. Men and women working as wardens walked the streets, checking there were no lights visible during the blackout. Any chink of light from a careless householder could guide the German bombers in their quest. The wardens also assisted at the shelters, issued gas masks and helped householders retrieve what they could from the ashes of their homes. Instantly recognizable in their dark boiler suits and tin helmets, their feet encased in heavy wellington boots, they were a friendly face in adversity.

But what if . . .?

He ordered another gin and his thoughts grew into an idea. He tapped his fingers on the wooden table in time to Jimmy Dorsey's 'Tangerine', which was playing on the wireless.

Surely when a bomb dropped on your house, if you survived you'd be so out of it and worried about your loved ones that to see a couple of ARP wardens in their instantly recognizable uniforms, sifting through the rubble, could only be a welcome sight?

Many householders had good stuff, money hidden in tins, heirlooms, mattresses with money inside. It wouldn't all get smashed to smithereens, would it?

He would need at least three men, boiler suits,

wellington boots and assorted tin helmets. With their official silver badges they'd be indistinguishable from the real thing. He'd also need a van. With petrol still rationed and black market petrol costing the earth he should be able to pick up a good little runabout for next to nothing, shouldn't he?

Den in Forton Road was a good fence for china, silver and jewellery. Stolen gear was never on display in his run-down little shop, he sent it further afield. Eric Mason in Ann's Hill Road would take small items of furniture, always in demand due to the bombings. And the odds and sods, clothing, kitchenware and such would find a home in the markets, not Gosport market, too close to home. Monty at Southampton would give him a good rate for bulk.

He'd need a store, wouldn't he? His own double garage at the back of his flat would do admirably. With trees either side of the road leading to it, the garage was secluded. Nosy parkers would have to work hard to find out what was going on. It would mean him leaving his MG outside on the road, but since his neighbours, those that owned cars, parked alongside the flats, he'd blend in beautifully.

His fingers began tapping quickly to The Song Spinners, 'Coming In On A Wing And A Prayer'. He'd decided in the pub that yet another gin was in order for the marvellous ruse he'd concocted. At this rate and with all his operations up and running, soon he should be rolling in money.

Now it was September and all Lawrence's plans *had* come together. But the funny thing about money, he thought, as he poured himself a whisky, was the more you had, the more you needed. His plans worked, but there were more people to pay out of the profits.

He sat down and opened the *Evening News*. He took off his glasses to read. These plain glass spectacles were part of his disguise and sometimes they were a hindrance.

'Nazi Atrocity in Maidenek'. It had been discovered that more than a million prisoners had been sent in cattle trucks to the concentration camp, enclosed with barbed wire and guarded by gun towers containing men with machine guns. They had been methodically stripped of all their possessions and their valuables went to Germany. In batches they were gassed. Their ashes were used as fertilizer.

Lawrence put down the newspaper and took another sip of his drink.

'My God,' he announced to the empty room. 'Some people have no feeling for their fellow man.'

*

'I want Joel. He knows where my things are.'

'Come on back to bed,' pleaded Pete. He ran his fingers through his bright hair. Joel should be back any time now, and wouldn't he be thankful to see him! Much as Pete admired Liliah's strength of mind, she was a handful and no mistake. He wished he knew what the hell she was on about.

He'd spent all morning with Frederick's solicitor. Yesterday they'd buried the old man in Ann's Hill Cemetery. He'd have informed Joel, if there'd been time to let him know, but planning a wartime funeral meant hardly a plan at all. When people died, they were buried whenever there was time for the ceremony.

Pete looked at the ruin around him that was Liliah's room. He was sick and tired of putting it to rights after she'd thrown everything aside in her search. He only wished he knew what it was she thought she'd lost. No, not lost, Liliah was sure something had been taken.

'Mrs Somerton, each one of my staff I'd trust with my life. From the carers to the domestics, not one would touch anything in any of the residents' rooms.' He'd got no further, for she pushed him aside and strode out into the passage where the wooden trolley was standing laden with fresh sheets, pillowcases, towels and cleaning materials.

He watched wide-eyed as she began throwing the clean bedding to the floor, as Belle the chambermaid came from the room next door with an armful of dirty washing and screamed as bedding went flying in all directions.

'Help me get her back into her room,' Pete yelled. Belle was picking up the sheets she'd dropped. 'Leave that!' he shouted. 'Grab her arms, but don't hurt her.'

Liliah pushed the girl aside as though she was a child and Belle stumbled, hitting her thigh on the trolley. She collapsed to the carpet in tears. Liliah immediately fell to her knees, gathering the girl in her bony arms.

'I'm so sorry,' she said. Tears sprang from her eyes. 'I'm so sorry.'

Pete looked at Liliah. She was a crumpled mess. Belle, unhurt but shook up, was patting Liliah's back. Pete put out a hand and Liliah stumbled to her feet, her eyes still drawn to Belle.

'I'm sorry, child,' she said. 'But I've no idea who I am without my papers. You do understand, don't you?'

Belle scrambled up. Pete watched amazed as the girl, leading Liliah by the hand, steered her back into her own room. Liliah climbed into bed and Belle tucked her in, after making sure she hadn't harmed herself in any way.

'Can you tell me about these papers?' Belle sat on the

side of the bed and held on to Liliah's hand. Pete sighed and began picking up Mrs Somerton's personal effects. A black diary, the leather scuffed and discoloured, was on the floor. Metal hair curlers, her silver-backed hairbrush and a jar of Pond's Cream, he picked them all up and set them on her dressing table.

Pete smiled at Belle. 'You all right?' he asked. Belle was smoothing Liliah's forehead and the woman was almost asleep, her head on the pillow, her breathing even and deep, her lashes fanned over her sallow cheeks.

Belle nodded. Liliah began mumbling about the papers. Pete picked up Liliah's dressing gown and hung it on the back of the door. Joel and Liliah were unlikely friends, but he understood her. If anyone could find out about these missing papers – if indeed there *were* missing papers – Pete was certain Joel could.

Chapter Eighteen

Michael 'Mac' MacKenzie shuffled the papers into a foolscap pile and sighed.

'Bloody paperwork,' he muttered and stared across his office and through the police station window, looking out over Church Path and the cockle pond in Walpole Park. He liked the job but not all its aspects, and he wasn't a typical Scot.

He had been born in Edinburgh, but his accent was more Hampshire Hog than Scottish. He hated the taste of whisky, but could drink brandy as though the vat might run dry. He was careless with money and he was a sucker for stray cats, spending a small fortune on feeding the three who had chosen to reside with him and the others who sat plaintively on his door-step wishing they could. He often bought fresh fish and cooked it for the moggies, saying, 'How can I give them leftovers when because of this bloody war, there's nothing left?'

The white paint that he'd used to retouch the window frames of his new house was evident by its smell and splotches on his hands. No one else had put in an offer on the semi-detached, terraced property. Probably because the wooden supports propping it up after the nineteen forty-three bomb blast gave it a lopsided look. But the large garden meant he could dig and plant to his heart's content while listening to his Billie Holiday records as loud as he wanted.

'Sir, you in today?' The curly-haired uniformed constable poked his head round the door of Mac's office. Mac slammed the pile of papers into a drawer of his desk.

'Out. So if you thought you'd got a day off from driving me around, forget it. I've been drafted down here from Winchester because the Hampshire police force has been amalgamated with your bloody lot, to help stamp out looting. That's not going to happen with you sitting on your arse, is it?'

Ben Chambers's face dropped.

'We're to be the *Hampshire Constabulary*.' He stared at his constable. 'Did you know there are precious few looters in Germany because they execute the buggers? We should do the same.'

'Yes, sir.'

His constable looked worn out. But then, with a four-month-old baby who didn't know the difference between night and day, who wouldn't?

The detective gave him a sudden smile that took ten years off his forty-year-old features. He caught sight of his reflection in the window. His red hair stood up in all directions, emphasizing the shadow on his lower face where he'd failed to shave. He turned away and stared at Ben.

'Had your breakfast?'

Ben looked to the parquet flooring. 'No, sir.'

Mac stared at him for a couple of seconds. 'Well, don't stand there like a moron, get the bloody car and we'll go down The Dive for a fry-up.'

'Joel, Joel.' Lizzie shook his shoulder and whispered, 'Joel, I think my waters have broken.'

Groggily he raised himself to a sitting position and blinked at Lizzie just as a contraction gripped her, making her groan.

He tried to think of the right questions to ask to make sure it wasn't a false alarm.

All he could come out with was, 'Are you sure?'

'I'm sure.' She was gritting her teeth. 'I've had back-ache all day but didn't want to worry—'

She rolled herself into a ball, rocking with pain, unable to finish the sentence. Finally she breathed heavily then said, 'I wanted to make sure . . .'

She grabbed his arm and her fingers dug into his flesh. 'Owwwww!'

With one fluid movement he leapt from the bed and flung the dividing line of pillows to the carpet. Into his trousers, and with the electric light switched on, he moved swiftly to Gladys's bedroom door, banging loudly and yelling as he rushed in, 'The baby's started! The baby's started!'

A head full of metal curlers appeared above the yellow counterpane and Gladys mouthed, 'Get the kettle on!' Then she clapped her hand across her mouth. 'Ain't got me teeth in!' He saw the tumbler of water with the false teeth grinning at him from the bedside table.

His head spinning, he half fell, half jumped down the stairs and filled the kettle then put it on the gas, hearing the reassuring pop of the flames.

He opened the back door and stood on the concrete in the dark. Soft rain was falling; he breathed deeply. He could hear Gladys and Lizzie upstairs. There was moaning and heavy panting, voices and the sound of moving furniture. He realized that although he had been told by Gladys to put the kettle on, he had no idea what to do with it. Should he make tea? Should he carry the hot water upstairs? Should he do both?

He worked with old people who frequently needed help in the night. He was perfectly calm and reassuring with them but this was different. Should he call the doctor? What doctor? Midwife? Yes, she'd need a midwife. Where was the nearest phone? Phone number? Best get back upstairs and ask.

Gladys had stripped the bed and a pile of wet sheets sat on the floor.

'Get rid of them,' she snapped. He could do that. Yes, he could do that. He gathered them up and tried not to look at Lizzie lying on her back, with her nightdress hiked up. Her face was covered in sweat and her hair was hanging limply around her face. She gave another yell and then a sound that made him shiver.

Gladys was bending over her, wiping her forehead and saying, 'You're doing fine, girl.'

She didn't look fine to him. The metallic smell of blood hung in the air.

'Pour some of that cold water into the basin!'

What cold water? Basin? Ah, the washing water in the tall jug. He threw down the sheets he was holding, went to the washstand and picked up the heavy jug. It clanged against the side of the large flowered basin.

'Mind that! It belonged to my mother!' Gladys turned and glared at him. 'And where's the tea?' She threw him the clean white pillowcase she was using to mop up Lizzie's sweat. 'Soak this!'

Glad of something tangible to do, he steeped the white cloth, wrung it out and passed it back to her.

'Shall I get someb—'

'Like who? She ain't registered with anyone here, you daft lump. And she's too far gone to take in the car to the War Memorial Hospital. Even if we could get her in there, place is full to bursting with war wounded. They been using the poorhouse by Alver Creek for births. Won't get her there in time.'

'What about Em?'

'No time.'

Lizzie was clutching Gladys's arms and grunting.

'Pant, love, pant.' Gladys began panting and Lizzie tried to emulate her until a scream came that practically shook the foundations of the small house. 'There, there,' continued Gladys, quite unperturbed.

Joel moved across the floor and got his foot tangled in the sheets; tripping over, he used the iron bedstead to steady himself. His weight shook the bed.

'Get rid of that bleedin' washin'!' shouted Gladys. 'And bring that tea!'

Downstairs, Joel sat on a stool in the scullery, his head in his hands. The wet bedding was piled on top of the copper. What if something happened to Lizzie and the baby? He sighed again and looked at the stinging, long, red burn on his hand. He'd forgotten to check the kettle for water and it had held so little it had almost burned dry. The metal sides were as hot as hell.

He'd started the process all over again, this time carefully filling the kettle.

Lizzie must have been in pain all day. She hadn't told him. It couldn't have helped that he'd allowed her to walk all that way to her mother's house – and all for nothing – as they'd not been able to get hold of Lily's papers. Was Lily Em's sister? Why didn't Lizzie say she was in the first stages of labour? Perhaps she hadn't realized it herself? It was, after all, her first baby.

He remembered that the range's fire had burned low. He went outside to the coal bunker and filled a metal bucket. September nights could be chilly and Gladys couldn't stand the cold. She had a coalman friend who frequently brought her a stolen sack of the precious stuff. The house should be kept warm for the baby.

Back in the kitchen, he took the range's top-plate off with the lifting iron and put in a shovelful of small bits of slack to liven it up. Then he made the tea and went upstairs again with two cups of tea on a tray, only to be greeted by Gladys: 'Jesus Christ! *She's* in no state to drink tea! One cup for me would have done!'

'I can't do right for doing wrong!' Joel said beneath his breath. He wasn't cross.

Gladys was in a flap and just as worried as he was.

Lizzie was threshing about. Her yelling began again and Joel's hands were shaking, his heart beating fast, the back of his neck wet with sweat. He didn't know what to do to ease her discomfort. Didn't some old biddies say having a baby was like going into the Vale of Death? Bloody old wives' tales. But he was praying silently, please don't let anything happen to his Lizzie.

'Nearly there,' Gladys said, through a lull in Lizzie's screams. 'She's crowned. Pant, pant!' He couldn't look at her, yelling orders to Lizzie. *No, he was scared to look.*

Then he made himself stare at the woman he loved giving birth to some other bloke's child. The sweat was streaming off Lizzie's face. Suddenly Joel couldn't stand it any longer.

He got up and moved close to the bed. 'Hold on to me, Lizzie, and do as Gladys says.'

Lizzie gripped his hand and looked at him and he knew he was lost.

'That's it, girl, you scream all you want,' he said softly.

A sound came from her throat like no other noise he'd heard before.

Gladys was busy at the other end and then, 'Here it comes!'

Lizzie shuddered and fell back.

'Joel!'

Lizzie was breathing hard and lying flat, her eyes closed, exhausted.

'Joel!'

He looked to where Gladys held the little mite in her hands. The small body was tinged with blue. He moved immediately to her side. Gladys had already wiped mucus off the little girl's face, but she wasn't breathing.

'Joel.' This time it was easy to hear Gladys's agonized use of his name.

He grabbed hold of the baby and laid it at the bottom of the bed where there was a flat surface. With his ear close to the tiny face he could hear the weak, infrequent whistling sound in the baby's nose.

'She's not breathing!' Gladys had tears in her eyes. Although she whispered the words, Lizzie must have heard.

'What's up with my baby?' She was struggling to move down the bloodied bed sheet.

'Keep Lizzie back from me.' Joel's voice was sharp. He turned back to the small form.

The baby lay unmoving.

Joel lowered his head until his mouth hovered over the tiny nose. Then he sucked and spat out mucus and blood. Again he gently sucked, and again hawked out the red and white slime. Carefully, once more, he listened at the tiny face, ignoring the shrill cries of Lizzie and Gladys. Then he looked at Lizzie and his heart almost split in two at her pain. To carry a child for nine months that was dying in front of her was surely the worst thing . . . He took a deep breath and sucked once more at the nose, no bigger than his little fingertip, and again the slime swept into his mouth.

Two small arms quivered. The baby's mouth opened beneath his lips, and the lustiest yell shot forth. So surprised was Joel that his eyes filled with tears as the tiny being, with eyes screwed shut, screamed.

Joel picked up the wriggling bloodied body and handed the slippery child to Lizzie, who with tears running down her cheeks rained kisses on her daughter.

Gladys sat on the edge of the bed staring at him.

'Well, I never,' she said. 'You saved that little one's life.' She shook her head and gazed at him adoringly. 'However did you think to do that?'

'I was so worried about Lizzie I couldn't think. Until I needed to . . .' He wiped his forehead with one hand.

'Sorry for spitting on the bed,' he said. 'As a medic I've had soldiers unable to breathe with their airways full of muck . . .'

Gladys looked as though she might ask him questions and he didn't want to get into discussing the horrors of war. He looked at Lizzie nuzzling her child and as though sensing his eyes on her, she looked up and mouthed, 'Thank you.'

The look in her eyes said so much more.

He thought he'd never been as happy as he was in that moment.

He walked the length of the bed and put out his hands to take the baby. 'Your afterbirth needs sorting,' he said. 'The cord needs cutting as well. Gladys, scissors?'

He looked down at the baby. 'You need a bath an' all,' he whispered. The baby's black hair was long enough for damp curls to be plastered to her head. He put his thumb inside her fist and her tiny fingers clutched tightly. A wave of something strange, the like of which he'd never felt before, swept over him and he knew although this wasn't his child, he would love her for evermore. He would die for her.

Half an hour later, Lizzie was washed and in one of Gladys's flannelette nighties. She'd offered a frilly concoction but Lizzie had declined it. The baby was clean and wrapped in a soft towel lying close to Lizzie, and all the soiled bedding was in soak; the rubbish had gone on the fire. All three were companionably drinking tea when Gladys said,

'What's her name?'

Joel stared at Lizzie who said, 'First of all I need to thank you, Joel. If it hadn't been for you my little one would be looking at a burial not a christening. I've never heard of a bloke being as much help as you was.'

Gladys broke in with, 'No, they think after they've first done their bit, it's women's work. You've been marvellous.'

Joel knew he was blushing. Male doctors attended births. Usually husbands kept out of the way. He thought of what had happened and how brave Lizzie had been. His heart was overflowing with love for her. 'I'll go and tell your mum first thing tomorrow,' he said. 'Then bring her back here after work in the car.'

'She'll be over the moon,' Gladys said, taking a slurp of tea. 'You ought to register the baby as well and get the midwife to call round.' She paused and smiled. 'While I'm at work tomorrow I'll be thinking about you and the baby all day.' A big smile lit her face. 'But you still ain't said what you're calling the little mite. Mind you, I can't see much of her daddy in her.' She stared at Joel, who felt uncomfortable beneath her gaze.

'No, that one's like her mum,' he said. Lizzie's face was pink with the beginnings of a blush.

'It's all that black hair,' said Gladys. Lizzie ran a hand through her own dark hair. She'd already told him about the baby's father's gypsy looks that had given him the nickname of Blackie.

'My mum's hair was dark,' said Lizzie. 'You must remember that.'

'I've forgotten what my natural colour is,' said Gladys, touching her bleached hair. 'But what about her name?'

Lizzie said, 'Her name's Jane, Janie, but her second name will be Pixie.'

Gladys put her hand to her mouth. 'Oh, my!'

Joel must have looked confused, for Lizzie said, 'Pamela, or Pixie as she was called, was Gladys's daughter. She died in a bomb blast near the Criterion picture house. She was a wonderful daughter, a great mother and had a happy marriage. If this little tot grows up to be half the woman Pixie was, I'll be more than happy. Is that all right with you, Gladys?'

But Gladys had her head in her hands and was crying.

She looked up. 'I can't thank you enough,' she said through teary eyes.

'Then it's settled. But there's something else. Will you be her godmother?'

'Oh, Lizzie, you don't know how happy that makes me . . .'

'Good,' Lizzie said. She gave a huge yawn. 'Having a baby certainly takes it out of you,' she smiled down at her daughter, 'but it's certainly worth it.' She stifled another yawn. 'We'll sort this christening as soon as possible. It's about time we had a bloody good old knees-up, war or no war!'

Chapter Nineteen

Em could feel her heart singing every time she thought about baby Janie. Joel had come knocking on the door telling her the news even before the alarm went this morning. Lily was still asleep. Em didn't wake her because she'd heard her get up in the night and wander downstairs, unable to sleep. Joel'd driven her round to Gladys's house for a quick peek before work, promising to return that evening for the pair of them.

'Some good things come out of the war,' she said to Lily. Both Em and Lily were in the rifle bullet shop today. Lily had been moved there because a girl had called in sick, and Em was 'Blue Band'.

Being a Blue Band meant Em had to check the girls working weren't wearing jewellery and hadn't hidden cigarettes or hairgrips in their hair, which meant searching them. She walked about the shop floor doing spot checks on the workers. It wasn't one of her favourite jobs, but it was less monotonous for her than Lily's.

Em stood behind her, watching her press detonators into bullets while sitting with the other women at a long bench. A machine operated a lengthy belt that moved along sliding the bullets down and the women pushed in the tiny detonators. Eventually the belt worked its way along the tables – the women turned out thousands of bullets at every shift. Em didn't know how Lily could stand doing the boring, repetitive work. She held her breath as Lily's hand shook while pressing down a detonator; she was a bag of nerves today. *Workers' Playtime* was on the wireless and even though it was loud, the noise of the machinery churning out the bullet belts was horrendous, so too was the smell of cordite.

'You coming to see the baby tonight?' Em was making notes on her clipboard, but she turned to Lily. 'Joel'll come and pick us up in the car.'

Lily shook her head. Em sniffed and frowned.

'I don't feel too good. It wouldn't be right if I passed on some germs, would it?'

Em sighed. She'd thought Lily would have been more excited about Lizzie's little girl. After all, she *was* her auntie, but she'd hardly mentioned Janie. Last Sunday when she'd taken the bus to Ann's Hill Cemetery to put fresh flowers on her mum's grave, nice yellow late roses, Lily had accompanied her, but Em thought she would have been more curious about her mother. She never asked anything about her father either. Em put it down to the fact that Lily had been brought up by foster parents.

'I think Joel's lovely, such a nice man. Most blokes would run a mile when a woman has a baby, not him. Mind you,' she confided, 'I'm not saying I wasn't a bit upset about my own daughter giving birth at Gladys's house.' She frowned again then said resignedly, 'Still, Gladys'll look after her.' She watched the girls working for a little longer, then moved on down the line.

Since Lily had been living with her, she hadn't seen so much of Gladys and she missed her. Her and Gladys used to have a right laugh. When they were working nights, they'd get up at lunchtime, and in the afternoons go to the tea dances at the Connaught Hall.

The place was always packed out with servicemen, mostly Americans. Em was sure some of the Americans were lonely and missed being at home with their families. You could always tell, especially when one of them produced a photo of his kiddies from his wallet for you to look at. It was nice just to be friends with some of them. Em sighed. She'd tried to get Lily to go dancing. She gone a couple of times and seemed to enjoy herself

– she even laughed at getting mixed up with dancing the wrong steps to the Dashing White Sergeant. But Lily wasn't like Gladys, who always wanted to joke with the men and get them to give her nylons.

Of course, dancing during the afternoon meant they couldn't have a proper drink because of going to work in the evenings, even though some of the men turned up with small bottles or hip flasks in their pockets. The women daren't go to Priddy's with the smell of alcohol on their breath. Not only was it forbidden, it was dangerous, and besides, Em had to set a good example.

Thoughts of baby Janie swam through Em's mind. All that black curly hair was gorgeous. She wasn't a bit like Joel with his floppy blond locks but Em could tell he was going to be a lovely dad. He couldn't take his eyes off his daughter. But wasn't it a shame his wife couldn't be found.

Gladys caught up with Em in the corridor. She'd been working in nitrates today and her fingers were itching where the acid had burned through to her fingertips. First cotton was soaked in acid, moving it around the pans with a fork-like implement to make sure it was fully immersed. Large plates were then put on top of the cotton to press the moisture out. Next it was rinsed with water to get rid of all the acid. She worked on a line with other girls, but it was heavy work and took two of them to squeeze the plates hard enough to make the brittle guncotton.

Of course the acid would splash. It got into clothes making holes in the material. If it got onto your skin and you went to see the nurse, she would put an antiseptic powder on it to soothe the burn. Then you went straight back to work on the line.

The brick building where the gunpowder was made was huge. Gladys was replacing Amy, one of the regular women who was sent to hospital yesterday with severe burns.

In one corner of the big room was a large barrel of water. Amy had accidentally splashed her face with acid. Screaming with pain she'd run to the barrel and tipped her head beneath the water. The girls had told Gladys her skin was puckered and red and she wouldn't stop screaming. Just kept on moving her face in the tub of water until the nurse came and took her away.

Gladys was pleased to see Em's face light up when she saw her. Then Em looked worried.

'It's not the baby, is it?'

Gladys laughed. 'No, she's a lovely little scrap and Lizzie's so good with her.'

Em frowned.

'It's Joel, he's got to go back to work. He can't stay down here any longer, he'll lose his job otherwise.'

'But he's coming to pick me up tonight,' Em said.

'Yes, that's all right, he's not going until tomorrow morning.'

'Lizzie too?'

'No. She's not fit to travel up there yet; she's staying at my house. Better really, because the doctor has seen her there. I went home at lunchtime. Everything's all right.' She could see her words reassured Em. She took a moment to scratch beneath her turban. 'We contacted the midwife and she's popping in. But what I wanted to ask you and Lily is, will she bring her bundle of papers along this evening so Joel and Lizzie can look through them?'

Em was staring at Gladys. 'Lily isn't coming tonight.'

Gladys was confused. 'Why not?'

'Says she don't feel right and doesn't want to pass anything on to the baby.'

'She looked all right to me, eating sarnies just now.' Gladys was indignant.

'Don't raise your voice to me! I'm only telling you what she said to me earlier.'

Gladys gave a deep sigh. 'Don't let's argue about

Lily any more, please, Em?' She felt her tears rise and hastily brushed them away but saw Em had spotted her discomfort.

Em said, 'Tell you what, she can't possibly mind me bringing her papers along if I promise to take good care of them. Of course my Lizzie and Joel want to know all about her.'

Gladys gave her a big smile. 'That's right. I wouldn't think she'd mind. After all, we know you're her sister. If she can't trust you with her documents, who can she trust?'

Just then a buzzer sounded. 'I'd better go,' said Em. 'Doing spot checks on the girls. I'll surprise those returning to the rifle bullet shop.'

Joel settled Em in the passenger seat but before starting up the car he asked, 'Is that Lily's stuff?'

'Yes,' Em said, shaking the brown carrier bag. 'I don't think she wanted to part with it. For a moment I thought she'd change her mind and come with me to keep an eye on it, but she's gone to bed. She's been ever so quiet and fidgety tonight.'

Joel was surprised Lily had parted with her papers so easily. He smiled, remembering how he and Lizzie had gone round to Em's house prepared to steal a look at them, when all they had to do was ask.

He couldn't say he didn't like the woman. He thought she was strange. She didn't seem at all interested in a family she was supposed to have taken such a long time to find.

'Baby all right?' Em broke into his thoughts.

'She's the prettiest little girl . . .'

'All right, proud dad.' Em laughed. 'You're going to miss the pair of them when you go back to Lyme Regis.'

'That's true. But we need money more than ever now. Though I'm glad Lizzie is staying here. She'd be on her own all day up there. At least here in Gosport with the midwife calling in and you and Gladys around, she won't get lonely.' He took a deep breath, then said, 'Can I smell cake?'

Em giggled like a young girl. 'I got hold of some raisins. A mate of mine has a son serving in North Africa and he sent her fruit. I'd saved a bit of sugar, been a while since I've been able to bake anything. It's a wartime fruit cake; I thought it'd be nice to celebrate Janie's birth.'

Joel thought how wonderfully kind Lizzie's mother was. Then he remembered the lies he'd told and a shadow hung over him. He wasn't the baby's father. While it was true he loved Lizzie and the little one, and he'd marry her tomorrow if he had the chance, and Lizzie had told him she cared for him. Still, if the lies he'd told had got Lizzie out of a hole and saved her mother from becoming the butt of jokes at Priddy's, then it was all worth it.

She asked him, 'Looking forward to going back to work?'

'I'd rather be with Lizzie,' he said. 'But babies cost money and Pete, a senior worker, has begged me to help with one of our ladies who's been very fretful of late.'

Em nodded. Joel thought about Pete's pleading. He had no idea why Mrs Somerton preferred him to attend to her, but that was the way it happened. It was similar to the way Fred had taken to him. A wave of sadness washed over him. It wouldn't be the same without the old man, but Pete and Marie had been right, a break away from his job had given him a new perspective on his work. And he'd enjoyed Lizzie's family and friends who'd made him feel so welcome. He'd driven past the Criterion picture house now and turned into Alma Street, parking outside the door of number fourteen.

Em was out of the car and banging on Gladys's door, the bag containing the cake and papers held tight in her hand.

'Bless you! Why didn't you just come in, the string's on the door.' Gladys pointed to the letter box. Joel could see the blush steal over Em's face. Gladys said, 'You're still my best friend. You don't have to stand on ceremony with me.'

She ushered the pair of them into the small house. Joel could smell baby's milk and talcum powder. Funny how someone so small could take over the place, he thought. Em's face was split in two with a big grin. She pulled out the cake and set it on the table and then piled the papers beside it.

Lizzie was sitting in the faded armchair in the kitchen, with Janie latched on to her breast. She looked the picture of contentment, he thought. She glanced up and gave him a broad smile that made his heart turn somersaults.

'Hello, Mum,' she said to Em. 'Yummy, cake. You're just in time to wind Janie.' She wrapped the woollen shawl around the tiny child and handed the baby to her mother, who pulled out a kitchen chair, sat down, then held the baby to her shoulder and began rubbing the child's back.

Joel laughed when a big burp filled the kitchen with sound. He realized if he could hear it so clearly it surely was a loud noise.

Gladys was in the scullery making tea.

Joel asked, 'You want a hand?'

She poked her head around the door and answered

him. 'Nah!' She looked at the cake. 'Oh, Em that must have taken much more than your sugar ration.'

Em said, 'You know how I love to bake.'

Gladys went back into the scullery then she called out, 'I got a message for you from Marlene who was in the Fox a while ago. She said Sam asked after you.'

Joel could see that Em was quite shaken. Lizzie had told him the publican was sweet on her mother.

'I don't have time to go gallivanting,' Em said.

'Well that's a pity because he's a nice man,' said Lizzie. Em sniffed and went on patting Janie's back.

'You don't have time to see him because you've been spending so much time with Lily,' said Lizzie.

'Actually, I don't think Lily's well,' said Em. 'She's been acting strange. It's like she doesn't care about anything. I had to watch her very carefully at work today. I'm sorry I got her the job. She lacks concentration.' She sniffed again.

Joel began sorting through Lily's papers. Lizzie pulled up a chair and made him sit down at the table then she perched on his lap. 'Not too heavy, am I?'

'What, a little thing like you?' He thought he'd never known such happiness as being part of this family, especially with the girl he loved on his knee.

Em, preoccupied with Janie, said, 'What are you doing?'

The papers were being divided into piles.

'I'm putting the letters in order of their dates so I get an idea of the timescale.' Lizzie began to help Joel. She was setting official letters in one pile and adding handwritten notes to a pile Joel had started. Joel looked at her and winked. She blushed, her neck going pink, her face reddening.

'Stop canoodling, you two.'

Joel looked at Em and winked at her for taking him to task. She giggled. 'Stop it,' she said, lifting the child and putting her nose to its nether regions. 'Pooh, who's a smelly girl, then?' She went over to the vacated armchair beneath the window and foraged with one hand in a big bag, producing a terry towelling nappy, some cream and a gauze square. 'We're gonna make you a nice clean girl again.'

Joel knew he was doing the right thing, leaving Lizzie with her mother and Gladys.

Lizzie had quite a pile of official letters and was now putting them in order of postmarked dates.

Joel's knees had gone to sleep but he would no more have told Lizzie to move than fly to the moon. Gladys had brought in a tray with a teapot and cups and saucers. The cake she put onto a plate and proceeded to cut it into slices.

'Eat and drink before you start going through them letters else the tea'll get cold,' Gladys said. Then, 'That Sam thinks the world of you, Em. Don't push him away, it ain't every day a good man comes along. And I know deep down you care a lot for him.' She watched her friend changing the baby. 'Funny how it all comes back.' Em passed her a dirty nappy. 'Coo, thanks,' Gladys said with a smile.

The two of them seemed perfectly at ease with each other again, thought Joel as he bit into the soft moistness of the cake. 'Umm!' he said. Em preened at his compliment and cuddled her granddaughter.

Chapter Twenty

Lawrence closed his car door and began walking across the road from the Queen's Hotel towards Em's house. He hadn't intended to pay Gloria a visit, but seeing Em climb in the car with the young man and drive away, he decided they'd probably be gone long enough for him to check whether Gloria had anything for him. He'd had a shock discovering just how many of the women Gloria had become involved with had been friendly with that woman he had fleeced. Who was she? She'd had lovely, long red hair . . . Her name escaped him. Mind you, his disguise was good enough to fool them and for that he was thankful. It didn't do to take chances.

Fifty pounds was enough this time. She didn't know it, but he'd hand it straight back to Gloria to return to Em. This was going to be the last of the small change, as he called it. Little sums borrowed and handed back within a day or so proved that Lily/Gloria could be trusted.

Fifty pounds was the proposed amount for next week. This wouldn't be going back to Em. Lily was going to tell Em that she owed a fair amount to a back-street moneylender. She'd borrowed the cash for repairs to a bomb-damaged house of hers that had a family living in it. The repairs needed to be done quickly, and the bank had been slow in paying out. This bloody war changed everything. The moneylender added so much interest that she refused to pay him and now he was going to hurt her if she didn't come up with the cash. She'd say the bank promised the money soon, just not soon enough for the loan shark. Surely Em wouldn't want her 'sister' hurt?

He'd leave the finer details to Gloria, the silly cow could make up any story she wanted as long as the money was forthcoming. Two thousand pounds would be in his hands within the next couple of weeks. Gloria would hand over the deeds to four houses in Ann's Hill Road, as surety.

Within the bundle of papers that Gloria had taken were the deeds to properties here and near Lyme Regis. The real Lily was a very wealthy woman. Her dead hus-band had left her well provided for, and her sister Em certainly wasn't short of a bob or two with her dead husband's insurance money and cash left her by her mother.

Remembering that Em always left the key strung behind the door he decided to surprise Gloria. He listened carefully at the letter box. The wireless was on but there were no other sounds. Gloria hadn't got in the car so she had to be home.

Carefully, he eased the key in the lock. She was sitting in the kitchen reading the local newspaper. At first he thought she was asleep with her eyes open. Then she looked up but didn't seem surprised by his presence. She put the newspaper on the floor. His forehead furrowed. She'd been reading the paper upside down!

She'd been crying. Her hair was wild, like she'd been raking her fingers through it. Her eyes, surrounded by dark shadows, darted constantly from him to the door then back again. How the hell had she completed a day working with dangerous materials in an armament factory? To him, she didn't look capable of doing anything except sleeping.

She took a deep breath then rose from the chair. In a flat voice she said, 'I have no money for you.'

The single slap he gave her took her off her feet and she stumbled backwards. Twisting her body, she was able to use her hands on the mantelpiece to save herself from falling into the unlit fire. He took a step forward but she was ready for him. Snatching the long poker from the fire set, she brandished it before her.

'Stop!'

He did. Staring at her in silence, wondering how she had dared to resist his advances. He made his words soft, inviting.

'So you didn't find the right time to ask Em for her money?'

She didn't move. 'There was time. I didn't ask her.'

He tried another tack. 'But you know I need the money so we can begin our new life together.'

'New life?' He saw her eyes had filled with tears. 'Or a continuation of our old one?'

Then she threw the poker down and it clattered into the fireplace.

'You don't understand. You never will,' she said.

He was staring at her. Her eyes were wild, her fingers twitching. She was demented, completely out of her mind. Only the sound of the mantel clock ticking and her heavy breathing broke the silence.

Lawrence realized nothing would be gained by hitting her again. She was already frightened of him.

'One week.' He shook his head. 'One week to come up with the cash, and I don't care how you get it.' He paused. 'If you don't have something for me, I will tell your so-called sister that you stole the papers from a woman in a nursing home so that you could defraud Em Earle from her savings by pretending to be her long-lost sister.'

'You wouldn't!' She was now rubbing at her face, like scratching at an imaginary insect bite.

'I would.' He knew now he had the upper hand once more. 'There's nothing to prove I was in on this scam. If you try to put any of the blame on me, I will deny everything.' He made a dismissive sound with his throat. 'Em'll know I'm right. Just look at the state of you, a right looney.' He moved towards her, grabbing both her wrists and turning her so she could see herself in the mirror above the mantelpiece. 'Is that the face of an honest woman?'

He saw her narrow her eyes at her reflection. It was obvious to him now that because Em had taken her into her heart and home, Gloria's conscience had rebelled at defrauding her and she had become unhinged.

He stepped back. 'One week,' he repeated.

As he walked down the passage and opened the front door, he found he was whistling happily along to the music from the wireless.

*

Gloria heard the door close. She ran down the passage and slid the bolt across then she stood with her back against the door. Sweat had broken out on her forehead and her hands were clammy. Please don't let him come back, she prayed. If Em knew Lawrence found his way into her house as many times as he had, she'd be mortified.

Then Gloria stared at the bolt. Her hand rose towards it and she pulled it back. What right had she to lock Em's door? When that nice young man Joel brought Em home she wouldn't be able to get in. She'd be angry with Gloria, pretending to be Lily.

But who was Lily? Lily was a fictitious name for a woman proclaiming falsely to be Em's sister. Liliah Somerton, the real sister of Em Earle, was living the rest of her days at Yew Trees Nursing Home in Lyme Regis, quite unaware that she, Gloria, had stolen her birth certificate, her marriage lines, property deeds and all the information Liliah had gathered together before her mind had started to falter; information from the authorities and letters from her mother that, when put together, told how Liliah's mother had tried to get her child returned to her, and had failed.

Gloria had been so in love with Lawrence Greyson that she'd allowed herself to be manipulated into stealing for him. Not just the old people's jewellery and money at Yew Trees, but Liliah Somerton's papers. She'd agreed to the scam so she could ask Em for large amounts of money, showing her the security she had in bricks and mortar in Gosport. Tears began to roll down her face.

Em had not only believed she was her sister but had taken her into her home, found her a job and was willingly sharing her family with her. A wonderful family and friends that shouldn't include a thief and liar like her.

She couldn't deceive Em any more.

Gloria was sobbing now. The past weeks had showed her how wrong she was to let Lawrence run her life. He didn't love her. All he cared about was himself. She'd thought she could change him and make him return to the wonderful man he'd been when they'd first met on The Cobb at Lyme Regis. He'd charmed her. But the real Lawrence was a monster.

She couldn't lie any more. It had got so she didn't know where the lies ended and the truth began. The days had melted into one long space where she couldn't tell the difference between being here in the house and working at the munitions factory. Today at Priddy's she'd been surprised to suddenly find herself pushing in tiny buttons she'd never seen in her life before. She'd had to steel herself to watch the other women and copy their actions. There were times when her hands shook so much that she wanted throw down the detonators and run from the building, away from Gosport. Go on running until she dropped from exhaustion.

She couldn't concentrate on anything. Even reading was difficult, for she forgot the words the moment she'd read them.

She hadn't wanted to coo over a pretty little baby that was nothing to do with her. She wasn't Janie's aunt. She hadn't wanted to say goodbye to Joel tonight. What was he to her? Nothing! Sure, she'd given him the bag full of letters, and why not? They didn't belong to her, they were the property of the real Liliah Somerton.

Gloria knew she'd upset Em by being unable to take flowers to her mother's grave. But that woman was Em's mother, not *her* parent. Her mother had dangled on the end of a rope, her tongue black, her eyes open, staring at nothing.

Gloria, tears still running unheeded, went over to the gas stove and lit the flame beneath the kettle.

A nice cup of tea would help her think more clearly. Tea always did that. It was a good pick-me-up.

Em would want to discuss the letters when she came home. She wiped her eyes but still the tears fell. Gloria cared so much for Em that to deceive her any longer was unthinkable. But Joel, unless he was a complete idiot, which he clearly wasn't, would recognize the name Liliah Somerton as being one of his patients at Yew Trees.

And yet she had shoved the bundle of letters at Em and said, 'Take them.'

Tonight when Em returned, Gloria's deception would be unveiled. Perhaps that was what she wanted? No more lies, no more trickery.

The kettle was boiling. She made a pot of tea and covered it with the knitted cosy.

Then she went out into the back garden, taking the torch from the drawer with her. There was no fear of the light being a warning to rogue enemy aircraft tonight. The government had eased up on the blackout.

In the shed, sending spiders scuttling, she found an old washing line. Near the lavatory the rowan tree leaves whispered to her in the darkness. A few late roses bloomed on the bush that straggled over the small brick outhouse. She put the torch on the cold earth and threw the length of rope in the air. It took three throws before it fell over a high branch and dropped back to the ground and she could knot it to the required height. She stood on the large pile of slates, stacked against the lavatory wall. They'd been gathered from the last bombing raid that had shaken the house, causing them to slide from the roof. She fastened the makeshift noose around her neck and jumped.

A vision of her mother swam before her eyes and she knew she would see her soon.

Chapter Twenty-One

'These are the facts,' Joel said. 'Liliah Somerton *is* your sister.'

A half-drunk cup of tea sat at his elbow. Em, with the baby asleep in her arms, was looking at him wide-eyed.

He put his hand on the pile of official missives. 'These prove Liliah Somerton was born in Hampshire the year before you. Exactly where, isn't clear. But your mother is her mother and apparently your father, her father. She was taken, brought up in various authority homes. When she became seventeen there are no more official documents concerning her whereabouts.' He paused. 'From your mother's letters, it's clear she loved Liliah very much and wanted to have her back with the family. No, more than wanted, she begged constantly. There's nothing explaining why they were parted.'

'Tell Mum about the other pile.' Lizzie, now sitting on a chair next to Joel, was misty-eyed. He turned and smiled at her. 'These communications have been sent to various people in the care system begging for news of Liliah. As the years have gone by, they explain your mother's circumstances, showing she could well afford to give a good home to her daughter. There appear to be more letters from your mother than replies.' He patted the pile. 'These are almost all in order. Some gaps, I'm afraid.' He sighed, took a long mouthful of tea and set the cup down on the saucer with a clatter. 'It looks,' he waved his hand over the table, 'as though all these communications came from one official source. Perhaps Liliah finally managed to get hold of the department who dealt with her, I don't know. The last letter is from the beginning of the war.'

'So Lily's my sister?' Em began a smile, which quickly faded when Joel said, 'I'm afraid not.'

Em's forehead creased with a frown, 'But you just said . . .'

Gladys got up from the chair she was sitting on and went behind Em and put her hand on her shoulder.

Lizzie broke in with, 'Lily isn't Liliah Somerton.'

The silence was deafening.

Em's eyes filled with tears. 'Take her,' she said, turning

to Gladys and placing the still-sleeping child in her friend's arms. She stood up and left the kitchen. Joel heard the sneck on the back door rise and felt the rush of cold air waft into the kitchen as Em went outside.

Lizzie made to get up, but Joel stilled her. 'Leave her; she needs to come to terms with this conclusion by herself. You'll confuse things. She's got fond of Lily, or whoever she is.'

Gladys said, 'Why?' Then she added, 'I mean, why has this happened?'

'Money's usually at the bottom of these deceptions.' Joel sighed. 'Has your mum got real money?'

He ran his fingers over some bundles of browning card and paper tied with faded green ribbon. 'Liliah is a very wealthy woman. She owns hundreds of pounds worth of properties. But it takes time to cash these in. The difficulty in selling property during wartime is that the owner and buyer never know if the building will still be standing by the time the sale has gone through.'

Lizzie sighed. 'Mum's got more money now than she's ever had before.'

Joel pointed to the deeds. 'Liliah – yes, her name is Liliah, not Lily – has houses here in Gosport, some land, and a house in Bere Regis, which is near Lyme Regis.' He paused. 'These were left to her by her husband.' He took hold of Lizzie's hands and said, 'I don't think this Lily planned this scam, if it is a scam, on her own.'

'I never liked her . . .' Gladys said. As if to agree with her, the canary started chirruping. With the child still in her arms, one-handed, Gladys neatly dropped a tea towel over the cage to shut the bird up.

'Maybe not, Gladys, but now Em needs her friends more than ever, and she certainly needs you!'

'OK, Joel, don't rub it in,' Gladys said sharply.

Joel heard the back door creak open and Em came in, wiping her eyes on a hanky. Her hair and clothes were damp like it had just started drizzling outside.

'Come and sit down, Em. I've got some more news for you, if you can stand it.'

'Can't be any worse, Joel.'

'I know where the real Liliah is.'

All eyes were on him. 'When I started looking through these letters I realized I'd seen them before. Or some very like them. They were in a large brown envelope in one of my charges' drawers in the home where I work.' He paused. 'I've never looked closely at this stuff before,' he stared across the table, 'because it wasn't mine to do so.' He took Em's hand. 'You do have a sister. She's at Yew Trees.'

Em put her hand to her mouth and stood there, her

eyes wide and staring. Gasps came from the rest of them.

'Em,' Joel said, 'she's a very sick lady. She may not even know who you are – she might have forgotten she was looking for her sister.' He looked away. 'She forgets a lot of things.'

Lizzie suddenly snapped to attention. 'But if she's only a year older than my mum, how come she's at Yew Trees?'

'She's unable to care for herself. But if you mean, why Yew Trees of all the places she could live . . . Her money obviously secured a place for her. We need to talk to Lily. She could shed some light . . .'

'Yes, we must find out what she's up to!' Gladys looked at Joel for affirmation. 'And how Lily has discovered the right people to swindle; that's if she intends to do so.'

'I agree,' he said. He began putting all the letters in a pile. 'What troubles me is she must have guessed we'd work out something wasn't right, so why did she allow you to have these, Em?' He put all the communications in the carrier bag.

'She's been very strange at home lately.' Em took the bag and sat it in front of her.

'And at work, Em,' Gladys piped up. She hoisted Janie to her shoulder and began rubbing the little girl's back.

Janie slept peacefully and Joel's heart swelled with love looking at her.

'Best I get her on her own and talk sensibly to her.' Em looked meaningfully at Gladys. Joel saw Em's eyes drift towards Janie.

'Give her to me, I expect she needs changing again. I never knew a little girl could pee so much.'

'She does whiff a bit,' Gladys said. 'But I need all the cuddles I can get.' She stared at Joel. 'Which reminds me, you're going back to work tomorrow, aren't you? What will happen when the real Liliah finds out she has a sister after all?'

'I can't just tell her. ' He sighed. 'I'll have a word with her doctor first. Every day her disposition changes and it really needs the right circumstances for her to find out about you, Em.' He looked at Em for affirmation. She nodded. He bent down and whispered to Lizzie, 'I wish I didn't have to . . .'

'I'll miss you, too,' she murmured shyly.

He kissed her forehead, knowing he was falling deeper and deeper in love with her all the time.

'Come on,' Em said. 'Get your coat on. I'll just go down to the lavatory, it'll save me going out in the cold when I get home. Then you can take me home, Joel.' She looked at the others. 'I don't think I'll say anything to Lily tonight. I need a clear head for work tomorrow. The day after is my day off, I'll cope better then.'

She kissed the baby and Lizzie and hugged Gladys. Their eyes met. Joel saw there was no need for words between the two women, who had been friends for so long.

Lizzie piped up, 'When all this is sorted out, I want to get Janie christened. I still want a big party like we used to have before the war. Perhaps we could start hoarding stuff to cook?'

Gladys said, 'Brilliant idea. The damned Germans have got to know who's boss sometime or other. The fighting can't last for ever. A combined Christmas and christening would be lovely.'

Lizzie cried, 'Wouldn't it just.'

Joel watched as a smile crept over Em's strained face. Then just as quickly the smile disappeared. 'If you think I'm spending good money to announce to all of Gosport that my beloved granddaughter is a bastard, you got another think coming, Lizzie Earle!'

It was a neighbour, Mrs Dooley from number twelve, shrieking hysterically, who woke Em long before she needed to get up for work.

With her dressing gown tied around her she ventured out into the back garden towards the shouting and screaming.

The body swung in the early morning September wind, but the rose barbs caught on Lily's dress and stopped it.

Em crept closer, her hand over her mouth. Red rose petals had caught in Lily's hair.

Mrs Dooley was still shouting, but Em turned a deaf ear to her. Instead she was aware of other back doors opening and a new cacophony of sounds as neighbours came out to see the spectacle.

'I thought she'd gone to bed. Made a pot of tea for me and gone to bed, leaving the light on for me.'

Mrs Dooley was at her side. 'Come in here.' Her neighbour pulled her away and into the small alley that ran at the rear of the houses. Em went with her without a murmur. Mrs Dooley pushed open her own back door and led Em into the scullery.

'My Bert's just back from calling the police.'

Her son was on early turn at Ashley's wallpaper factory. Mrs Dooley never let him out of the house without a proper breakfast inside him and the air was thick with the smell of fried bread. A cup of greasy-looking tea was pressed in front of Em on the small table where the dirty breakfast dishes were piled. Em stared at the congealed fat on the plates and felt her stomach rebel.

'The coppers won't be long.' Mrs Dooley heaved her considerable girth onto a chair that didn't look strong enough to hold her. Em could see the stains on her wrap-around pinny had been there some time. 'Did you have any idea she'd do that?'

Em shook her head. She couldn't speak. Now it suddenly made sense why Lily had handed over the letters. She wanted the truth out in the open. She knew she was going to end it all.

Mrs Dooley picked up the cup and put it to Em's lips as though she was a child. 'There's sugar in it, sugar's good for shock.'

Em couldn't help but take a mouthful of tea. But as soon as the hot liquid touched her lips she leapt up, ran to the back door and vomited onto the concrete.

Loud knocking echoed through the house.

'That'll be the police, love.' The woman patted Em on the shoulder and went to answer her front door. Em leaned forward and vomited again. She used her sleeve to wipe her mouth and the strands of hair that had fallen over her face and were coated with sick. When she stood up she was looking at a tall man with red hair and a uniformed police constable at his side.

'MacKenzie,' he said, putting his hand forward to shake hers. 'Mrs Earle, do you mind coming back with us to your house to identify your sister?'

Chapter Twenty-Two

Mac stared at his shoes. His legs were stretched out across the desk and his chair tipped back. He needed a new pair of brogues. Brown ones would be nice. He sighed. It'd been a long time since anyone had been able to pick and choose what shoes they wanted. Bloody war! He cursed softly, then looked towards the door of his office as it opened.

Ben Chambers said, 'No foul play. She hanged herself.'

'She might have committed suicide, but I'd like to know what made her do it.' He stared at the constable. 'You coming in? Or are you going to carry on talking round the door?'

Constable Chambers stepped inside the office and closed the door behind him. 'It's a lot to take in, all that about her pretending to be someone else, sir.'

Mac said, 'Especially as she never asked her supposed sister for anything.'

'I reckon there was someone else behind it.'

'Oh, you do, do you, Ben?' He saw he'd made the constable look flustered. 'I do, too,' he admitted. 'Did you get anywhere talking to that young bloke from the care home?'

'I believe him when he says he's no idea who was behind the trick that was being played on Mrs Earle, sir.'

'You've got to admit it's funny though, that the real sister lives at the home he works in.' Mac took his feet off the table. 'Still, there's been no actual offence. The old dear has all her papers back again and Gloria hanged herself. No foul play. End of story. Now, if we could find out who's behind the ARP buggers fleecing the poor sods who've just copped a bomb blast, it would be a feather in our caps. That V2 that landed on the grocer's in the town, taking down the walls of the jeweller's next to it, made it easy for them to take exactly what they wanted.' Mac got out of his chair and began pacing up and down the office.

After a while he said, 'I'm going to pay a visit to the knocking shop at the ferry. The powers that be don't want that as a blot on Gosport's landscape. We've got to find the owner who pimps the girls and shut the place down. You'd better book out a car. I'm not leaving mine anywhere near the public lavatories down there to get vandalized. People are getting to know my vehicle.'

He thought of his pride and joy, his Rover Streamline Coupe. When he'd still had a wife she'd accused him of loving the car more than her. He still had the car, but not his wife.

'We could walk, sir?'

Ben quickly realized he should never have suggested that. The door closed behind the constable before Mac could utter another word.

Mac had loved Ellie; never messed her about. It wasn't her fault she couldn't cope with the loneliness of being a policeman's wife. He drummed his fingers on the table top. Maybe it would have been different if they'd had kiddies? Three miscarriages in three years was a lot to ask of any woman. Especially when he was busy trying to climb the greasy pole. That bank job where the teller got killed had finished his marriage. She'd wanted him by her side when the baby came early, and by the time the stakeout was over, Ellie had lost the child.

He always believed Ellie would come back, but she never did. Now she was settled down with a market gardener and they had a little girl. Another reason he was glad to get away from Edinburgh.

He wasn't a monk, though. There had been a couple

of women who'd excited him. A few he'd woken up in bed with, without being able to remember their names. But the bloody job was his wife. He was married to it.

He leafed through some papers on his desk. He had to be careful with this brothel. It was rumoured to be frequented by a couple of local coppers of whom he wasn't worthy to lick their boots. It wouldn't do for him to be careless. Not at all.

The first thing Mac noticed as he opened the door was that the place had had a fresh coat of paint.

'Looks a lot better than the last time I was here,' Ben said, as they began climbing the stairs.

'And I thought you were a happily married man.'

Mac turned and looked at Ben as he stepped on to the top landing. The poor bloke was blushing.

'I . . . I . . .'

'I know you were here on business.' Mac laughed and opened the door in front of him. He announced that he was a detective, but he wasn't prepared for the welcome from the red-headed angel before him.

'Can I help you two?' She leaned back on the chair behind the desk and crossed her legs at the knees, which caused her tight skirt to ride up. He swore he could see a hint of black suspender and creamy thigh, but maybe that was simply wishful thinking.

Mac gulped. 'Who are you?' he asked.

'Name's Marlene. I do a bit of tidying up.' The woman got up and stepped towards him, putting out a hand to shake his. 'We've not met before, have we?'

He shook his head. She barely reached his shoulder, but there was an inner strength about her that he immediately warmed to. Her hand was cool without being clammy and he liked the way she wore the utility suit of navy wool with the sparkling white blouse beneath, showing off her full-bosomed yet slim figure. But it was her hair that took his breath away, long and glossy almost the colour of autumn leaves. He had red hair. Scottish men were often blessed with fiery locks and he was no exception. But he loved red hair on a woman.

'Mac,' he almost stuttered. 'Detective MacKenzie, Michael,' he added. Then, 'Plain clothes.' He could have kicked himself. It was obvious that he was plain clothes – he was wearing a long coat with a suit beneath it. He didn't open his mouth to introduce the constable at his side for he thought he'd balls that up, too.

'What can I do for you?'

She let her hand drop and moved back behind the desk. His eyes roved around the room. A few chairs against a wall. A small table with a vase of flowers and a wireless, a window covered with a pretty net curtain, a wardrobe in the corner, and two doors, both closed. He could see the kitchen area to the side of the desk. The small sink was gleaming white and four willow-patterned cups with matching saucers had been washed and left to drain on the board.

The last time he'd been here, a few months ago, to sort out an altercation that had got way out of hand between a couple of blokes, the place had been a rat-hole. Now he couldn't believe the transformation. Fresh paint and a smell of lavender polish assailed his senses.

'So you're working here?' He looked at her.

'Depends what you mean by working. I work at the armament factory. But I pop in here to tidy up.' She waved her arm around. 'If the phone rings I answer it, I make cups of tea sometimes for my friends, Carla and Ruby.' She paused and looked him up and down. He swore she liked what she saw. 'Would you like a cup of tea? I'm sorry I don't have anything stronger.'

Mac nodded. 'A cuppa would be most welcome, wouldn't it, Ben?'

Ben shifted from one foot to the other. He clearly, thought Mac, believed this polite scenario was a farce! Nevertheless Ben muttered, 'I'd love a cup.'

He watched her as she went out into the tiny kitchen and shook the kettle to check for water then lit the gas on the stove.

'These friends of yours . . . Do they entertain gentlemen?'

She turned and smiled. 'I've no idea what they do when the door's closed, and you wouldn't expect me to tell you, would you, Mac?'

He knew then that she and he were on the same wavelength. She was the girls' maid. She gave him a smile that made his spine tingle.

Marlene was an extremely clever woman who appeared to be aware of the laws concerning brothels. The law stated it was illegal for women to solicit on the streets. They weren't on the street but in an exceptionally clean flat. What went on in private premises was of no concern to him. Mac knew he'd have his work cut out finding who was behind this set-up. A pimp living off prostitute's earnings wasn't a nice person.

Unless he was proved wrong, Marlene wasn't committing a crime, and neither were her 'friends'. She'd been quick to point out she had regular employment. He suddenly realized he was more than a little relieved about that.

Mac walked over to the doorway and watched her deft

movements as she made tea. There were no rings on her fingers. He'd already told Ben to relax and smiled at his constable sprawled on a chair, legs stretched out, eyes closed. He guessed another sleepless night with his little one had been on the cards. Briefly, he wondered what it would be like to have a continuation of his line. He and his wife had wanted children but the strain of the still-birth and the miscarriages had been almost more than he could bear. Perhaps it had been a good thing there'd been no little ones, in view of the break-up.

The wireless was playing softly in the background, but it didn't disguise the laughter he could hear coming from behind one of the closed doors. Marlene brought out the tea tray and set it on the desk.

'Black, white?' She handed him the tea with just a little milk. Ben was snoring gently. Mac looked at his constable and shrugged. Asleep on duty? Mac was a hard taskmaster, but he was also human.

'Who's your boss?' He took a mouthful of tea.

'If I told you I've absolutely no idea, would you believe me?'

'I'd find it difficult. But stranger things have happened.' She really did have the most gorgeous green eyes, he thought.

'I can assure you it's perfectly true.'

For a moment they sipped tea, making polite conversation. The door to one of the rooms opened and a very beautiful young woman wearing a frothy concoction of a slip that was held up with a glittery brooch beneath her ample bosoms, sailed out holding the hand of a paunchy elderly gentleman, who stopped suddenly and stared hard at Mac. Mac swallowed his tea with difficulty and tried not to choke.

'Ah, MacKenzie.' The man's face turned the colour of beetroot and he stepped away from the woman, treading on Ben's foot. Ben immediately woke with a howl of protest, but upon seeing who had woken him, quickly stood to attention.

'Sir! Sir . . . Sorry, sir!' Ben's face too, was red.

Mac saw the look that passed between Marlene and the girl and the smile that followed. He too wanted to laugh. He now saw the reason Marlene had pressed them both to stay for tea.

'I'm just visiting my, my niece . . .' The man's words came out as though strangled.

'And I'm having tea with my new friend, sir.' Mac held his cup in the air but glanced across at Marlene. She had her hand in front of her mouth, trying not to laugh. She took a deep breath and said calmly, 'I believe you three are all in the same line of business?'

The paunchy man poked his finger in his collar as though he was feeling the heat and said, 'Quite so.'

Mac watched as the dark-haired girl slipped her arm through the man's arm and whispered loud enough for everyone to hear, 'Saturday?'

He tried to disentangle himself. Nodding his head he said, 'Yes.' Then he looked at Mac. 'I'm taking Carla, my niece,' he added, 'to the theatre. Saturday,' he added. He managed to move free from Carla and got to the door before he added, 'I'd like you to pop along to my office when you've a moment tomorrow, MacKenzie.' He cleared his throat. 'Any time, at your convenience.'

Mac put his empty cup down on its saucer and said, 'Yes, sir.' When he looked up the man had gone. He could hear footsteps tripping down the stairs to the street, then the clatter of the front door as it slammed shut.

'You knew Chief Superintendent Andrew Metcalfe was in there.' Mac looked at the open door. Part of an unmade bed was clearly visible.

'Of course. I simply thought I'd show you we have a higher class of visitor now this place has been tarted up.'

Ben seemed to come alive. 'That was . . . That was . . .'

'Stop repeating yourself, Constable. Yes, that was our superior officer,' Mac said.

'He never said a word about me sleeping on duty . . .'

'He was hardly in a position to do anything about that, Ben,' smiled Mac. 'So think yourself lucky.'

He turned towards Marlene, who was collecting the cups and setting them back on the tray. Carla had gone into the kitchen and refilled the kettle. Mac put a hand on Marlene's arm. 'I've not finished with you,' he said.

She looked into his eyes, picked up the tray and went towards the kitchen, turning towards him. She smiled and said, 'No, I didn't think you had.'

He was still chuckling when he and Ben went downstairs and out into the street.

Chapter Twenty-Three

Liliah Somerton was asleep when Joel quietly placed a cup of tea on her bedside table. In sleep she looked younger. He studied her face, and now he could see the similarities between her and Em Earle, her real sister. The widow's peak above her high forehead, the long ear lobes, the full lower lip and the straight nose. Both women had a penchant for dangly earrings. Liliah wore plain gold drops and he'd never seen her without them. Em wore Victorian gold and jet. But she removed them for work.

He gently shook her arm, which she had flung outside the covers in her sleep. She opened her eyes. Poor love, he thought, as he smelled the urine rising from the sheets. Incontinence was one of the prices she paid, along with memory loss. The room smelled musty and he went across to the window, pulled back the curtains, and opened it. Sharp, cold sunlight streamed in.

'Joel.'

He smiled at her. She'd remembered his name.

'I've a cup of tea here, just as you like it, strong with no sugar.'

He helped her sit up and folded the pillows at her back so she wouldn't slip down the bed. Then he raised the cup to her lips. He had to remind himself she was of a similar age to that of Lizzie's mum, for she smelled of old woman and sleep and looked years older than Em.

'Mrs Somerton?' She drank gratefully, greedily. Then she looked at him.

'Is that who I am?' Her eyes were milky and vague. With one hand he smoothed her thin hair away from her face.

He nodded, set the cup back on the saucer then said, 'I've got papers that belong to you.' He could almost see her memory returning.

'I couldn't find them.'

'I know,' he said, reaching behind him and spilling the letters and cards on the bed in front of her.

'Not mine! Mine were in a blue, blue . . .' She paused, searching for the word, which eluded her.

'The blue folder tore, but the papers are all there in this brown bag.'

He helped her hands pull the letters from the depths

of the bag. A sigh of relief shook her body and a smile hovered as she recognized the coloured ribbons on the property deeds. There were tears in her eyes as she looked up at him and said, 'I only had the diary.'

'What diary?'

'Mummy's diary.' She was cross now, as though he should know what she was talking about. Was it possible that she had her and Em's mother's diary? Surely it would be in *Em's* possession? Her mother had lived with Em. How did Liliah come by it?

Liliah was eagerly sifting through the letters, oblivious now to Joel. He put his hand on the papers to gain her attention.

'Where is the diary, Mrs Somerton?'

'In the drawer, of course.' Her voice was sharp, snappy almost. 'Where my handkerchiefs are.'

'May I see it?' Joel asked.

'Of course, Joel,' she said sweetly. The sharpness in her voice had disappeared almost as soon as it had begun. 'It's in the Bible,' she said happily. 'Joel, did you know that?'

So far this morning her dialogue had made sense. It was a good day. God help him, but he wondered if sometimes it suited her to be difficult.

He smiled at her, rose from the chair at the side of

her bed and went to the chest of drawers. Amongst the embroidered handkerchiefs was a leather-bound diary. He took it out and as he lifted it, a note fell from the pages. He looked at Liliah, immersed in searching through the letters. Then he picked up the note and couldn't help himself as he deciphered the writing.

FOR WHEN YOU ARE OLD ENOUGH TO UNDERSTAND, LILIAH MY LOVE.

He stared at the copperplate writing. From reading her mother's letters he knew it was the same. Whoever had stolen Liliah's papers had left the diary.

Joel flicked through the brown-edged pages. In places the writing was in pencil and barely visible. Some pages were blank. On others a thick pen had been used. It appeared to be a five-year diary, but the entries weren't consistent. He could tell by the broken brass clip that there had once been a small lock attached.

'Mrs Somerton, may I look at this?'

Liliah looked up and frowned. 'It's mine.'

'I'll take care . . .'

'Yes, you will, Joel.' She looked at her letters on the bed. 'I am Liliah Somerton, Joel.'

He put the diary in his pocket and closed the drawer.

There were so many unanswered questions, perhaps the diary held the answers.

'Liliah Somerton, we must get someone in to help you get washed and dressed.' He smiled at her. He suddenly realized he hadn't asked her the question he had come to her room to speak to her about. He picked up her frail hand, hoping the touch of another human being would soften the shock of what he was about to say.

'Liliah, would you like to see your sister?'

It seemed as though she had great difficulty in allowing his words to register. Her eyes searched for his. He nodded assuredly. Those eyes now filled with tears, and he felt his hand being squeezed until she almost inflicted pain on him. Her breathing was practically at a standstill, yet she asked in a tiny voice,

'Really?'

'Yes.'

Joel had spent a long time upon his return to Yew Trees talking to the duty doctor about the possibility of Em travelling from Gosport to Lyme Regis to see Liliah. It had been decided that the sisters needed to meet, but that Joel should be present, along with the medical practitioner in case Liliah became upset. It was no mean feat to meet someone she had been trying to find for years.

Liliah was staring at him as though he was God. He

could almost see her mind trying to make sense of the words, as though she had misheard or dreamed the conversation. She said quite calmly, 'I would.' Then, 'Does she know of me?'

'She does now.'

'I would like that.' Liliah lay back amongst the pillows and closed her eyes. Her hand slipped from Joel's palm. Before he had time to leave the room, she said, 'I would like that very much, Joel.'

Joel took her cup and saucer with him and went down to the kitchen. It wouldn't be long before Liliah Somerton would be dressed for the new day; once she had had breakfasted she would be able to sit in the lounge. Despite the sun, it was too cold to venture out in the gardens. Later, he'd phone Em at work and arrange for her to come down to Lyme Regis. Maybe Lizzie would want to come back? He missed Lizzie and the little one so much.

Marie was at the sink, peeling potatoes. 'Nice to have you back,' she said. The wireless played softly; he could smell meat pies cooking. He wondered how much actual meat they'd contain, but Marie always seemed to make a little go a long way.

He smiled at her and then poured himself a cup of tea from the big urn. It was breakfast time and at every mealtime the urn was used. A teapot sufficed at other occasions.

'Liliah Somerton's being got ready to face a new day,' he said, sitting at the table. The newspaper which Pete had abandoned had the headlines, 'First German City Falls to Allies'. He read on, 'Aachen suffers German looters'.

'Look at this, Marie, the Nazis are stealing from their own people.'

'We've got looters as well,' she chided. 'Despicable people. Though I believe it's worse in the south-east.'

He drank his tea, remembering being at the police station at Gosport with Em. The police had called at Gladys's house before he'd left for Gosport to tell Em's daughter, Lizzie, about the hanging and to propose that someone go and stay with Em. Finding Gloria like that had been a terrible shock for her. Joel had promptly postponed his return to Yew Trees. Now that time had passed, he was beginning to take in what the police had discovered.

They'd found out that Gloria had worked at Yew Trees. Accused of stealing from some of the elderly, she left of her own accord; the theft was unproven, and she dropped out of sight. She then pretended to be Liliah, probably in the hopes of stealing money from Em, and in due course Liliah herself. But this was only supposition.

The false identity card and ration book given to Em suggested a well-thought-out plan; perhaps a little too clever for Gloria alone to come up with. Her own documents, showing her true identity, were discovered hidden in her bedroom drawer.

The Gosport detective, Mac MacKenzie, thought there was probably someone else involved. There was no proof, and now Gloria was dead. But one good thing had come out of it all. Em definitely had a sister.

'She can be a bugger when you're not around.' Joel turned at Marie's voice. He knew instinctively she meant Liliah. He was fond of the woman. He reminded himself again that he shouldn't get involved in the clients' lives, but he couldn't help it. He thought about Fred. It still hurt to remember the old man. If it wasn't for the war, funeral parlours would be able to keep to their promised burial dates. It still rankled Joel that he had been unable to attend Fred's funeral.

He patted the diary in his pocket. Of course, he could say this was none of his business, put the diary back in Liliah's drawer and walk away. But it involved Lizzie and he was in love with her. He needed a visit to Gosport with Em, and Lizzie, of course, to see what else could be discovered about Liliah's past. Perhaps the diary would shed its secrets.

'She'll be happy when she meets her sister,' Marie said. 'Close the window, Joel, the rain's coming in.'

Summer was a memory. The sun had turned to dark clouds and heavy rain. He pulled the metal window closed and locked it. He should be helping with breakfast. Quite a few of the inmates, now that they were up and dressed, needed feeding like babies. The more mobile could congregate in the dining room and eat at the tables. Pete was on breakfast duty today.

Joel decided to look at the photographs hanging on the wall of the long corridor as he walked towards the dining room. He could hear the murmur of voices and the clatter of crockery. The smell of crispy bacon made his stomach growl with hunger.

It didn't take him long to find Gloria's smiling face amongst the pictures of staff that had been photographed yearly. She looked ridiculously carefree. How awful that her life should end like that. Someone had to have had a hand in this. Someone, besides Gloria, was responsible for all that had happened. He would try his hardest to discover the culprit.

Mac was off duty and he'd given himself a choice of calling in on Marlene, or going home and fixing the shed door, which was falling off its hinges. Marlene won.

It wasn't the first time he'd visited her – something drew him like a moth to a flame. As he pushed open the top door, he saw her sitting at the desk writing in a large notebook. As she saw him she quickly shut the book and put down the pen.

'What brings you here?'

She was alone in the room, but he could hear noises and music coming from behind the two doors. A large spray of autumn foliage with chrysanthemum flowers was displayed on her desk. The leaves gave off the fragrance of pine trees. She had a cup of tea, steaming next to the ledger.

'Thought I'd see if I could scrounge a cuppa.'

'The Dive's open.' She named the café near the bus station. She looked at him with her marvellous green eyes and his stomach flipped.

He leaned forward over the desk. 'But you're here.'

'I don't wait on fellers,' she said. Those eyes flashed dangerously. 'But the tea in the pot's fresh.' She waved towards the kitchen, then got up and went to the door, sliding the bolt across. 'The girls are on their last appointments for this evening. We could all do with an early night. Two of us have already been working today, at the armament factory.'

He loped towards the kitchen and poured himself a drink.

'I'd rather have a brandy,' he said.

'Naughty! Aren't you on duty?'

'No.'

'In that case, there's a bottle of brandy in the cupboard above the sink. I'll have one as well.'

He took a mouthful of tea before searching for tumblers. His mother had brought him up never to be wasteful, so he'd drink the tea as well. He poured two good measures and took them to her desk.

'Did you ever speak with Handy Andy?'

He looked at her and frowned. 'Handy Andy?'

'Carla says he has more arms than an octopus.'

'Of course.' He tapped the side of his head. 'Chief Superintendent Andrew Metcalfe.' He cast his mind back to his first visit, when his superior had rolled from the room with Carla. 'I did.' He laughed. 'The naughty old bugger made me promise never to tell anyone I'd caught him here.'

'Actually, he's very fond of Carla.'

'I don't suppose his wife knows how fond.'

'Have you met her?' She sipped at her drink.

'Yes. And I don't blame him for having a bit on the side.' He remembered the loud-voiced dragon of a woman who chaired several committees and made sure her point of view was always heard, and acted upon. 'He's a good bloke.'

Marlene drank back the rest of her brandy. Mac liked a woman who drank spirits straight up. None of those fancy cocktail things prettied up with bits of fruit.

She sat back and stared at him. When she spoke, it was like she'd rehearsed what she was going to say.

'I know you're out to get hold of the man who runs this place. I won't help you, for two reasons. One, I need the money I'm getting for being here and so do the girls. Carla has a daughter. Ruby wants enough money behind her to start somewhere anew, maybe abroad.' She smiled at him. 'That's when we get planes that allow us to fly again.'

Air travel had been curtailed for most people because of the war. Marlene saying, 'Andy wants to set Carla up in a flat,' broke his thoughts. 'I think the daft bugger has fallen for her.'

He thought of Carla and her long dark hair, her exotic looks. It wouldn't be hard to fall for a woman like that.

'And your second reason?'

'That's easy. I don't know who's behind this operation. Ruby hands over the books and profits. He trusts her, no one else. Obviously needing the cut she's earned, she'll keep her mouth shut on the little she knows.'

'This place will eventually have to be shut down,' he said. He tapped his glass on the table. 'What will you do then?'

'I want my life back.' The hardness in her voice surprised him. 'Doing this job, dealing with the men who visit, has changed me. I'm a different woman to the one who was broken by the bastard that fleeced me of my home and money.' She held out her glass. 'I think another drink's in order, don't you?'

He could feel her eyes on him as he took the two tumblers and went out to the kitchen.

'You want to talk about it?' He set the glass in front of her. While he'd been gone she'd put away the ledger and pen. Now, she sat in the chair looking composed and incredibly beautiful in a black outfit with the jacket undone and a white blouse unbuttoned sufficiently for him to wonder what desirable things lay beneath.

She reached across and took the glass. 'I met this handsome man at an auction, we became friends and he lent me money to build up the gold business. I always paid him back immediately I had the profits.' She paused. He could tell that talking about it wasn't comfortable for her. 'He had a nice car, a lovely home and things got serious between us. I was naive. He said he needed money to tide him over a building deal, and I readily went into debt for him.' She suddenly laughed, bitterly. 'We were engaged, with me wearing a ring from my own stock, can you believe that?'

She stared at him. For a few seconds all that could be heard were the murmurings from the rooms opposite and the wireless softly playing a tune sung by that skinny, good-looking young Italian, Frank Sinatra.

'Anyway, he left me penniless. I lost the deeds to my house, my beloved market stall, and owed money left, right and centre. I still owe money. The good wages at the armament factory are a godsend. Working here is the icing on the cake, it lets me send money to my mum in Littlehampton. She's staying with her sister, while looking after my little girl.' Marlene gave a big sigh.

'And this was Samuel Golden?' Marlene nodded. 'I've heard of him,' he said. 'A slippery customer. You weren't the first woman he'd stolen from—'

'I know that now,' she interrupted. 'Your lot never caught him.' She drank back the rest of her brandy.

Just then, one of the bedroom doors opened and Carla stepped out in a silky dressing gown with its belt tied tightly around her slim waist. Behind her, a young man walked into the office. He stared at Mac, then at Marlene, but seemed reluctant to leave.

Carla got up, went to the door and slid back the bolt. She held the door open.

'Any problems, you come right back,' she whispered loud enough for Mac to hear. The young man moved and Mac noticed his limp. The man leaned forward and kissed Carla on the forehead.

'Thank you,' he said. Mac heard him clatter down the stairs.

'Any tea left?' Carla made for the kitchen. There was the rattle of cups and water running into the kettle. She poked her head around the doorpost. 'He'll be all right now,' she said. 'Getting married at the weekend and scared he couldn't do his duty because he'd copped a mine in France. He's been worried sick. I'd say his girl's going to be a lucky woman!'

Mac smiled. 'One down, one to go,' he said, and pointed towards the other closed bedroom door. 'If I wait, can I take you out for a bite to eat?'

Marlene stared at the clock. 'It's late, it's wartime.'

'Go on, you miserable cow,' said Carla. 'Go out with him.'

'I know a place,' Mac said. Marlene nodded and smiled at him and his heart soared heavenwards.

Chapter Twenty-Four

'Look, old chap, d'you want the car or not?' Pete said. He was, as usual, reading. Now he folded the newspaper and put it on the kitchen table. 'You'll get more use out of it than my brother who, quite frankly, could do with the money.'

Joel thought about the little Austin that he drove regularly down to Gosport. It was a good runner. He hated asking to borrow the vehicle and with Gladys able to get hold of black market petrol, he might just as well buy it.

'Done,' he said, when Pete named his brother's asking price. 'I haven't got the cash on me but he can have it at the end of the week.' Pete shook his hand, and the deal was done.

'His wife's having another nipper,' Pete said, as if that explained everything. He picked up a novel and began flicking through the pages. John Steinbeck's *Once There Was a War*. Looked like good reading, thought Joel.

The place was quiet. Most patients were napping, some were in the lounge listening to the wireless, and even Dolly was quiet after having them up half the night. She'd left her room and climbed in bed with a new resident; the elderly air force pilot, with a medal for bravery, was scared out of his wits by Dolly's ample flesh.

'D'you want to earn a few bob extra this weekend?' Joel looked at Pete, who had abandoned the book and was running his fingers through his orange hair while fiddling with the knob on the wireless.

'You want me to do your shift so you can go and see your Lizzie?'

Joel nodded. He liked the way Pete had said 'your Lizzie'. He wished she was his.

He felt he'd done his part in being a substitute father for Janie and was now no longer needed. Lizzie's mother and Gladys had accepted Lizzie and the child and the time for neighbours' wagging tongues had passed. His sole use at the moment was in delivering the diary to Gosport so it could be read, and the secret that Em's mother had taken to her grave exposed at last.

Both Pete and Marie were well aware of Liliah

Somerton's quest for her sister. Joel had decided nothing good could come of exposing all the facts, as he knew them, to the owners of Yew Trees. The residents may very well feel threatened if they thought the carers might steal from them.

The doctor was on hand in case Liliah became upset at her first meeting with her sister. Pete and Marie were both enthusiastic when they discovered Liliah's relative had been found and were eager to do all they could to help. Marie had insisted on making a few extra scones and teacakes for Em's arrival. Joel marvelled that she'd got hold of the ingredients and knew Em would be touched by Marie's kindness.

Pete was still twiddling the knob on the large oval Bakelite wireless. Strange noises came from the speaker as stations came and went.

'How about it, then?' Joel needed an answer.

'Course.' Pete looked up. 'Check the oven, will you? Wouldn't do for Marie's Woolton Pie to burn, would it? It's been in there for twenty minutes already.' Pete had been left looking after the dinner while Marie popped to the shops.

Joel took the frayed oven glove and opened the oven door to a gust of hot air that enveloped him, just as the wireless latched on to a news announcement. Joel saw the white crust still needed browning so he closed the door.

'Yes!' Pete let out a shout that made Joel jump. 'Listen!'

'RAF Lancaster bombers have sunk the last major German warship The Tirpitz in Tromsø Fjord in Norway. The Germans had said that she was unsinkable.'

The announcer's voice was grave, but Pete grabbed hold of Joel's hands and pulled him into a silly dance.

'Good ol' Barnes Wallis and his bombs,' shouted Pete. 'The unsinkable has been bloody sunk!'

Marie's voice cut through the noise as she dumped a brown carrier bag of shopping on the table and proceeded to take off her coat. Her face was red after coming in from the cold outside.

'Told you to look after me pie, and this is what you get up to, you daft beggars!'

Marlene took off her clothes, letting them drop one by one on to the old velvet armchair beneath the window. A bowl of hot water was on the kitchen table and a towel lay warming over the fender in front of the fire. Her precious bar of Lux soap sat in a saucer. If it was good enough for Veronica Lake, it was good enough for her. The range was lit and the heat warmed her body. The rag rug was cosy beneath her toes. Slowly, she began to wash herself all over. The soap slid over her skin, its scented freshness making her feel less tired. This was a luxury, washing in front of the fire. Usually, she washed outside in the cold scullery where the draughts came through the ill-fitting back door and chilled her to the bone.

She thought of Mac's house and the bathroom he had installed. A gleaming white tub, and a small wash-basin in the corner with a cupboard beneath it. The toilet was inside the house, separate from the bathroom. He was fond of making things, was Mac. She smiled to herself.

Single-handedly he was in the process of transforming his house into a home. He wasn't overly tidy and he allowed his cats to sleep upstairs on the bed. Why, she'd even caught him cooking a piece of cod for them! But her mother reckoned any man who loved animals was a good man.

The wireless was playing Glenn Miller and she hummed along as she towelled her body dry.

They'd been out together a few times now. She liked being with him. He'd managed so far to kiss her on the cheek and on the forehead when saying goodnight. She'd amazed herself by realizing she wanted more than chaste kisses. But she felt *he* didn't need to take things further yet and she liked that about him. Marlene still had issues with trust.

Once he'd promised to collect her from the flat at the ferry but though she'd waited, he hadn't turned up. Her first thought was that he had decided not to bother, that men were like that. She'd gone home to bed and tossed and turned, wondering what she'd done wrong. The next afternoon he'd been waiting outside Priddy's with a bunch of wilted Michaelmas daisies in his hands as she'd finished her shift. He was full of apologies.

He explained that there'd been a break-in in the town and he'd been required to visit the young thief's home, where some of the stolen stuff was recovered. The relief she felt that it was his job that had kept him from her was enormous.

Finishing up, she put on her long flannelette night-dress and took the bowl outside to the scullery. As she watched the water swirl down the sink's plughole, she realized she spent a big part of each day thinking about the red-haired man who'd entered her life.

When the kettle had boiled, she filled the stone hot-water bottle and took it upstairs, tucking it down deep in the bed.

She knew she was a different person from the Marlene who had allowed Samuel Golden to walk all over her in the name of love. She'd gone through a period of shame, believing that she'd deserved to be treated badly. But working with the girls at Priddy's had shown her laughter was a tonic to banish even the most difficult times. And she'd forced herself to work towards the goal of paying off the debts Samuel Golden had left her with. Being in the flat with Carla and Ruby had opened her eyes to their attitudes to men. Carla reckoned men were like buses. Miss one and two came along together. But she admired them both for using men's money for services rendered, while retaining their independence.

She'd not only filled the hot-water bottle but she'd made a pot of tea and now she poured herself a cup before collecting her dirty clothes and sorting them, ready for washing before work at Priddy's in the morning.

Marlene stirred her tea. Working with the girls made her smile. Men wanted sex. That's all it was and if they couldn't get it at home, they were willing to pay for it at the flat; even though she stipulated that johnnies must be worn to protect the girls. Men wanted straightforward sex and sometimes sex that wasn't really sex at all. Some men expected more than ordinary sex and as long as Carla and Ruby agreed, Marlene was also agreeable. But she drew the line at any man who wanted to hurt her girls. Some men were like naughty boys.

Mr Humber liked being shouted at while he stood in the corner of the bedroom naked. Edward wanted Carla to fasten a collar around his neck and take him for a naked walk in the Ferry Gardens. Since it was important that he walked on all fours, two nights a week Carla stayed late so they'd not be discovered by anyone who was actually walking a dog. Some men were lonely and simply wanted to talk. Donald liked Ruby to walk over him in her red court shoes. The men were all pretty harmless and enjoyed a cup of tea afterwards. And, of course, there were men from the forces, Americans, Canadians, nice boys away from home who paid well and tipped her.

Marlene kept records of them and their payments. Two ledgers, one for herself and one for the mysterious Mr X, who collected his share of the profits from Ruby.

If anyone had asked her a few months ago if she ever thought she'd be happy again, she would have bitten their hand off. But she *was* happy. Both jobs had given her back her confidence – the confidence she'd had in bucket-loads when she owned her own market stall – and that Samuel Golden had destroyed. She'd get that stall back one day, she vowed, and pay her debts. Most of all she wanted her beloved daughter, Jeannie, and her mother home with her.

Marlene drank some of her tea and toasted her legs

in front of the range. She believed in karma. What goes around comes around. One day Samuel Golden would get what was coming to him. She wasn't the only woman he'd deceived, the police had told her that, they just couldn't catch the slippery customer. She hoped she would meet him again one day, face to face, and tell him exactly what she thought of him.

She decided she'd finish sorting the clothes in the morning. She took the clock from the mantelpiece, wound it, and set the alarm. Then she put it on the kitchen table ready to take upstairs with her.

Looking in the mirror above the kitchen range, she saw that hard work had thinned her face. But she was still an attractive woman. She pushed back her hair that earlier she'd brushed, leaning forward so that it fell down in ripples of red and gold, the hairbrush pulling from root to tips. Mac loved her hair. Once he'd asked her if he could brush it. She'd liked the feel of his strong hands wielding the brush.

Deep down, Marlene knew she could love him. All she had to do was rid herself of the fear that he might hurt her as Samuel Golden had done.

Lizzie put her hands over her ears. Janie was crying. Gladys patted the baby's back. Janie was clutched to her breast, her head resting on Gladys's shoulder but straining with every lungful of powerful sound she uttered. The noise was relentless. The evening news on the wireless had been drowned out by the baby's cries.

'I can't hear myself think,' Lizzie said. 'You want me to take her?' She gave a deep sigh.

'If I don't know what to do with a kiddie now, I never will,' came the terse reply. 'Joel's coming down tomorrow.'

'Did he phone Priddy's to let you know?'

Gladys nodded, then got up and began walking around the kitchen, still patting Janie's back. 'He's got to wait seven years before he can marry you, you know.'

Lizzie was now folding up the nappies that had dried over the fireguard. She paused and tried to get her head around what Gladys was talking about. Of course, the lie. Oh dear, it was one thing telling an untruth, but another living with it.

'I know,' she said, then went on folding the terry towelling squares. The thing was, she had grown to love Joel. She'd been out with many men, including the father of Janie, Blackie Bristow, whom she *thought* she had loved but she'd come to realize that Joel was special. And she was sure he loved her: but enough to marry her? He'd never mentioned marriage. *Never.* And there was no real reason why he couldn't ask her to be his wife, was there?

They could get round the lie by saying they'd discovered his wife had been declared dead in the bomb blast. That would mean another lie. *But if he really loved her . . .*

Of course, there was the obvious – that she was *soiled goods*. Most men wanted to be the first feller to make love to their wives, but she was no longer a virgin and she had a daughter to prove it. 'I couldn't bear it if he left me.' The words flowed from her mouth before she realized she'd said them.

Gladys stopped walking. Miraculously, the baby stopped crying and gave an almighty belch of wind that seemed too large for such a little body!

'There, there,' Gladys cooed. 'It was all that nasty windy-pindy that was making you cry, wasn't it?' She looked at Lizzie, a frown etched across her forehead. 'Why would Joel leave you when you've given him a lovely daughter?' She unlatched the child from her shoulder and Lizzie saw her blue cardigan now sported a milky sick mark across its back. Gladys sniffed loudly, held out the child in front of her and said, 'Both ends. It's come out both ends.'

Lizzie sat back in the armchair by the window and said, 'Give her to me.'

With the baby handed over to her mother, Gladys gathered a pot of Vaseline, a dry nappy and a gauze square and set them within reach of Lizzie, who had already begun undressing Janie.

'Answer me,' Gladys said. 'Why would Joel think about leaving you?'

'I'm being silly,' said Lizzie. 'I shouldn't have opened my mouth.'

Deftly she stripped away the offending nappy and cleaned Janie. She saw Gladys watching her.

'Anyone can see that man loves you.'

'And I love him,' Lizzie said. 'Perhaps it's because we're apart and I miss him.'

'Go back to Lyme Regis with him, then.'

Lizzie shook her head. 'He'll be at work. Sometimes he does night shifts. I'll be honest with you, Gladys, I don't think I could take being on my own in the prefab. I know it's a lovely home, but . . .'

'He's lucky to have a job. Anyway, you won't be on your own, you got the baby.'

Lizzie felt the tears rise. She pulled down the long white nightie Janie wore and cuddled her. 'I like being here with you, Gladys.'

It was true, she was happy now she was home again in Gosport, with her mother just up the road. But she couldn't get it out of her head that Joel might decide to get on with his life now the lie had served its purpose.

Even if he truly cared for her, how could they conduct a love affair with him in one part of the country and her in another?

She looked down at Janie lying in her arms, almost asleep now. Gladys had taken the dirty nappy out to the scullery, Lizzie could hear the tap running.

'I'm making tea,' Gladys called. 'Joel's bringing down a diary belonging to Liliah Somerton. It might help your mum make sense of what happened and why Liliah ended up being fostered. He wants to take your mum to meet her. And us, he said.'

Lizzie's heart lifted at the thought of seeing Joel again. And her mum had been so down lately – since Lily, or rather Gloria, had died – a family get-together might be just what she needed. But it would be difficult for Em meeting a sister she never knew she had.

'There's one thing I'm not sure about, Glad. If Liliah Somerton had all those papers and the diary, why that she didn't contact Mum before?'

'I've thought about that. The poor woman isn't in any fit state to search any longer for her sister. But somebody was, and I don't believe it was Lily that found your mum. See, there are organizations like the Salvation Army that can trace people if you've got information for them to go on – Liliah might not have known about that.

'When Liliah's documents were stolen, I believe there was someone else besides Lily who was behind all this. Joel said he would do all he could to find out the truth, and I believe him. He's a damn good bloke to do all this for your mum. Though I suspect it's all for you, really.'

'Do you think so?' Lizzie got up, the baby in her arms quivering at the movement, then settling again. At the scullery door she watched Gladys rinsing out the teapot. 'I do love him, you know.'

Gladys turned and faced her. 'Then tell him, you silly cow. And once you've told him, tell him again!'

Chapter Twenty-Five

Lawrence Greyson closed the padlock on his lock-up. The van he'd picked up for a song was a godsend. So was the access, for a price of course, to unlimited black market petrol.

Above him, the sky was as black as ink and the air smelled of cordite. High over the trees to the left of the garage, an orange glow lit the sky like an early sunrise. The German bombers had struck quickly and accurately. Gosport's High Street had taken a battering and a shipyard near the floating bridge was still burning.

'Toys,' said the man at his side. 'Can you shift 'em?'

'I can get rid of anything,' Lawrence said. 'Call round tomorrow night and you'll get your share of the money.'

The man coughed and shifted his weight from one foot to the other. 'The prams and cots should be all right once they're cleaned up . . .' Lawrence had noted the brick dust. The stuff would be polished to perfection before it was moved on.

'Yeah, but you don't have to worry about that. Leave it to me.'

Lawrence pushed open his back gate and stood facing the man. 'Tomorrow.'

He unlocked the shed. Inside, the man removed his tin hat and stepped awkwardly out of his navy-coloured dungarees after removing his boots. The toy elephant fell to the wooden floor with a light thwump and was quickly snatched up, but Lawrence had spotted the man's mistake.

'I told you never to take any of the goods. What the hell are you playing at?' Lawrence's voice rose in the cold night air. He wasn't shouting. He didn't dare draw attention to himself, but his tone was like cold steel. He scooped up the clothes and hat and jammed them in a sack while the man struggled into his own clothes and shoes.

'D'you know how long it's been since ordinary people can afford toys? I just thought . . .' The stuffed toy sat on the workbench.

'You just thought taking a stolen toy wouldn't arouse suspicion?' He jammed the cloth animal into the bag along with the bloke's boiler suit and threw the sack further into the darkness. He grabbed the man's overcoat from the back of the door.

'Christ! I gotta three-year-old who'd love that thing . . .'

'You got a three-year-old who wouldn't want his dad in the nick for looting.' Lawrence turned away from him in disgust. 'It gets recognized, you get caught, I go down with you, and I'm not going down for anyone.'

'Sorry. I didn't think . . .'

Lawrence sighed. 'That's the trouble between us: I think, you don't.' He stared at the man before him. 'Piss off before I really get angry.' The man turned, shrugging himself into his coat. The tall gate closed behind him and Lawrence walked up the back garden path to the kitchen door of his ground-floor flat. Before he turned the key, he stood listening to the near silence. Trees rustled in the light wind, a cat miaowed further along the row of houses and he breathed a sigh of relief.

As he let himself in he wondered if he'd been too hard on his mate. Everything was hard to come by, because of this bloody war. Surely a stolen toy elephant given to a kiddie couldn't bring his whole operation down?

He took off his own tin ARP hat and his clothes. His dressing gown was hanging over a kitchen chair and he put it on. In a while he'd have a bath and get rid of the brick dust and stink of burning that clung to him. He pushed open the door to his drawing room and poured himself a large brandy from the bottle on the table. Before he drank he took off his spectacles and gave them a polish. He'd be glad when he moved on and could get rid of this disguise. The glasses pinched the bridge of his nose but he could hardly stop wearing them outside now, could he?

Tomorrow, Roy Sanders would come round with his van, give him a price for the stuff and take it away. He took a sip of the brandy and rolled it around on his tongue. He swallowed and felt the warmth line his throat. He took a further swallow and sighed contentedly. He had a good thing going and he didn't want it spoiled by a bloody toy elephant.

Joel knocked on Gladys's Alma Street door. He'd been told many times to use the key on the string, but still didn't feel right doing so.

Lizzie opened the door and threw her arms around him, then stepped back.

'That's a lovely welcome,' he said.

'Sorry to sweep you off your feet, but I'm so glad to see you.' She smelled of poppies, he thought. And she'd done something to her hair; it was curled under at the ends with a lovely sweeping fringe.

'You look, er, lovely,' he said. He wasn't very good at giving compliments.

'Get in out of the cold,' she said, pulling him into the passage. 'Gladys'll be moaning about letting all the heat out.'

As if on cue, Gladys shouted, 'You coming in or not?'

After closing the door and taking off his heavy coat, he picked up the brown carrier bag he'd brought in from the car and walked into the warm kitchen.

The baby was asleep in the pram, Gladys was sitting with her feet in a bowl of water and Em was knitting something small with white wool. For the baby, he guessed. He saw Lizzie had been reading at the kitchen table. Agatha Christie's *The Body in the Library*. The range gave out a good heat and the wireless was playing softly, big band dance music.

'Hello, everyone,' he said, putting the carrier bag on the table. 'I hope you're not offended but Marie wondered if I'd like to bring this down.' He produced a deep-dish pie and set it on the table. The crust was golden brown. Then he foraged inside his bag again and came out with a bag of home-made ginger biscuits. 'Marie sometimes doesn't get it right when cooking. She thinks everyone will eat loads but often the oldies only want tiny portions. She hopes you don't mind?'

'Don't mind! I could bite her hand off,' said Gladys. She took a foot out of the bowl and wetly stepped across to the table, lifting the pie. 'There's meat in there, I can smell it!' She smiled at Joel. 'I'll write a note thanking her. Let's have the biscuits with a cuppa.'

She grabbed a towel off the back of a kitchen chair and began wiping her feet, then encased them in her pom-pom slippers.

'I'll stick the kettle on.' Em put down her knitting and she got up and went into the scullery.

Joel followed her. 'You worried about meeting Liliah?'

She gave him a half-smile. 'I'm terrified.'

'I'll be with you,' he said, watching as she rinsed the teapot. 'I hope you don't mind,' he said, 'but I've been doing a few nights at the home and while it's been quiet I thought I'd try to decipher some of the writing in the diary.'

'How did you get on with that?'

'It's taken me ages to sort out the story, but it would take longer if we sat around the table trying to work out the different types of writing; some is in pencil, some in ink and the rest is barely legible. It looks as if the diary had got very wet and pages became stuck together.'

The diary had required careful handling, for the thread holding the pages had snapped and some had been sewn together again with black twine. Some pages were so brittle that they flaked and fell when he touched them. Other pages had been folded and in time the creases had become permanent; that also made the writing difficult to read.

As he had deciphered the sentences he had become as one with the person spilling her heart out on the paper. It soon became clear that this was no ordinary woman and the reflective passages allowed him entry into her mind and, later, her thoughts, some of which were heartbreaking.

'I'll begin when we're comfortable,' he said, taking a sheaf of paper from his inside jacket pocket. He looked at Em. 'Do you want me to give you a hand with the tea?'

She shook her head. 'Go on in and get warm, I'm just coming.'

He went past Lizzie's chair and paused, putting his hand on her shoulder. He so wanted to sweep her up in his arms and kiss her properly, as he would have done if the lie were the truth. She smiled as he touched her. He gave a small sigh, if only she knew . . .

Gladys moved the tray over on the table. 'Come on, Joel, let's find out what the past holds.' She looked at Em. 'Or would *you* rather read what Joel's got in his hands? After all, it's your mother's story.'

Em frowned and picked up her knitting again. 'I got no secrets from you, Glad. You sort out the tea, I made it.'

Joel saw a smile pass between them, which said in spite of all that had happened they were best friends.

'Right,' Joel said. 'Any questions, try and save them until the end.'

He looked at them waiting for him to start. He gave a small cough to clear his throat, then began speaking.

'Your dad, Alfie, was married to a woman named Helen Scott. Her brother Ronald was a bad egg. Ronald was feared by the people in Bermondsey, London. The police were always trying to pin something on him, but he was a right slippery customer. Alfie had a job in a kiosk selling newspapers. He was an honest man who tried to make his marriage work, but Helen would go off with anyone who asked her. Her brother thought the sun shone from her eyes.

'Alfie met a young chambermaid, Sally—'

A gasp came from Em. 'Mum,' she muttered.

Joel continued, 'Of course, Alfie was older than Sally and Ronald would have killed him if he'd discovered him cheating on his sister. So, they met in secret, Alfie and Sally. One afternoon they went to the pictures. Alfie came out of the auditorium to go to the lavatory just in time to see Ronald forcing the woman in the cash desk to hand over the takings. A couple of his men were standing by, watching out. The woman refused and Ronald, who'd got into the small kiosk, hit her. Alfie saw her fall, strike her head and knew she was a goner. Alfie also knew he'd been spotted, for he heard Ronald shout "Get him" to his cronies. Alfie, back in the cinema, grabbed Sally and they disappeared out of the side door.'

Em was holding her hand to her mouth but no one else stirred, all engrossed in his story.

'Alfie knew Ronald would, in all probability, kill him. Alfie could use his fists but Ronald wouldn't hesitate to use a knife. He'd done it before.' He paused. 'There's a note referring to Ronald killing a man in a knife fight over a girl. Ronald got away with that by saying he was defending himself when the man drew his weapon first.' He shuffled the pages then began to read once more. 'Alfie was a liability. Not just because he had witnessed the cashier's demise, but it also wouldn't take Ronald long to discover he had a girlfriend.

'Alfie had fallen in love with the girl and didn't want her hurt. That night he slept in the garden shed at the big house where Sally worked. To be honest, he was terrified to go home to his wife and with good reason, but he also wanted to be around Sally in case Ronald came calling. Sally proposed they run away together, to somewhere where they could both get work, maybe the seaside, somewhere like Brighton or Southsea.'

Joel picked up his cup and took a long swallow of tea. When he had first pieced together the story he had been astounded at what this young girl was willing to do for the man she loved. Now, as he looked round the table, he could see they were all impatient for him to continue, so he finished the tea quickly and began again.

'So they went on the run. But with hardly any money between them, it was difficult. They met up with some travellers. Alfie wanted to go to the police, make a clean breast of everything, but Sally persuaded him otherwise. She said Ronald would say he was in with them, part of their gang. She didn't want to be parted from Alfie. She begged him to stay with the travellers. Moving from place to place and making just about enough money to eat, she was happy. At first, they shared a van with an elderly woman, who seemed to command respect from the other travellers and who'd taken a shine to Sally. They had a sort of tent made with branches and canvas that they slept in. Alfie was good with his fists, so at fairgrounds he challenged the public to "Have a Go" at knocking him out. He made good money at that, although Sally hated seeing him with bruises. Sally made peg dollies and pegs out of wood and bits of tin and told fortunes from tea leaves in cups.' He paused and looked at his rapt audience.

'Then a family bought a new vardo, or caravan, and Alfie and Sally moved into their very own home, the old caravan. Sally was pregnant.' Gladys started coughing and Lizzie made her drink some more tea. 'Sorry,' she said.

'The pregnancy didn't go well. Sally was sick a lot. She wouldn't go to a hospital or a doctor because they didn't have the money. The fear of Ronald discovering them was a constant threat. The women helped her when her time came and she and the baby were looked after with potions made by the old woman. The baby was sickly. Liliah, for that was the baby girl's name, wouldn't take her mother's milk. A wet nurse fed her, one of the other travellers who had given birth just before Sally. The van was draughty and let in water. Liliah got so sick that Alfie wouldn't listen to Sally's protestations, and took the baby to the hospital in Bath. They kept the baby in. Because the couple had no marriage lines, no birth certificate for Liliah, not even a proper address, the authorities at the hospital wouldn't let the baby go back to the caravan. Liliah got better but still they refused to let Sally and Alfie take her.'

Here, Joel paused and looked around at them. 'This

is where the letters start. There's one from the hospital to the children's officer saying Liliah was "at risk". However, the baby *was* eventually allowed to go back with her mother. There was no denying Sally loved her child.

'The travellers had moved on, and Alfie and Sally caught them up. Alfie was trying to save money for a rental deposit on a house. He thought it was time they had a proper home. Weeks passed, Liliah got sick again, a chesty cough that wracked the little girl's body and resulted in another hospital stay. When Liliah was barely five months old, she contracted measles with complications in her chest again. Sally took her to the local doctor, they were near Basingstoke now. Sally was again pregnant. The doctor admitted Liliah to hospital. Both Sally and Alfie visited every day. There's a lot of letters from this period onwards from Sally to the authorities and replies from them to her. They were short of money because they travelled each day to be with Liliah. This time, when Liliah was better, the hospital refused to allow her back, saying that they were living in "unsuitable conditions". The hospital even sent a Mrs James to look at where Sally and Alfie were living. She made a point of saying there was no food in the caravan and that the place was damp. Liliah was to be fostered out until such time as her parents could provide decent housing.

'The child was sent to a children's home near Winchester with a view to her living with a couple from nearby Alresford. Sally and Alfie had no say in the matter. The authorities threw everything they could at the couple, even stating they were "unmarried and unfit to look after Liliah". The travellers moved down to Wickham for the annual horse fair. Wickham isn't too far from Winchester, so Sally and Alfie went with them. They visited St Cuthbert's where Liliah was, and were turned away. They might disrupt the child "who was settling in nicely", they were told.'

Joel paused again. This time he wiped a tear from one eye. There wasn't a sound in the kitchen except the ticking of the mantel clock.

'A letter was sent to them, care of Wickham post office which was Sally's postal address. She'd kept the authorities in the know about every movement the travellers made and, where possible, gave forwarding addresses. This communication stated that the couple from Alresford weren't able to take Liliah. Sally went back to St Cuthbert's, but they told her the child was no longer there.

'Alfie, through contacts at the horse fair, got the offer of a house in Gosport. He borrowed the deposit and he and Sally moved in. Then began a deluge of letters from Sally and Alfie wanting to know where their child was. They had a comfortable home and wanted Liliah back.

'Sally gave birth to Em. The letters never stopped.'

Joel handed the pages over to Em. Then he took the diary out of his pocket and put it on the table. 'You can check if you want, but that's the story. I can't leave you the diary, Em, it belongs to Liliah.'

Silence reigned in the small kitchen. It seemed to Joel as if all of them were thinking deeply about the story he'd told.

'There aren't any details of Liliah's life afterwards. She told me once she'd been brought up in the country. Perhaps she'll be able to tell you more. Sometimes her thoughts are jumbled, so maybe not. The correspondence between Sally and the authorities went on for years. It seems that somehow Liliah "disappeared".' He looked at Em. 'You say that your parents never spoke of Liliah?'

Em shook her head. 'Never,' she said, wiping the back of her hand across her eyes.

'The letters show that they never gave up hope.'

'I'll put the kettle on again,' said Gladys, pulling her handkerchief from her sleeve. A small cry issued from the pram and Lizzie got to her feet, ready to tend to Janie.

'I never expected that,' Em said. 'Never in my wildest imaginings!' She paused. 'Liliah will be able to tell us her side of it,' she began.

'As I said, I wouldn't be too sure of that,' said Joel. 'You must remember that though she's only a little older than you, life hasn't been kind to her. Her memory is shot to pieces, but she has been searching for you since before the war. The war robbed her of her husband. Her illness escalated, leaving her practically a shell of a woman. Liliah doesn't like to be parted from the letters and documents you saw previously. They tell her who she is.'

He could hear Gladys rattling the cups as she washed them and the hiss of the gas as the kettle boiled. He looked round at Lizzie but her face was inscrutable. Janie had settled again.

He thought how good it would feel to be in bed with Lizzie soon, even if there had to be a line of pillows between them.

Em's voice broke into his thoughts.

'We were a close family,' she said. 'Sitting around the kitchen table in the evenings, doing jigsaw puzzles or reading – both Mum and Dad were avid readers. But never once did either of them mention that I had a sister, never.'

'Can't you imagine how heartbroken they must have been to have lost their beloved firstborn?' Lizzie said, looking at Janie. 'At some point the letters sent to the authorities and the copies of the replies had been gathered together and put in a folder.'

'In the meantime, lives are altered and people are moved on.'

'Like fish slipping through nets,' said Gladys, putting down the tray on the table. The teapot spout steamed. Gladys looked at the bag of biscuits. 'About time we started on these,' she said.

Janie started grumbling.

Joel said, 'Give her to me, I expect she needs changing.'

Lizzie brought her daughter over to him.

He held her, gazing at her tiny features that were going to grow until she became an even more precious and beautiful girl. 'She might look lovely, but she smells bad.' He wrinkled his nose. 'I'll change her,' he said. 'You pass me all the stuff.'

'Can you?' Lizzie frowned.

'I look after elderly people who wear nappies, just bigger ones. Changing this little one will be a welcome relief.'

Chapter Twenty-Six

'We decided it would be better if you two met in Liliah's room, where she feels at ease.'

Em looked at the doctor, then at Joel, and nodded. 'She wants Joel to be with her, I hope you don't mind,' the white-coated doctor added. 'And this first meeting should be short.'

Em was glad Joel was going to be there.

The three of them stopped outside a door, which was ajar. The doctor knocked politely, pushed the door open and they entered.

The woman in the bed was practically skeletal, but her blue eyes were bright. Em gasped at how much Liliah resembled her mother, with her straight nose and the same high forehead.

The doctor pulled a chair over so Em could sit down beside the bed.

'Well, here she is, Liliah.' Joel tried to inject a little humour into the tense moment. Liliah looked up at him and smiled. Em could sense a bond between them. She hoped it was a good day for Liliah, with her thoughts in order and her mind open to talking to her. She put out her hand and touched the paper-thin fingers of her sister. This woman had been searching for her, her only relative. What if she disappointed her? Joel had told her of Liliah's health problems, but she'd not been prepared for this husk of a woman. Still, Em thought, there was plenty a person could say without actually speaking.

'I'm Em. We both have the same parents . . .'

There were tears in Liliah's eyes.

Em tried again. 'Last night we read the diary Mum left you.' She could feel Liliah's gaze taking in every part of her. Her blue utility costume, washed so many times it was almost shapeless, her black high heels, her blue felt hat with the feather on the side.

Em looked around the room. A dressing gown hung over the end of the bed. There was a chest of drawers, a couple of chairs and a window that looked out over the garden. The curtains were frilled and matched the bed quilt. It smelled of lavender and old lady. Yet Liliah wasn't old, she was barely a year older than Em herself.

Life had done this to Liliah; it had made her old before her time.

Em looked into Liliah's face, unknown but not unfamiliar.

'I think Mum would be happy to see us like this,' she said. Liliah's hand tightened its frail grip on Em's fingers. She sighed deeply.

'I think so,' said Liliah.

Marlene pushed her plate aside. 'Well, I haven't had such a good meal for ages,' she said. 'Where did you manage to get chops?'

Mac winked at her. 'That's a perk of being a copper. Even people who haven't done anything wrong want to keep on the best side of the law.'

She shook her head and he got up from the table, gathering the empty plates. 'I've got pudding,' he announced proudly. 'It's from a tin, got it off the Canadians when they were in port. I made some custard, but it's a bit lumpy.' She laughed as he left the kitchen, taking the plates into the scullery.

There was a big Welsh dresser to one side of the room, the table in the centre and an armchair frayed at the arm-rests beneath the window. The black-leaded grate looked like it could do with a clean, but the fire burned merrily and the place looked comfortable enough considering Mac was in the throes of redecorating. Newspaper was spread out on the dresser and paintbrushes soaked in tins and broken cups. The old lino on the floor was covered with white spots of distemper from the newly whitened ceiling.

'I'll get him in the end, you know.' His voice carried through to her.

'Who?' Marlene knew very well who he meant, but she wanted to play dumb enough for him to explain.

'Your boss.' She could hear him scraping a pan. The smell of vanilla floated into the room.

'Well, you'll not get his whereabouts and identity from me – I've told you; I need the job too much. When I've finally paid my creditors I'll be working towards buying a cheap van and some stock, so I can get on my feet again . . .' She paused. She didn't want him to think she was harping on about how badly Samuel Golden had treated her. 'Anyway, if we close down what will your superior officers do to get their jollies?'

'They'll have to find somewhere else, won't they? Honour among cops and all that, I'll make sure no one discovers their little love nests. I'll have to.' His voice echoed from the scullery.

Marlene liked that about him; that he cared about people.

Mac came in with two dishes piled high with a suspiciously yellow mountain of pudding, covered with pale lumps. 'It tastes better than it looks,' he said, setting down the plate in front of her. She poked it with a fork, then took a tentative mouthful.

'It's nice,' she said.

'Suet pudding, it said on the tin.'

'I believe you.' He put out a hand as he sat down opposite her and covered her fingers just as she was about to take a mouthful. 'You don't want me to eat it?'

He let his hand drop and sighed. For a while they ate. The only sounds were the clacking of spoons and forks against china and the fire throwing out sparks.

Marlene sat back on her chair and said, 'I'm absolutely full.'

Mac said, 'It'll cost you.'

'I can pay, but not in money.'

'You've thought this over very carefully, haven't you?'

Marlene said, 'It's time, don't you think?' She got up from her chair and moved towards him. 'I wanted you the moment you entered the office, but I was scared.'

Standing in front of him, she felt his arms go around her waist and he rested his head against her stomach. 'I want nothing from you except yourself,' Mac said.

She knew this man was nothing like Samuel Golden. He was honest, kind and had waited until she was ready. They didn't move. She felt what she could only describe as her spirit spiralling with his in the peacefulness that surrounded them.

He rose and she felt his strong arms hold her close to his heart. His eyes were upon her, his face filled with kindness and she saw his love for her. He tipped her chin towards him and with her face in his large hands, he kissed her again and again.

Marlene felt as if he was tucking her heart inside his soul.

'You're beautiful,' he said. He began kissing her face, her cheeks, her nose, then pulled her long hair back so he could kiss around her throat. Suddenly, Marlene was crying.

Mac wiped the tears from her face with his thumbs. 'I'm not going to hurt you, or deceive you,' he said.

'No, I don't believe you will,' Marlene said. She took his hand and led him out of the kitchen and up the stairs, their shoes clacking on the bare wood. Remains of flowered wallpaper curled in strips down the walls.

The bed was rumpled, like he'd got out of it and gone straight to work. She looked back at him and smiled. Even in here signs of decorating dominated the room:

two of the walls were hung with leafy paper and there was a smell of paint in the air, clean and fresh.

He was breathless as he watched her undress. Naked, she lay back on the candlewick bedspread as he took off his clothes. Then he leaned over her, brushing stray strands of her hair from her face. The room was a tip, a decorator's nightmare. But to Marlene it was the room where the rest of her life was about to happen.

'It's been a long time . . .'

'Woman, you're doing fine.'

Against her softness he was hard and full. She touched his beautiful, sensitive mouth with her lips as he moved over her, his body moulding exactly into the curved hollow of her hips. He pressed into her, deeper and deeper, kissing her so that she was crushed into him.

'Hold me tight,' he murmured as he moved inside her, so easily she was sure they'd been made for each other, like parts of a jigsaw.

His hands traced over her hips, his back arching and she answered with rising thrusts of her own. There was the taste of salt on her lips from his body then a roaring inside her coming from some hidden place, as his sweat mixed with her tears that Mac kissed from her cheeks.

Then her body remembered and acted as though she'd never forgotten. Each memory started a chain reaction of new pleasures until another, louder cry leaped from Marlene's throat.

'Oh, yes, my love.' Mac's breath was hot against her neck as his urgency peaked. A moment so intense it felt like exquisite pain as he thrust inside her. And then he turned, his cries muffled against the pillow. Long ragged sounds were torn from him; then finally, peace for them both.

Mac held her for a long time, in silence.

Marlene lay still. The room was dark; she knew this was the beginning of something that was like nothing she'd experienced before. She turned her head to see Mac grinning at her with sheer pleasure.

'I'm glad I've got another tin of that suet pudding,' he said.

The knock at his door was loud enough for him to hear despite the sound of people shouting outside. The siren had screamed and already people were running for cover.

Lawrence Greyson let Colin in and they went together through the back and down to the shed where the gear was kept.

'On your own?' Lawrence didn't mind that there were just the two of them – it meant more profits if only a couple of them posed as ARP wardens.

The air was thick with dust and the smell of burning that hung over the nearby village.

Colin sometimes took the empty van home with him, so he was always the first to arrive and pick up Lawrence. Lawrence knew he used the vehicle for his own personal use, but he didn't care as long as it was always filled with petrol when he needed it.

It didn't take them long to rig themselves out in their uniforms.

'Don't go into the village,' commanded Lawrence. Through the window of the shed he could see flames licking skyward near the church. 'Retired people.' He spoke as if that meant everything. He knew the middle classes believed in banks, so although their furnishings were decent, they seldom kept money and jewellery at home.

The streets were now still. People were either at home in their Anderson shelters or tucked into Morrisons. Possibly most were safer in the communal shelters, but not always. In the van he turned to Colin: 'You read about the bomb, that V2 landing on the shopping centre in Lewisham?' Colin, his eyes on the road ahead, shook his head. 'Couple of months back it was. Penetrated an air-raid shelter, it did. Fifty-one dead and loads injured.'

Colin turned and stared at him. 'It's called Doodlebug

Alley. The south,' he said. 'We got most of our airfields and factories down here.'

'Go into the town,' said Lawrence. 'As long as the bombs keep falling, we're in business.'

He thought suddenly of the elderly woman in the flat above him. She'd knocked on his door asking him to help with her kitchen tap that wouldn't stop dripping. He'd helped her, of course, a regular Sir Galahad. After all, a simple washer change took no time at all. Sitting in her living room, looking around while nursing a cup of tea, had been an eye-opener to his way of thinking about the middle classes. She had some very nice bits of stuff laid out on tables and shelves. An onyx table lighter just happened to fall into his pocket. Got a few notes for that, he did.

Through the windscreen he watched as sudden flares in the distance meant that Portsmouth was getting a hammering. Searchlights toured the skies, looking for the planes. He pushed his spectacles up on his nose.

There was something exciting about being outside while the bombing went on. At any second it could be his last moment on this earth. He didn't do the things he did simply for the money, it was for the thrill of it all as well, the kicks. Like the women. He picked them up and discarded them like old socks, simply because he could.

'Try the High Street,' he said. He spoke loudly as the

noise outside the van was horrendous – it felt almost as if they were cocooned in the small space of the motor.

He saw what he was looking for, and could hardly believe his luck. A jeweller! Who would have thought the Jerries would be so gracious as to give him two jewellers in the space of a few weeks. Gold was easy to pocket and everyone liked it. As was jewellery and watches, an absolute godsend just before Christmas. He'd be able to sell the stuff on quickly. His spirits rose and he began humming a tune to himself. *The holly and the ivy* . . .

'You see what I see?'

Gadd's the greengrocer was in ruins, flames issuing from the top floor. Woolworth's had lost a side wall and the counters were festooned with broken goods and dusty bricks. There was no fire there, but it was creeping along at a fair rate from Gadd's as the wind blew fingers of flames along the roof towards the jeweller's.

'No fire in the jeweller's yet,' said Colin, as though reading his mind. 'I'll park here.'

The van would be a good distance away. 'If the ambulances and fire engines want to get closer we might get hemmed in.' He paused and looked at Lawrence fearfully. 'There's not going to be dead people, is there?' Colin got the creeps if he thought there were people in the buildings.

One night they'd encountered the body of a young man. There wasn't a mark on him when Lawrence discovered him lying in the smoking rubble, but he was as dead as a doornail. Colin was upset about it for ages afterwards.

Colin jumped down from the van. 'C'mon, let's see what we can salvage before the all-clear goes. Don't tread on anything still burning. These welly boots could shrivel up on your feet.'

Lawrence held his scarf over his mouth so he could breathe as they walked back towards the jeweller. The air was foul. For once he was grateful for his spectacles, as they gave him some relief from the smoke. Once inside the shop, his eyes scoured the ground for treasures that might have fallen from shelves. Dusty velvet pillows of rings and bracelets lay amongst the broken glass shop counters. The alarm was magically still working, and the shrill penetrating sound blasted his ears as it competed with the drone of the overhead planes.

'Look at that,' Colin tugged on his arm. 'Only the bloody safe!'

A small square safe with the door off its hinges sat on the floor at the rear of the shop. With one bound Lawrence was on it. It was too heavy to move, but there was no need. Small boxes tumbled from it as Colin explored the contents. He held up a sheaf of white notes. 'Bloody fivers,' he said. 'What's in the boxes?'

Lawrence used his thumbnail to flip one open. 'Fuckin' 'ell!'

Colin was at his shoulder. 'Diamonds!' The tiny stones glittered. 'Must be worth a fortune.'

'Stuff 'em inside your jumper,' said Lawrence. He leaned across Colin and scooped small bags from the shelves and jammed them into his pockets.

A noise above them made Lawrence look up. He could see the sky, the stars bright like the diamonds. Another yawning creak came from on high. Flames were picking their way downwards. The chimney seemed to sway, or was it a trick of his eyes? Then came the siren. The all-clear was moaning its mournful song. Lawrence stared hard at the chimney stack, mesmerized.

'Let's get out, it's not safe.'

He heard a vehicle draw up close. Lawrence pressed himself back into the shattered doorway of Woolworth's, alongside the jeweller's, grabbing hold of Colin. It wouldn't do to be seen running away. Not two ARP men.

The sudden crash added to the chaos of voices and the noise of the fire engine now trundling over the uneven ground, its bell loudly clanging. Dust hurled its way upwards from the fallen chimney. Bricks and cement sprayed everywhere after hitting the floor of the shop. The decorative clay pots dropped, rolled, smashed and then lay still amongst the debris that now covered the safe.

'Whew! We could have been under that,' Colin said from the safety of the pavement. He wiped his forehead. Even in the dull light, Lawrence could see the sweat running down Colin's face from beneath his tin hat.

People seemed to have appeared from nowhere. Then Lawrence saw the lorry halt in the road and three men emerge dressed as ARP wardens. Real wardens.

'C'mon,' he said. He stepped into the fray with Colin following. The firemen had set up hoses to the standpipes and were concentrating on spraying the ashes and the surrounding shops. Lawrence moved swiftly through the people, some of whom had just come to gawp. His heart was thumping inside his chest.

'Oy! You!' Automatically he turned. A fireman was staring at him. Sweat seemed to seep out of Lawrence's every pore. He looked the man full in the face and watched as the man's mouth moved. 'You see anyone inside the building, mate?'

It took a while for Lawrence to find his voice. 'No,' he said. He felt like a balloon that had deflated.

Half an hour later they were outside his shed, where

Lawrence insisted the clothes and boots be kept. His flat was in darkness, as were the other homes around him.

'Close call,' said Colin. He had paper money stuffed everywhere on his person and he was now tipping it all into a cardboard box. 'I was scared of leaving a trail of fivers as I walked,' he said. 'We've hit the jackpot tonight.'

Lawrence wanted a drink, the larger the better. He knew he'd be a fool to take all this stuff into his flat at this time of night. What if he dropped notes on the garden path and only discovered he'd done so in the morning? What if he trod diamonds into the concrete? Suppose someone saw him staggering up to the kitchen with a box of loot? It only wanted one nosy parker to see him acting suspiciously. Best to leave the lot in the shed overnight.

Colin had a fistful of notes. 'I'll take this to tide me over,' he said. 'I'll come round in the morning and we'll see what we've got then.'

Lawrence took the money out of his hand. 'No! I got to look at it, suppose it's marked?'

Colin allowed him to take the money but he glared. 'It's all right for you. You haven't got a wife always needing stuff.'

'Don't tell me your troubles, mate. What's the matter,

after all this time you decided you don't trust me? You think the split is going to go more my way?'

Colin shuffled from one foot to the other. 'No . . .'

Lawrence let out a long sigh. 'Come round tomorrow, mate.' He knew he'd got the upper hand when Colin turned, picked up his coat that he'd left there earlier in the evening and put it on. He had a bit of difficulty with the arms, but soon he wound his scarf about his neck and gave Lawrence a sudden grin.

'Eleven?'

'Make it later, the evening would be better. I can take the pretty stuff down to Den in the morning, see what he'll cough up for that,' said Lawrence.

Chapter Twenty-Seven

'These prefabs are fantastic,' said Gladys. 'Makes you realize what old-fashioned houses we have.' She was sitting on the sofa, a screwed-up ball of newspaper on its arm.

She looked at Em for reassurance, who nodded. 'We've got prefabs in Gosport, too,' she said. Now it was Gladys's turn to agree with her.

'Anyone want anything else to eat? Another cup of tea?' Joel looked at them expectantly. Lizzie was in her bedroom with the baby and he was eager to go and talk to her.

Gladys patted her stomach. 'I'm full to the brim with fish and chips. Good thing they ain't rationed.'

'So am I,' said Em, hauling herself out of the easy chair. 'And that bottle of stout went down a treat. We've got an early start in the morning back to Gosport, so I think I'll turn in, if that's all right? You coming, Glad?'

Joel said a silent prayer. Ever since he and Em had returned from Yew Trees they'd discussed endlessly what had gone on between Em and her new-found sister. The lives of both of them had been disentangled, discussed and dissected with the end result being tears, sadness, wonderment and now, hope for the future.

With the doctor's prompting, Em and he had discovered Liliah had had a good life despite the unhappiness of her formative years. She'd done well at school, gone on to university and had travelled the world. She'd had romances, so she said, but preferred being alone until she'd met her future husband in the services. They'd married and she'd been extremely happy until he'd died. Sadly, throughout her life, she'd suffered from her nerves. Some days 'up', some days 'down', but there was no denying her happiness at meeting Em. It was as if she'd been given a new lease on life and had shed twenty years.

'I'm going to ask for more time off when I get back to Priddy's, and then I'll come and spend more time with Liliah,' Joel heard Em say.

He'd been amazed that Liliah had been forthcoming with her questions and had appeared totally in command of herself. What's more, the two women got on like a house on fire. Em knew how to give Liliah time to gather her thoughts before she spoke and was ready to help her sister understand her life with their mother. Joel was surprised that Em had taken family photographs with her. Liliah had never seen a photo of her mother so it was a poignant moment, especially when she realized how like her mother she looked.

When the doctor decided it was time for Em to leave, as Em rose from her chair at the side of the bed, Liliah had begged her to return soon.

'Will you put me up, Joel? I'll come up on the train,' she'd called.

'You can stay in my prefab any time, Em,' he'd replied.

He got up and began gathering the newspaper that had contained the fish and chips. He screwed it into a large ball and then started collecting the empty beer bottles. He smiled to himself. They'd eaten a hearty meal with bread and butter, beer, and some of Marie's rice pudding. She'd baked a dish especially for Joel to give them.

Just then the door opened and Lizzie stood on the step. 'Janie's asleep now,' she said. 'I feel as though I've been pulled through a hedge backwards.' She put up a hand to smooth her hair.

'Well, you certainly don't look like it,' Joel said, moving towards her and planting a kiss on the top of her head.

She gave him a hesitant smile. He didn't want to give her a silly little kiss. He wanted to crush her to him and kiss the living daylights out of her!

He was supposed to be her lover. Only he wasn't! And now, because Em and Gladys were sharing the room he usually slept in, he had to sleep with Lizzie and not lay a finger on her! He sighed as he took the bottles and put them outside by the back step. The newspaper went in the bin and he banged the metal lid hard down to seal it shut – that cat at number seven was a terror for sneaking edible bits from bins. Anyway, the noise helped him release a little frustration.

'It's not going to be for ever.' Lizzie's voice surprised him – she'd followed him out to the garden.

'If you only knew . . .'

'Knew what? That you're fed up with pretending, that you're only doing it for my sake?'

He looked at her sheepishly. Her perfume was wafting over him, poppies, strong, sensual. He cleared his throat. How could he tell her what he really wanted? That he didn't want to pretend any more. He wanted her! He'd always wanted her! But he didn't want her to laugh at him and tell him he was being ridiculous. The truth was, he didn't know what he could do to show her he loved her. Everything he'd done was because he cared. He'd proposed the lie to make it easier for her to see her mother, because he loved her. And what next? Would she simply drift from his life now Liliah and Em were reunited?

He didn't want to take her back to Gosport tomorrow. He wanted her here, with him. But that was impossible. With Janie so tiny, Lizzie needed her mother and Gladys near her for advice and help.

Lizzie said, 'Well?'

So she wanted an answer. Of course he was fed up with the pretence.

He sighed. 'Yes, I've had enough of lying to everyone . . .'

A dark shadow seemed to cloud her face. 'It won't be for much longer,' she said. Her voice was hard.

'But—' His voice dwindled as she interrupted.

'We'll all be back in Gosport tomorrow night,' she said. 'Your life will be your own again. Thank you for all you've done.' Then she hesitated as though about to say something more. He waited. There was another moment's silence then she said curtly, 'I'm going to bed.'

The door clicked as she swept inside, leaving him staring at the stars, the black and white cat from number seven sitting by the gate watching him.

'Well, Joel, you made a right mess of that,' he muttered

to himself as he followed Lizzie into the empty kitchen. He took out a bottle of pale ale from the small crate in the cupboard and pulled off the top. There were no sounds from the living room, so he guessed everyone had gone to bed. He sat down at the kitchen table and put the bottle to his lips.

When it was empty, he started on a second one.

Lizzie heard Joel softly open the bedroom door. Em and Gladys had finally stopped talking in the next room and gone to sleep. She tried hard not to breathe. Her head was whirling with things she wanted to say to him. She kept quite still. Janie was fast asleep, but every so often a tiny snuffle whistled down her nose. It was one of those things that Lizzie listened for to let her know all was well in Janie's sleepy world. She thought of Joel and how he had brought life back into her child. Without him, there would be no baby sleeping contentedly in her cot, just a few feet away.

The pillows were lined at her back. She'd put them there, but not because she wanted to. It was a habit, that in view of the words she and Joel had exchanged earlier, she thought she'd better not break.

What she wanted to do was throw the pillows on the floor and grasp Joel to her. But if he pushed her away she wouldn't be able to stand it. He'd made it clear tonight that he was fed up with the charade, hadn't he?

Trouble was, Lizzie hadn't bargained on falling in love with him.

Back when she'd been serving behind the bar, Joel had been the answer to her prayers with the lie that he loved her and was the father of her unborn child. The lie that he couldn't marry her because he already had a missing wife was an invention that had enabled her to go home to Gosport. She could be with her mother without either of them being ridiculed for her unmarried state.

But she hadn't known then what a wonderful man he was.

How stupid she'd been to assume he fancied her. He was simply a good man who liked his job and the people around him. Look how he'd cared for that old man who had died. And what about Liliah? For her peace of mind, he'd proved Liliah *did* have a sister. Her mother wouldn't be sleeping contentedly in the next room, after visiting the sister she never knew she had, if he wasn't a diligent and dedicated carer. So why on earth would a good man like Joel want a woman like her who had produced Blackie Bristow's bastard?

She felt the bed quiver as he kicked it in the dark. 'Bugger!' She could sense him rubbing his foot. His exclamation had been muted. She heard his clothes fall to the lino. Usually he folded them and piled them on the chair, but not tonight.

The bed sagged as he climbed on. A wave of alcohol swept over her. There'd been a few bottles of beer left in the cupboard when she'd come to bed. She doubted they were there now.

He muttered, 'Bloody things' and threw the pillows on the floor where they landed with soft thumps. For a moment her heart lifted. Then he was lying on his back, breathing heavily. She sighed.

She'd intended to apologize for her abrupt behaviour in the garden. Lizzie wanted to tell him she loved him. It wasn't going to matter that he didn't care for her.

A snore told her that Joel was already asleep.

A tear crept out from beneath Lizzie's lashes and ran down her cheek.

"I'm sorry, Em, there's no question of you having more time off.' Rupert Scrivenor, her boss, shuffled the papers on his desk. A waft of cologne swept over her. 'Look here.' He waved a hand over a printed page. 'This is an order for anti-tank mines. You know I can't tell you where they're going, but it's a rush job. It's all hands on deck for this.'

'Not even a couple of days? I've just met my sister . . .'

He shook his head. 'Get the girls to send out this order and you can have all the time you need.'

She stared at him, at his piercing blue eyes, his fair hair, his immaculate suit. He was a good man; he would have given her time off had it been possible. She nodded. Fair enough, this bloody war had to be won, didn't it? And, since D-Day they all knew they were winning, but if they slackened off in their efforts . . . Her eyes moved on to the poster on his wall. 'A concealed mistake is a crime. It may cost a brave man his life.' Safety slogans were everywhere. She nodded again and closed the door behind her.

Over in the brick building, Em watched the women working on the order. Gladys was among them, standing next to Milly, a relatively new worker at Priddy's. Gladys took her eyes away from the tray she was filling with detonators. Em shook her head so that Gladys knew she hadn't been granted the time off.

She saw Gladys sigh as her attention slid back to the detonators. The wireless was playing; *Workers' Playtime* cheering everyone up. Standing by Milly's side, Em couldn't believe her eyes as she watched the detonator fall from Milly's hand into the tray.

She was lifted off her feet and hit the cement floor

with a weight flattening her body. The noise after the initial terrific bang included screams, shouts, cries and a crumbling sound. Then there was light, a brightness. Her sight was blurred, there was a ringing in her ears and she felt unreal, like she was in a dream.

The heaviness on top of her was oozing a red substance that was trickling over her skin, her arms and her face. A moan came from above her. An outstretched arm that didn't belong to her was slung across her shoulder, covered in scratches and oozing droplets of blood. She recognized the hand, the ringless fingers of Gladys. Gladys was lying on top of her. It was Gladys moaning.

Em wriggled sideways. She didn't feel hurt. There was blood and mess covering the concrete floor and sliding down the side of the workbench, which was now a V-shape where it had broken in half.

A woman said, 'Don't worry, help's coming.'

Worry? Why should she worry? Gladys moaned again. Em slid through the gore and was surprised that she could move her arms, her legs. She held on to the wooden base that was all that was left of the bench, to find her legs were like jelly. But she pushed herself upright. She looked down.

'Ohhh!' Gladys's boiler suit had disappeared from

her back. Bits of navy blue material were stuck in the bloodied mess where her skin should be. Gladys was lying in pools of blood that covered every surface. Em dropped to her knees, smoothing hair that obstructed Gladys's sight. The hair came away in her hand.

Gladys had her eyes open. There was blood coming from her nose and ears. Em smoothed her cheek. 'I'm here,' she said. Gladys closed her eyes. Em knew she was out of it.

Again she struggled to her feet. The floor was slippery.

Milly had disintegrated. One of her work boots was on the floor lying on its side, clean and empty. The smell of raw meat pervaded the air.

There were sirens now, loud and coming closer. They hurt her ears. She looked up and saw the sky. Bits of tin were lifting in the November wind. She saw a door hanging off its hinges, the windows of the hut had blown out. Electricity fittings were hanging, swinging crazily in the wind. Everything was covered with dust. A fireman reached the open doorway where women were huddled, crying.

'Over here.' Her voice seemed to belong to someone else.

The men picked their way through fallen debris and when they reached Gladys, Em began to cry. 'She threw herself on top of me to save me,' she said. 'Don't let her die.'

'Can you walk?' The ambulance man looked kind. Em nodded. She didn't know whether she could walk or not, but it was Gladys she was thinking about, not herself. 'Leave her to us, love.' He looked nice, Em thought, like he had a wife and kiddies and he loved them . . . 'Let's try and get you to the ambulance, love. We're coming for your mate.'

But Em couldn't move. She was shaking like she was dancing without music. She looked around and decided no one else was hurt, she could tell by the number of women sitting, crying, outside on the grass. She could see now that the wall had gone. All her charges were there. Except for Milly. 'Milly Watkins was working this bench,' she said, grabbing at the ambulance man's sleeve as he tried to pull out the stretcher. The man nodded. 'Get to the ambulance,' he repeated. This time Em took a step forward, then another, and collapsed in the dust.

Lizzie held tightly to Janie as she walked down the white corridor. The smell of disinfectant was strong. She could understand why people hated hospitals. The news of Gladys's injuries had been relayed to her from Mr

Scrivenor himself. He'd called round in his gleaming car just as she'd been bathing Janie.

'Your mother is fine, shaken up, but fine. If you like I can take you to the War Memorial Hospital to collect her. They wanted to keep her in overnight, but she won't hear of it. She also needs some clothes. They disposed of hers. I'll drive you to Em's to collect some more.'

Lizzie was too upset to answer him. All she could think about was Gladys and her mother and the friendship they shared. She finished bathing Janie and got her ready to leave.

Tears filled her eyes as she put clean underwear, a skirt and her mother's favourite blue jumper into a carrier bag. Mr Scrivenor drove them to Bury Road. He offered to come and wait with her until they could collect her mother and see Gladys, and then drive them home again, but she didn't want that. She'd make her own way home, she told him. And she could take care of her mother. She knew he'd spoken to the doctors and there didn't seem any point in him sitting, waiting. He had work in the morning.

Her mother looked very small, sitting up in bed. She was in a long ward surrounded by women of all ages. The nurse said her mother had suffered from shock.

'Oh, Lizzie,' Em said. 'She pushed me out of the way

and took the brunt of the explosion. It's all my fault.' She started crying again. Her eyes were red and beneath them puffy bags added years to her age.

Lizzie settled Janie in Em's arms then cuddled the both of them.

'Stop it, it's not your fault, she did it because she loves you.' She foraged in her coat pocket for a handkerchief and gave it to her mother. 'What's happening to Gladys?'

In between sniffs and tears, Lizzie heard that Gladys was to be moved to the Queen Victoria Hospital at East Grinstead. Lizzie pulled the blue cotton curtain round the bed. 'We need to get home,' she said. 'But first we must see Gladys.' Em relinquished Janie and began dressing.

'It's the best place to treat her burns,' she said, struggling into her knickers. 'They can do things there that the hospitals round here aren't equipped to do. How long she's there depends on her. The doctor said the main worry would be if her skin becomes infected. They've given her injections for pain relief and we can see her when she wakes.'

Em began to cry again, the handkerchief pressed to her eyes. 'I'm not going nowhere until I've spoken to her.'

Lizzie put her arms around her mother. 'Quite right.'

Em looked at her and nodded. 'They kept saying how

lucky I was. Milly wasn't so lucky. I'm going to have nightmares for ever about her,' she said. 'Blown to smithereens.' She shuddered. 'It would have been the same for me if Gladys hadn't acted so quickly.'

Janie whimpered from her place in the depths of the starched, white sheets. Lizzie picked her up. She opened her eyes, dark blue, so like Blackie's eyes. Lizzie marvelled that people hadn't commented on how like Blackie she was, with that cap of dark curls. She rocked Janie and soon her eyes closed again.

When her mother was dressed, she pulled back the curtain and placed her child in her mother's arms again. 'Take her for a bit. She likes you cuddling her.' Anything, she thought, anything to take her mind off the dreadful scenes her mother had witnessed at Priddy's. She told Em to sit holding Janie while she found a nurse to let them know they needed to find Gladys.

As she walked along the polished corridor Lizzie knew that she was trapped. How could she go to Lyme Regis now, even if Joel wanted her to, and leave her mother when she needed her most? Not that Joel had asked her, but then he wouldn't, would he? And oh, how she wanted him at this moment. She knew she had to tell him about the accident. She'd phone Yew Trees, yes, that's what she would do.

But not until her mother had seen Gladys and set her mind at rest.

The small room in the corridor held three young nurses drinking well-earned cups of tea. Lizzie could have killed for a cup herself. With information seeping out of her ears Lizzie promised to bring back her mother if anything untoward happened. Shock was a very funny thing, she was told. With a nurse in tow, Lizzie returned to the ward where she found her mother jiggling Janie on her knees.

'You talking to your nan?' Lizzie smiled at Em. She was speaking to Janie, who was opening and closing her mouth. 'You talking to me?'

Lizzie had guessed rightly that having the baby with her would help Em bear up under the strain of believing she was to blame for Gladys's burns. No, there was no way Lizzie could return to Lyme Regis now.

Her mother looked at the blue-and-white-clothed nurse, then wordlessly they followed her down the corridor, out over the central gardens, back into a ward then into a single room.

Gladys was attached to a tall, square, freestanding object by a variety of wires. There was a humming noise coming from the machine.

'You can stay for a few moments, but she needs her

rest,' the nurse said at the door as she left in a rustle of starched petticoats. Amazingly, Gladys was propped on her side. Lizzie noticed the grey parting in her bleached hair and she wanted to gather her up and hold her tight. Her mother was standing at her bedside looking down at her friend.

'Hello,' croaked Gladys. Lizzie bent and kissed her forehead because it was one of the only parts of her that was not covered. A white cloth was resting on her back and Lizzie couldn't see how bad the burns were.

Em said, 'You saved my life.' There were tears in her eyes again.

'Don't want to lose you, do I?' Gladys's voice was fragmented. Her forehead creased with suffering.

'Are you in much pain?' Lizzie hoisted Janie to her shoulder, and with difficulty bent down to Gladys's level so that Gladys could kiss the baby.

'They've given me stuff and I'm all floaty.'

'Do you need anything from home?'

Gladys tried to shake her head, but despite her bravery Lizzie could see it hurt her.

Em touched Gladys's fingers and let her hand linger on the sheet. No words were exchanged, but Lizzie knew that touch held great meaning.

The sound of rubber soles arrived and with them a

voice that said, 'You have to leave now. She'll be taken to East Grinstead tonight.'

'I'll come as soon as I can,' Em said to Gladys. Her cheeks were wet. Lizzie used one hand to press her baby to her, the other to rise and grab her mother's arm.

'We have to go,' she murmured, almost pushing Em towards the door.

'Look after my canary, don't let anything happen to him,' Gladys said.

Em looked back at Gladys whose eyes had closed. 'I will,' she said. Then, 'Gladys, you've had that canary for ever and I ain't ever heard you call him by name. What's he called?'

'Called? Called?' Gladys's voice rose. 'He's a bleedin' canary, what's he want a name for?'

Chapter Twenty-Eight

'Where's Lizzie?' Joel had never expected Em to step on the platform without Lizzie and the baby in tow. His heart plummeted. Around them, people chattered while carrying suitcases and greeting loved ones. The smell of steam filled the station and porters pushed trolleys piled high with luggage. The loudspeaker announced the arrival of another train and Em said,

'It's difficult packing stuff up for a little one just for a couple of days,' she said. 'And someone's got to feed that canary Gladys dotes on.'

Joel tried to make out he understood. 'Of course,' he said. 'And kiddies like continuity, don't they? Not being pushed around from pillar to post.' He took her bag from her and together they walked the length of the platform, then out of the station into the fresh air.

He didn't feel like smiling but he did his best. 'Liliah's

looking forward to seeing you,' he said. 'But before we talk about her, how's Gladys?'

He was grateful he'd been informed about Gladys. She was a good friend to him, and it had been hard not to drop everything and drive down to Lizzie and Em. But Gladys had been whisked away from Gosport and he was worried about Lizzie's attitude towards him. He didn't want to push his nose in where it wasn't wanted.

'Actually, she's as well as can be expected.' Em pulled her coat around her, the wind was cold. A skinny sun was trying its best to shine, but grey clouds were winning the battle. 'Perhaps that's what they say to everyone who phones up asking about their loved ones,' she said.

'But is she going to get better?'

'It all depends on whether the wounds become infected.' Em sounded knowledgeable. 'They keep on pumping her full of stuff and she sleeps a lot.' Joel heard the break in her voice and when he looked at her he saw that her eyes were full of tears.

'I'm sorry,' he said. 'Talking like this is reminding you all over again, isn't it?'

'All I keep thinking is that if Gladys hadn't pushed us both to the floor, we'd be dead.'

'You don't have to leave so soon, you know, Em,' Joel

said, thinking a few more days away from Gosport might make all the difference.

'Oh, I do, love. They're holding a special service for Milly. She had a family, you know. Besides, the order for the anti-tank mines still has to be cleared. Those workshops are ruined but already other premises have been opened up. As ol' Scrivenor says, we're fighting a war that we're going to win, by hook or by crook.' She looked at him. 'I asked for time off to come and see Liliah and he wouldn't grant it. Now I've got the time off, but by Christ, at what cost!'

He didn't speak again until they reached his car. 'I wish Lizzie had come,' he said.

'I don't,' Em sighed. 'She's been a right misery ever since you've been gone and I'm glad of this couple of days away from her and her long face.'

Joel put her bag on the back seat and helped Em into the passenger side. He caught a whiff of the violet perfume she liked. As he started up the engine he asked, 'When d'you want to see Liliah, tonight or tomorrow?' He was thinking about Lizzie being miserable. Could it possibly be because she missed him?

'Later,' she said, 'if she's not too tired.'

Em closed her eyes. He saw how weary she was, so didn't speak until he pulled up outside the lay-by near the prefab. He shook her shoulder gently.

'We're here,' he said.

'Get that kettle on, Joel, I'm gasping for a cuppa,' she said.

He made her eat a sandwich with her tea, then packed her off for a bath and a lie down. He was working a night shift and they'd decided she could ride in to Yew Trees with him. It was too cold and dark for Em to wander through the town by herself.

'I'll be home about six in the morning and I promise I'll be as quiet as I can,' he said. There was some of Lizzie's bath salts left, a sachet of Amami shampoo and plenty of hot water from the fire's back boiler.

'You spoil me,' Em said, disappearing into the bathroom.

Joel did a few chores. He'd got shopping in to cook a breakfast in the morning for Em and as he'd already had a sleep earlier that day, he settled down in the living room with *The High Window* by Raymond Chandler, another book Pete had passed on to him.

But he kept reading the same line over and over again. What was the real reason Lizzie had allowed Em to travel on her own when she clearly needed company? Was it her way of telling him that she didn't need him any longer? If so, why didn't she tell him face to face? By staying in Gosport she was making it pretty plain that she no longer considered the prefab her home. He tried to put thoughts of her out of his head. Finally, he laid the book down and sat staring at the fire.

He should have had the guts to tell her before that he loved her. It might have made her think differently about him. When he first set eyes on her serving behind the bar, he had been attracted immediately. Yet he'd let time slip by, even though he thought that despite her pregnancy she was radiant – or maybe because of it. And now, with the bloom of motherhood on her, she was magnificent. Her long hair was shiny as a raven's wing and those dark eyes haunted him; all he ever wanted in a woman. And Janie was an added bonus! If Lizzie was finished with him, he'd never see Janie again. He sighed. That little girl was a marvel and he loved her like she was his own child.

Joel put his head in his hands and tried to stop the tears that threatened.

He told himself real men didn't cry.

The toilet chain flushed. Joel sat up straight in the chair. Where had the time gone? He looked at the mantel clock. He sniffed away his heartache. It was time to put the kettle on again. Em would need a cup of tea before he took her to Yew Trees.

*

Pete caught him up in the corridor. 'Despite everything, those two are getting on like a house on fire.' He ran his fingers through his orange hair, which only made it more untidy. 'She's been a perfect sweetheart this past few days.' He nodded back at Liliah's room. The two sisters were alone but the door was open. Joel heard Em laugh. It did his heart good to hear that sound. Em was taking the explosion badly. Today in the newspaper he'd read of a bomb blast at an RAF dump near Burton upon Trent. Ninety people had died. What a terrible tragedy, he thought sadly. 'You all right?' Pete asked him.

'Yes,' he said. 'You know what it's like, nights always mess up sleep patterns.' It wasn't exactly a lie, but he didn't want to talk to Pete about Lizzie. Maybe later he'd have a chat with Em and see if she could shed any light on the matter.

'She's got a soft spot for you,' Pete said.

Joel watched him scoop up the dead flower petals from the vase of yellow chrysanthemums on a side table. Because of the heat in Yew Trees, flowers didn't last long.

'Who has?'

'Liliah.'

Joel laughed. Then he nodded. 'Me and her always got on well.' For some reason he thought of Fred. 'There's always a couple of the oldies who get under the skin.' He looked at Pete. 'I know you tell me not to get involved with them but . . .' He pushed thoughts of the old man away before it made him maudlin. 'Liliah is a tough bird,' he said. 'She's come through a lot in her life and still manages a smile . . .'

'A smile for you maybe. But for the rest of us, she gives us hell.'

Joel smiled. Liliah had got under his skin. It was to her room he gravitated when he came to work.

'You've made her happy, Joel. Found her sister, given her something to live for.'

Joel was embarrassed by the conversation now. He was glad they'd reached the kitchen. He could smell coffee. Not the good stuff, but nevertheless his taste buds tingled.

On the side was a plate with a teacloth over it. He picked up a corner and peeked at a couple of well-filled sandwiches and a pasty, one of Marie's home-made ones. It was his supper, to be eaten after he'd taken Em back to the prefab.

'I'm hanging around until you get back,' Pete said.

'Who else is on tonight?'

'Young Barbara, and Judy, that new blonde nurse.' Pete exaggeratedly licked his lips. Judy was an eyeful, almost all the men lusted after her. 'Dr Allen is on call.'

Joel nodded. He pointed to a paperback on the table. 'That for me?'

'Just finished it, mate. James Holland, *Fortress Malta: An Island Under Siege*. Once you pick it up, you won't put it down.'

'Thanks,' Joel said. Usually the nights were pretty quiet, unless one or the other of the patients decided to wander. Night times were when Dollie decided to play up. Joel did plenty of walkabouts to make sure everything was as it should be.

Footsteps could be heard outside the kitchen. Em poked her head around the door. 'Hello? I'm not intruding, am I?'

'Ready to leave?' Pete untangled himself and a newspaper from an armchair. 'Want a cuppa?'

'No, no,' Em said. 'Liliah's asleep. I thought it time I went.'

Joel put down the book he'd been thumbing through. 'Is she all right?'

'Oh, yes. She disappeared inside herself once or twice, but made me laugh at some of the antics she got up to when she was on ambulance duty.'

'It was lovely to hear you two talking away nineteen to the dozen,' said Pete.

'All right if I take Em home to the prefab?'

Pete nodded then settled down again in the armchair. He produced another book from his back pocket.

Joel walked Em to the coat-stand and they both dressed for the cold outside.

November snowflakes fluttered down in the freezing night air. Joel's breath misted as soon as it left his lips.

In the car, Em asked, 'What was she like?'

'Who?' Joel had no idea who Em was talking about.

'Your wife? Do you still think about her?' He turned and Em was looking at him.

Joel's heart dropped. Jesus, would this lie never end? It was like throwing a stone in water, the rings got wider and wider.

'I try not to think about her.' That at any rate was true. He blurted out, 'I love Lizzie.'

He felt Em's hand on his arm. 'And she loves you.'

He dared a questioning look at her. 'Really? Do you really think so?'

'If you ask me, that's why she's such a pain in the arse. She wants to be with you.'

'I want to be with her.'

'What's stopping you then? You got with each other long enough to make our Janie.' He was staring at the road but he could feel Em looking at him, waiting for an answer. 'C'mon, I'm not stupid, I know something's not right,' she pressed.

'My job's here, my home's here, but Lizzie feels more secure in Gosport.' He didn't add that he thought his part in her life was over and done with. 'And she seems to have changed towards me since the baby's birth.'

'Have you ever stopped to think she might be tired? Babies come with sleepless nights.'

He hadn't thought a great deal about that, mainly because they were apart so much.

He pulled up in the lay-by outside the prefab, turned off the engine then leaned across and opened the door so Em could get out. Earlier he'd given her a spare key.

Em climbed out, then she turned round and said, 'She was in love once before with a black-market bloke who didn't treat her right. Her own father was an arsehole. She don't know how to accept being loved for herself. Tell her you love her. Then tell her again.'

He watched her walk up the concrete path and open the door. She turned and waved. He returned the gesture and started up the car again.

Lizzie's mother knew her better than anyone. He had a lot to think about.

Chapter Twenty-Nine

'I think you'll be interested in something I've got for you, sir.'

Mac looked up from the bane of his life, paperwork. He set down his pen and stared up at Ben Chambers.

'Anything'll be more interesting than this lot.' Ben's eyes had the familiar dark bags below them that signalled more sleepless nights, but there was no disguising the grin that split his good-natured face from ear to ear. Mac sat back on his chair so the rear legs tipped. 'Come on, you going to tell me, or just stand there like a Cheshire cat?'

'A phone call came in this morning from the pawn shop, Hillier's, in Stoke Road. A couple of brand new diamond rings were taken in as pledges first thing. The woman behind the counter gave the bloke a pawn ticket and some cash. When old man Hillier came in he checked against the "stolen" list and found they matched the stuff that disappeared the other night from the jeweller's in the town.'

Mac stood up. 'Don't suppose she remembers the bloke?' His heart started pumping fast. Two ARP blokes had been seen climbing into a van and leaving just when the genuine helpers were arriving. No one got the number of the van.

'Better than that, sir. The bloke gave his own name and address for the pawn ticket.'

It took a moment for Ben's words to sink in. 'I don't believe it!' He advanced a couple of steps towards Ben and clapped him on the shoulders. 'Don't stand there, get a car, we'll give him a visit.'

Ben's smile was infectious. 'The car's downstairs.'

Mac pushed past him with a smile bigger than the constable's, saying, 'Come on then, what we waiting for?'

Two hours later, Ben pulled up in front of the white-painted building that housed Lawrence Greyson's ground-floor flat. The other police car tucked itself in behind Ben's car.

Mac knocked on the glossy Regency green-painted door. Two minutes later Mac and Ben were sitting comfortably in Lawrence Greyson's drawing room.

'I'm not sure you have the right to be tramping all

over my home.' Mac saw him grimace as a constable tipped out a drawer on to the polished table, then swept everything back in haphazardly.

Mac waved a paper. 'This says I do,' he said. 'But it would be less troublesome for you if you just told me where the stuff is.'

'Stuff? What stuff?' Lawrence Greyson laughed. 'Whatever you're looking for, you'll not find it here.'

Mac stared at the dark-haired man wearing glasses. He didn't like his public school voice, he didn't like his good looks and most of all he disliked the man, for he knew this bastard had taken Marlene's hard-earned money. Even without proof, Mac knew this was the man behind a great deal of Gosport's crime.

'Nice place you've got here.' Mac thought about his own small house. Never could he aspire to live somewhere like this. He couldn't even afford the rent on his wages. Who said crime didn't pay?

There was a crash, the sound of tinkling glass. 'Whoops,' Mac said.

Lawrence Greyson leapt to his feet. 'If you . . .' The sound of heavy shoes trampling about continued.

'If we what? Accidentally break something while in the pursuance of duty?'

Lawrence Greyson sat back down in the armchair, his face black with anger.

'Is this a random search?' He looked up.

'Not at all,' said Ben Chambers, after a nod from Mac. 'Colin Thomas – I believe he's a friend of yours? – has told us all about the jeweller's you both robbed the other night.'

Mac saw the anger flit across Greyson's eyes.

Ben walked over to the sideboard that had already been searched. The pile of drawers stacked on the Turkish carpet looked ready to topple. Ben felt around the back of the unit. Then he tried again, and pulled out a package that had been taped to the underside.

'Break in! I did no such thing!'

'Didn't need to, did you? Not when you were both posing as ARP wardens, filling your pockets with stolen goods and money from the safe.' Ben turned the package over in his hands.

'I don't know any Colin Thomas and I certainly wouldn't break in anywhere.'

'Colin Thomas says you did.' Mac grinned at him.

Lawrence Greyson looked as if he knew it was all over.

'Not only that,' said Ben, 'he pawned a couple of rings. Would you believe he put his own name on the pawn ticket?' The man's eyes were flickering wildly as he digested this information and realized why the police had come to his flat. He knew that he was well and truly nicked as he saw the taped package being handed to the detective.

Mac started to laugh. 'You should have given him a bigger cut, there would have been no need for him to steal from you then, would there?' The look on Greyson's face was priceless, a dead giveaway. Mac sighed. They hadn't come up with any proof yet. Until then, Greyson could go on denying everything. He stared into the man's face. He wanted to go over to him and give him a good kicking for what he'd put Marlene through. But that was more than his job was worth. Again, until he had proof, it was all hearsay.

Mac opened the package. Several pieces of card fell to the carpet. Mac picked them up.

'What have we here? Medical cards in different names?' Mac thumbed through the other bits of paper. 'Birth certificates.' He held up three passports and grinned at Laurence Greyson. One of the passports was for a blond-haired man named Samuel Golden. Mac was silent, staring at the photograph of the man as he'd looked when he'd robbed Marlene.

He heard the back door open. A blast of cold November air swept through to the drawing room. Quick footsteps and a uniformed policeman stood before Mac, holding a pair of wellingtons and a couple of dark blue boiler suits with insignias pinned to the lapels.

'Found in the shed, sir.'

'Gotcha!' Mac said. 'Well done,' he said to the policeman. 'Come across anything else?' A shake of his head meant nothing else had been found. Mac rose from his seat and said, 'I'm taking you in for questioning. You can join your mate Colin who you don't know.'

Lawrence Greyson sighed.

'I'm glad you're back.' Pete looked up from his book. 'Mrs Somerton woke up and asked for you.' Joel thought he looked worried and on edge. His fingers tapped on the table top. 'The doctor's with her now,' he said.

Joel said, 'I expect the excitement of Em coming today was a bit much. Liliah has no visitors for ages, then becomes the centre of attention.' All the same a prickle of worry set its claws in him.

He waited while Pete showed him a note of everything that needed to be attended to before Marie arrived early the next morning. As soon as Joel turned away, Pete blurted out, 'Mrs Somerton's taken a turn for the worse.'

Without another word, Joel sprinted along the corridor and up to Liliah's room.

As he entered, Dr Sprall, the locum, put his fingers to his lips, motioning Joel to quietness. Liliah was very still, hardly making a mound in the white bed. Theodore Sprall took his stethoscope from his ears, stood away from Liliah and said, 'Very sudden.'

Joel knelt down on the floor so that his face was close to Liliah's and looked at her. Her breathing was ragged, like she was taking great gasps of air into her throat; her skin was translucent. He could smell that old lady fragrance tinged with lavender.

'Is it just a bad turn?' He turned towards the white-coated man.

The doctor shook his grey-haired head and put his hand on Joel's shoulder. Joel saw he wanted to talk to him, so he rose. He was still looking at Liliah and his heart was heavy. He went outside with the doctor, who pulled the door closed. It suddenly entered Joel's head that Liliah would hate the door being shut and he turned and pushed it open a fraction.

'We can talk now,' the doctor said, leading him along the corridor and adjusting his spectacles on his nose where they had slid down. 'She's had a massive heart attack. She's in and out of consciousness—'

Joel broke in. 'Shouldn't she be in hospital? Is an ambulance on its way?'

'Slow down, else you'll be the next patient.'

Joel took a deep breath, 'She was fine, earlier, happy . . .'

'Then you should be glad for her, much better for her to go quickly than linger for months.' He stared at Joel then put his hand on his shoulder. 'You should know that.'

Yes, he understood, but Joel had become fond of Liliah and it was like it had been with Fred, all over again. He loved them, then lost them. He put his hands over his face, not wanting the doctor to see him cry as they walked back towards the room.

He murmured, 'Is she in pain?' A shake of the doctor's head gave him his answer.

'I've given her something. It's simply a matter of time.' The doctor pushed open the door and Joel followed him inside. Liliah hadn't moved. He thought of Em.

'Her sister's at my home, would it be a good idea to go and fetch her?'

'If you want.'

Joel left the room and hurried down to the kitchen. 'Will you take the car and go to the prefab and get Em?' Joel was thanking God for black market petrol as he found the car's keys in his jacket pocket and handed them to Pete.

'All right,' Pete said, setting down his book and taking

the keys. 'You'd better warn the other carers on duty that I'm going to be missing for half an hour.' Joel didn't wait for him to leave before he ran back upstairs to Liliah's room. He could hear the rasping breaths from the corridor. The doctor was still hovering and as Joel entered he moved a chair to the side of the bed so he could sit near her.

He hated the sounds she was making. The strangled gasping for air that rattled in her chest. On and on it went. Joel sat with his hand covering hers. Her skin was cold, like she was already dead. The minutes ticked by, thoughts flowed aimlessly around his brain, all the while accompanied by the coarse sounds of her breath.

He was watching her when her eyelids fluttered open. His heart lurched. Perhaps it was going to be all right? Her eyes held his. Her thin mouth moved and her voice was soft. 'Joel?' He waited for her to speak again and when she did she said, 'It's in the Bible, did you know that?' The deep breath she had taken to enable her to speak faded away to nothingness.

Joel was still holding her hand when Dr Sprall said, 'She's gone, Joel.'

Em was crying. She hadn't touched the tea that Sally, one of the carers, had made for her. Joel didn't know what to do. His head was full of cotton wool and he kept seeing pictures in his mind of Liliah in happier times.

Pete hadn't left Yew Trees yet. He and the doctor, between them, had made the necessary phone calls and Liliah Somerton was due to be taken from the home to another resting place.

'I wish I could have been in time to talk to her . . .' Em's eyes were red-rimmed. She'd had to be dragged forcibly away from Liliah's body.

'You made her very happy,' Pete said, running his fingers through his red hair. To Joel he said, 'I think, mate, a few days off would do you the world of good. Why don't you take Em back to Gosport? What with her friend Gladys, the accident at Priddy's, and now this, she's in no fit state to get on a train by herself.'

Joel took a mouthful of his tea. If he stayed here, at the home, it would be a constant reminder of Liliah, which he could do without. More than anything he longed to be in Gladys's small house with Lizzie at his side. But would she welcome his presence?

'I've already had a word with the funeral parlour. They can't do the necessary until next week. Come back then.' Pete was insistent.

'You'll be shorthanded . . .'

'We can get in a temporary carer. You're no good moping around like a wet sock.'

Em seemed to wake up. 'Please, Joel? I'd really appreciate it if you'd take me home in the car.' She gave him a bit of a smile. 'The bloke Gladys gets the petrol from has left a few cans and bottles . . .'

Joel sighed. 'It seems my mind has been made up for me.' He didn't care where he was, but he really did want to be away from Yew Trees. Liliah and Fred were fighting inside his head for supremacy in his thoughts and he felt like his brain was going to explode with grief. 'Can you really manage?' he asked Pete. 'Besides, you shouldn't be here, you should be at home.'

'Call it overtime,' Pete said. 'As a senior staff member I'd have been called in anyway. As your boss I'm telling you to go.'

Chapter Thirty

Marlene leant on one elbow and looked down at Mac. Perspiration glistened on his forehead and top lip and his red hair was in damp tendrils, flattened against his head. Small stubbles of beard tried to escape through his chin.

'Will you let me see him?'

'We've just had glorious sex and already you're thinking of someone else?' He grinned at her, pushed the sheet aside and threw his naked legs out of bed. 'I'm making tea, want some?'

'Not if you've only got condensed milk to put in it.'

'Go without, then.' He turned round, bent down and kissed her on the tip of her nose. 'Because I spend most of my time at the cop shop, fresh milk doesn't last.'

After he'd left the bedroom she looked around. Every room in his house was in the process of refurbishment. Planks of wood stood against the wall, and a pile of books leaned precariously on two pots of green paint. Despite materials being hard to come by, Mac seemed to be able to influence shopkeepers to sell to him. It was like charming birds from the trees.

He wasn't the tidiest of men. Clothes hung on nails banged in the back of the door and she could see one of his work shoes lying by the paint pots, the other near the wardrobe. But she loved him for it. Marlene could hear him singing tunelessly downstairs while he rattled cups. She knew if she stayed where she was, in bed, he would bring her up a cup of tea and she would drink it, condensed milk and all. She smiled to herself; maybe he would even come back to bed!

Mac put the chipped mug of creamy sweet tea on the tea chest next to her side of the bed and after setting down his own mug, unbuttoned and allowed his trousers to fall to the floor before climbing back in bed. She snuggled up to him. He smelled of sex, fresh musky perspiration and his skin was cool. He hadn't yet got around to lighting the fire in the range downstairs.

Marlene shivered. 'You're cold,' she said.

'It's three weeks to Christmas, so what d'you expect, woman? There's frost on the grass outside.' He wriggled his hands in the bed and touched her warm skin.

'Ohhh!' she cried. 'Spoilsport.' But she didn't brush

his probing fingers away. Instead, she said, 'You haven't answered me. Can I see him?'

'Only if you make love to me. Now. This very minute.' He pulled her towards him and began kissing her. She could feel his hardness growing and she lay pliable, happy and ready for him to make her deliriously happy.

Afterwards, sated, she lay in his arms.

'I think I've fallen in love with you,' he said.

She laughed. 'Don't say anything you might regret later,' she warned. Marlene was happy. Happier than she'd been for a long time, and it was all because of this red-headed man. She'd kept no secrets from him, and he'd told her his innermost feelings about his marriage, its break-up and the pain that had taken a long time to heal.

He said, 'If you want to come into work with me I'll arrange a meeting with Samuel Golden, that's who you knew him as, but his birth certificate says he's Bert Yates.'

Marlene giggled. 'No wonder he decided on a different name.'

'He'll be taken to Winchester prison later this morning then held there until the case against him can be proven, which it can, and they've got a date for trial.' He smoothed her hair away from her face. 'He's admitted running the brothel, so you need to get the girls away from there. No one except him will be charged but if you let me have the books you've kept, they'll help convict him for living off immoral earnings. Ruby'll testify she passed on the profits.

'We've broken the little racket he had going with a fence. His looting days are over. The men who worked with him sang their hearts out. And for some reason, or maybe because I allowed him to believe it would be better to have any other crimes taken into consideration, we now know he was behind the death of Gloria.' He rubbed his hand across his bristly chin. 'He can't be charged for her suicide but he'd got quite a racket going with the poor woman stealing from the elderly. She hanged herself sooner than steal from Em Earle.'

Marlene, eyes wide, said, 'I'd no idea he was such a rotter. I thought . . .'

'You thought he deceived women by taking their money. That's only the tip of the iceberg.'

'Will I have to testify against him for that?'

'Not sure yet. Probably, but you're only one of the women he's defrauded.'

Marlene shook her head. 'Are there many?'

Mac nodded. 'We've got to contact them, but he's been very helpful. Of course it's to his own advantage to tell us everything. He's extremely angry that one of his men stole from him and that's when we became involved. Naturally, he wants to get back at them.' He paused and picked up his cup and drank. 'Funny thing, Marlene, love, is I can see the attraction for women in going with a bloke like him. It wasn't his money, but the women trusted this good-looking, well-spoken man.' He paused. 'As you made a complaint against him for stealing from you, there's every possibility you'll be called when his case comes up. How would you feel . . .'

He was out of bed now and pulling on a pair of trousers that had seen better days. His chest was bare, despite the cold air. Small curls of red hair rested against his skin. Freckles covered his body, and she loved all of them.

'No need to ask, Mac. He ruined me, I want vengeance. Not just for me, but for the other women he's deceived.'

Mac bent and kissed the top of her head. 'Get a move on, get yourself decent.'

He got as far as the bedroom door, 'I'll make some toast while you're getting ready. Can't go out in the cold with nothing inside you.'

Marlene said, 'Does Em know you've got him in for questioning?'

'She does now. We need as much evidence against him

as possible and there were times when he went to her house to see Gloria, and was seen there.'

Marlene hoped with all her heart that Samuel Golden, or whoever he was, got everything that was coming to him.

'I'm glad we've all come together to see Gladys,' Em said. She was regretting wearing her high heels as they tramped up the gravel driveway from the bus stop. She'd told herself that she was to be bright and happy while in Gladys's company. It wouldn't do to allow her grief about her sister's death to overwhelm her. Gladys needed happy visitors.

The Queen Victoria Hospital at East Grinstead, in the heart of Sussex, sprawled over the countryside. The Plastic Surgery and Burns Unit was famous for helping the war wounded, not only to recover but also to gain confidence to re-enter the world outside, living with scars.

Gladys was in Ward Two, which was devoted to women and children with burns received during the air raids.

The hospital grounds were neat and well cared for. It was too late now for flowers, the frosts had seen to that, but wooden seats placed in strategic settings caught the best of the weak sun that was trying to emerge. Em could smell the freshness of the countryside and it raised her spirits.

Joel carried Janie, warmly wrapped in a shawl, and Lizzie walked at his side carrying the bag of baby paraphernalia that accompanied her daughter everywhere.

'It would have been so much easier to have come by car,' Joel grumbled. Em knew that in the kitchen at Alma Street, several gallons of black market petrol, its red dye having disappeared during the gas mask straining process, sat alongside the wall. However, there had been a few problems with obtaining the petrol as it wasn't as plentiful at source as it had been. Joel knew he had to reserve it for important driving, and whilst a visit to Gladys was a priority, they decided it was better to use public transport. Joel wasn't really so cross as he made out. All along he'd felt guilty at using more than the allocated petrol allowance that other car owners had to make do with.

The hospital already had a Christmassy feel to it, with sprays of holly berries and branches of evergreen tucked into long-necked vases on tables everywhere and placed behind pictures hanging on the walls. Polish and disinfectant smells vied for supremacy and smiling faces greeted them in every corridor.

Em's heels clicked on the wooden floor as a nurse

showed them to Gladys's room where she sat up in bed.

'You look so well,' exclaimed Lizzie. Gladys's back was festooned with loose white cotton. Pinpricks of blood showed through the material.

'The food is very good,' Gladys said. 'And it's nice not having to cook it myself.'

Em put the bunch of chrysanthemums she'd bought in the market on top of Gladys's locker. 'What have they told you?'

'That you telephoned and explained about your sister dying.' She put out her hands and gripped Em's fingers. 'I'm really sorry.' She paused. 'It's so unfair that you've only just found her and now . . .'

Em looked into her best friend's eyes. 'Thank you,' she whispered. She nodded her head in the direction of Joel. 'He'd known her longer than I did and he's cut up something terrible.' For a moment she was silent, then she remembered she was supposed to be cheering Gladys up. 'What have they said about your burns?'

'That they are grade two, whatever that means.' She was wearing a gown belonging to the hospital, but back to front so her modesty was kept. 'So far there's no infection.' She gave a toothy grin. 'They keep pumping me full of stuff to stop that,' she said. 'I'd give anything to be able to lie down properly. I have to sleep on my tummy. But if it hadn't been for that other girl taking the full brunt of the blast, I certainly wouldn't be here.'

'And if it hadn't been for you, I wouldn't be here.'

'Shut up, Em, change the bloomin' record.'

'Well, you haven't lost your sense of humour,' Lizzie said.

'How can I? By rights with this lot,' she tossed her head meaning the burns on her back, 'I should be in terrible pain and nearly at wits' end. But they keep putting needles in me and I want to giggle and laugh. It's like being down the Fox and feeling tiddly on a Saturday night.' She looked at Janie. ''Ere, let's have a look at that little darling.' Gladys cooed and aaahhed over the still sleeping child. 'I bet you wish you two could get married, don't you?'

Em saw Joel and Lizzie exchange glances. They were sitting on chairs Joel had found outside in the corridor. Em could see there was still something amiss in Joel and Lizzie's relationship. Neither answered Gladys's probing.

Em said quickly, to change the subject, 'Guess who's going to court for his part in all the looting that's been going on in Gosport?' Em saw the look on Joel's face as the women began talking animatedly. 'Why don't you take Janie out into the gardens for a bit of fresh air, Joel?'

The look of relief on his face made her smile. Em knew men got fed up quickly when women started chatting. Joel held the baby carefully to his breast as he escaped.

Gladys pricked up her ears at the talk about looting. Em related all she'd found out about the man they'd known as Samuel Golden. Then she told her friend as much as she'd heard from Mac about his part in forcing Gloria to pretend to be her sister. And that her friend Marlene had been duped by him. 'I hope he gets what's coming to him,' said Gladys.

'I'm sure he will,' Lizzie said. 'And you don't have to worry about your canary, he's fine. I'm staying at your house until you come home,' she added. Inevitably the gossip got around to Marlene, Mac and the closure of the knocking shop, as Gladys called it.

'But what about those two nice girls?' Gladys always wanted to know the ins and outs of everything.

'Marlene told me that the dark-haired one, Carla, has got a flat in Forton Road; Mac's boss is really fond of her and her little girl. He pays the rent and she don't go on the game no more now,' Em said. 'Which is a good thing, as her little girl is getting older and might start asking questions. I really like Carla.'

'Ain't he married?' Gladys was indignant.

'He is. But his wife's been such a cow to him all these

years that you can't begrudge the poor bloke a bit of happiness, now, can you?' Gladys nodded sagely.

'What about the young one?' The words sprang from Gladys's mouth. Em reckoned she was starved of news from Gosport and needed to make up for it by asking as many questions as she could before they left.

Em knew Ruby had decided to give up prostitution, as one of her regulars wanted her to be his proper girl-friend. He was a bit older than her but had a nice house in Stubbington, a village near Gosport, and a good job on the railways. Ruby had decided that after several years of trying not to have babies that she would like to settle down and become a mother. She apparently had agreed to tell the police about delivering the brothel money to her boss, Mr X.

The talking and laughing went on until a nurse brought round a trolley with tea and cakes.

Joel returned with Janie, saying it was getting too cold outside in the gardens for her now. Gladys smothered the little girl in kisses and Lizzie changed her child's nappy, ready for the trip home again.

'I asked a doctor when you could come home, Gladys,' Joel said, after swallowing a mouthful of tea. 'It'll be a while yet, apparently. He said you're safer in here. It really is important that your back heals cleanly.'

'I don't mind being in here as long as you'll all come back and see me,' Gladys said. Em saw the tears sparkling in her eyes. 'But I do miss me canary. I'd give anything to see him hop about and hear him chatter.'

Chapter Thirty-One

Marlene sat on the hard wooden chair and stared around the room. It smelled of stale milk and sweat. The walls were bare and the locked window looked out towards the back of the station, where several police cars were parked and bicycles were lined up for beat bobbies.

She'd worn her boots, which were almost hidden beneath her grey slacks with the wide-bottomed legs. Her long grey coat with a belt tightly tied over her pink jumper completed her outfit. She'd plaited her hair and it hung in a long rope down her back.

Mac had told her to wait while he mustered Samuel Golden from the cells. She looked at the table between her and another chair opposite. Someone had obviously got fed up with waiting and had dug their initials into the wood.

It crossed her mind that she hadn't been searched before entering the small room. Mac had asked her if she had anything on her that might possibly be of use to the prisoner. She had denied hiding anything on her person and had left her handbag outside with the duty sergeant at the main desk.

Footsteps echoed along the corridor and then the door swung open. Mac entered first and smiled at her. Behind him, handcuffed to the young constable Marlene had come to know as Ben, was a man Marlene wouldn't have recognized as Samuel Golden. She would have passed him in the street without a second glance.

Dark hair, with grey at the roots and wearing horn-rimmed spectacles, he stared at her, dismissed her then crumpled into the seat on the opposite side of the table. Ben twisted his hand so that the handcuffs were easier to manage while he stood and the prisoner sat.

Marlene could hear the tap-tap of Samuel Golden's foot beneath the table.

A shiver ran down her spine as he looked across at her. His eyes narrowed.

Mac pressed his hand on the back of her chair near her shoulder blade. Through her coat she felt the warmth and it gave her the courage to speak.

'When you left me to wake up alone in your bedroom,

penniless, when I realized what you'd done to me, I wanted to kill myself.'

He gave a deep breath that ran out slowly. 'Bit dramatic, darling. It's only money.'

The arrogance of the man! 'But it was my money, money I'd worked hard for, money that should have done my child some good!'

'You weren't thinking of your child when you were in my bed enjoying my favours. You loved every minute of our time together.' He gave a sickly smile. 'I remember *that* very well.'

She shook her head, felt the heat rise from her neck and over her face. Why had she never realized before how the tone of his voice irritated her; that precise pronouncement of vowels so different from her own Gosport slangy drawl. It wasn't normal. Perhaps he'd practised for years to come up with the vocal sounds he thought would charm women, make them believe he'd gone to fee-paying schools as a child, then on to university. And his sarcasm? No decent man would say those things to a woman. But he wasn't a decent man, was he?

'You've conned so many women, why?'

'Because I can, dear. You're all so stupid as to think you can emerge from the cesspits and rise to the middle-classes. You were willing to pay me to give you a life you could never aspire to on your own.'

She let his words sink in. Marlene realized it was no good appealing to his sensitive side, he had none. Mac had told her he'd sung like a canary when he'd been told it would be to his advantage to help the police.

'Did Gloria try to better herself, or did she do your bidding because she loved you?'

He stared at her. 'Ah, the silly cow who hanged herself?' He nodded and looked thoughtful as though he had difficulty in remembering the woman. 'She was weak.' His lip curled in disgust.

Marlene turned away and blinked to stop her tears.

She thought of the looting. What he'd done there was no different to stealing from defenceless women.

'Didn't you ever stop to think about the people you were stealing from when you looted from ordinary houses? Didn't it ever occur to you to help them in their hour of need? Maybe search for people in those ruins instead of stealing from them?'

'Look after number one.' He smiled at her. She felt sick. What had she hoped to accomplish by seeing him? This was the man who'd stolen her livelihood, caused her to be separated from her mother and her child; and made her work harder than she'd ever worked before to pay back money she'd borrowed to give to him. What did she expect? That he'd fall to his knees, beg her to forgive him?

She turned her head away from him again. What doesn't kill you makes you stronger.

What this excuse for a man sitting in front of her *had* done for her was to strengthen her. Make her mentally more powerful than she'd ever been before!

She rose from her chair. 'You're going to prison for a long time. You deserve it.'

Marlene looked at Mac, who smiled at her and stepped towards the door. Then she turned back to the man sitting at the table who had seemed to shrink with every moment he spent in that room.

His life was over. Hers was just beginning.

'I should be thanking you for everything,' she said.

'You know what I think?'

Lizzie turned her head away from the sink where she was washing up cups and stared at him. 'And what do you think?' The wind outside was rustling the leaves in the privet hedges and whistling through the crevices where the shed was broken. But in the small scullery it was like being cocooned from the storm.

Joel said, 'Your mother is giving us time to sort out

whatever is wrong. So I think we should do just that.' He saw her move her head, tilting it to listen for any sound from Janie, who was fast asleep in her pram. Earlier when he'd looked at the sleeping child in the kitchen, he had felt his heart about to burst with love for the tiny being. The thought of not being in her life as she matured to adulthood was like a knife in his gut.

Lizzie put the last cup on the wooden draining board and emptied out the enamelled bowl of dirty water.

'And is there something wrong?'

He picked up the tea towel and handed it to her. She wiped her hands and put the cloth down on the copper.

'Well, for a start, every time I ask a question you answer it with another question.'

'And that makes things wrong?' She pushed her long hair back over her shoulder.

'See what I mean?' he said. Lizzie went over to the kettle, lifted it, shook it, then took a Swan Vesta match and lit the gas, settling the kettle on top of the flames. The rain was pelting against the windows, leaving rivulets of water running down. Joel took a deep breath. 'I'm not going back to work at Yew Trees.'

She turned towards him. For a while there was silence between them, their souls reaching towards each other.

'I think I understand why,' she said. Her dark eyes were soft with kindness.

'Do you? Do you really, Lizzie?'

She nodded. 'It broke your heart when Fred died and now you've had to go through it all again . . .'

'That's exactly it,' he said. 'I can't take any more of getting close to people then losing them.'

Again, there was a silence. It was like that one sentence he had spoken had many meanings. She turned away. 'You'll go back for the funeral?'

'Of course. Your mum'll need someone with her. But I'd go to say goodbye to Liliah anyway . . .'

Lizzie moved away from the stove and stood in front of him. 'I've got something to say to you, and if you're planning on a new start away from here, I'd better get it off my chest.' She was so close he could feel her breath on his face. The scent of poppies from her perfume was heady, as was the heat from her warm skin. He held on to her eyes as she stared at him. From in the kitchen the canary started chirruping and jumping from its perch to the sides of its cage.

'When we began this charade and you pretended Janie was yours I thought it was because you had some feelings for me. The lie we told my mum and Gladys about you having a wife who'd gone missing suited my purpose very well. I liked you . . .' He opened his mouth to speak, but she said, 'Let me finish.' She took a deep breath. 'It seemed to be working out well. Gladys and Mum began to care about you and I . . . I . . .' She paused. Her words came out in a jumble. 'I fell for you. I tried not to show it because I didn't want you to think I was foolish. After all, you were doing me a favour, that's all. And as the time went on and you didn't make a move on me, I realized how silly I was being in allowing my feelings to come to the surface.'

She put her hands over face. But it was too late, he'd seen the wetness of tears on her cheeks. 'There we were, pretending we were a couple so Mum and Gladys wouldn't think anything was wrong. After all, my mum has had her fair share of upsets what with my dad dying last year. He used to knock her about. She pretended everything was all right, but everyone was talking about her behind her back, and I knew how hurt she was. So when you suggested we pretend we were in love, I jumped at the chance of coming home without having all the tittle-tattle from the neighbours about me being pregnant and unmarried directed at Mum.'

The kettle began its mournful cry. Lizzie walked over and turned the gas down low. She'd already rinsed the teapot so she swirled hot water to warm it then spooned in the tea. Joel watched her quick movements. There was so much he wanted to ask and say, but he didn't dare interrupt her. If he'd had the courage she had they could have had this conversation ages ago. Now he wanted an end to all this heartache. An end to the pretence of being someone he wasn't.

Lizzie pulled the cosy on the pot, left it on the draining board then faced him again.

'Look,' she said. He could see how difficult it was for her to get the words out. 'I'm glad you're making a fresh start. But I don't want you to leave Gosport without knowing that I love you.' She stood quite still, looking at him.

Again he opened his mouth, but she shook her head and put her hand on his arm as a warning. 'Listen. I love the way you are with Janie. I know I made a mistake by getting pregnant but the result is I love my daughter. I'd go through fire and flood for that little girl.' She paused. Another deep breath followed and her voice rose with emotion. 'If I had my way, she'd be your daughter and I'd be asking you to marry me . . .'

'Yes,' he cried.

She frowned as though not understanding. He smiled at her. 'Yes,' he said again. 'Yes, I'll marry you.'

He watched the smile creep from her lips to her cheeks and her eyes and then Lizzie's whole face lit up.

'I love you,' he said. 'I thought you didn't have any use for me now I'd served my purpose with the lie. I've been so miserable thinking we'd have to live separate lives . . .'

She didn't let him get any more words out, for she was in his arms and her mouth was on his, stopping him from speaking.

'I love you,' he said again, eventually. But then he pushed her away. 'But I can't marry you now.'

Lizzie's eyes flashed. 'But why not, if you love me?'

'How can I keep a wife and child without a job?' He looked down at his feet. 'I meant what I said. I can't take it any more at Yew Trees. I lost Fred, then Liliah. I'll go mad if I stay there.'

He knew she understood. Lizzie was living in Gladys's house and her mother chipped in with money for house-keeping because they both knew that as soon as Janie could be left with a childminder, Lizzie would be at work, somewhere, anywhere. That was what families did. They looked after their own. But he was too much of a man to allow them to keep him.

'I've got some back pay to come,' he said. 'I want to be with you and Janie. Life's too short to be apart any longer. We'll marry as soon as I have a job . . .'

Lizzie didn't let him finish for her mouth was on his again, until she pulled away and said, 'I think we should go to bed, and throw out that line of pillows that separates us.'

'You are quite a bossy lady,' he said. 'And I like it. But what about the pot of tea you've just made?'

'The tea will keep.'

He agreed with her, and the tuneful song that came from the canary showed that he did too.

Chapter Thirty-Two

'I hope there's going to be enough food.' Em stared at the sheet-covered trestle tables at the side of the wall in Sloane Stanley Hall. They were weighed down with sausage rolls, more roll than sausage, mince pies, plates of Spam thinly cut, bowls of peaches, courtesy of Mac's American buddy from Denver, egg sandwiches (dried egg flavoured with plenty of pepper), paste sandwiches and a magnificent cake, also from Mac's friend. A small barrel of beer had been tapped and there was plenty of orange juice for the little ones.

'There's enough for an army,' said Gladys. She was in a wheelchair. She'd been allowed home for the weekend, still weak and able to walk only for short distances. 'I wish I could dance.' She looked wistfully at the crowded floor where couples were smooching.

The small band played on the stage. Mr Pout, the

dark-suited conductor wearing white gloves, was moving his baton to 'Have Yourself A Merry Little Christmas'.

'The next time you come home will be for good,' said Em, bending down and brushing back Gladys's hair from her face. She saw it had grown back, but the roots needed bleaching and she decided she'd buy some peroxide from the chemist in the morning. 'You sure I look all right in this blue dress?' It was an old dress, but she'd put some bias binding along the threadbare edges and changed the buttons that went from neck to hem.

'You look lovely, Em. And I'm sure Sam will think so too.'

Em had invited the manager from the Fox public house to the do. Once upon a time they'd been close, but things had cooled between them after Lizzie had left home and Lily had appeared on the scene. Em had now decided it was time to get on with her life again, after all that had happened with Liliah. She was excited about seeing Sam and hoped he'd forgive her for neglecting him.

'I never thought Joel and his mate Pete would get all the bunting up in time,' Gladys said. The hall was decked out in red, green and white garlands made of crêpe paper, cut in strips and twisted. A Christmas tree stood on the stage, leaning slightly to one side, and already the pine needles had begun to fall. Lizzie had spent ages making pretend presents out of wallpaper-covered matchboxes and decorations from milk bottle tops for the tree.

Joel was holding Janie, who now managed to hold her head up without wobbling and seemed to be taking an interest in everything going on about her. She could also stand in his lap, so strong were her little legs.

'I heard he nearly broke down at Liliah's funeral.'

Em stared at her friend. 'He was a pillar of strength to me. He told them he wasn't staying on at Yew Trees. They understood. That man's got a heart of gold,' she said.

'Heart of gold,' repeated Gladys. 'And you got a bit of gold as well, what with Liliah's will.'

Em thought about the money she'd inherited. When all the dues were paid it was a good sum to go into the post office in case of a rainy day. Thinking of Liliah was like a knife being plunged into her heart. How cruel was life to take away a sister she'd just begun to love? She hadn't wanted money, she'd wanted Liliah.

'I can marry Lizzie now,' Joel had told Em. Fred's money had seen to that. There was cash enough for a deposit on a vacant property in Alma Street a few doors away from Gladys. And when Em had told him there could be a job for him at Priddy's, he'd whirled her around like a dervish.

'They make a nice couple, don't they?' Em broke out of her thoughts and looked over to where Marlene was dancing with Mac, who was holding her more than a little close. His hand was also a lot lower on her bottom than it should be.

'I wish I had hair like hers,' answered Gladys. Marlene's glorious red mane was hanging loose down her back. In the electric light it glinted and glistened like a flowing river on a summer's day.

'Yeah, well you might have had better hair if you hadn't dyed it so much,' said Em. 'One day you'll rot your head!'

Gladys turned her nose up in disgust. 'I heard Marlene's opening her stall again in the New Year.' She paused. 'She's already been to a couple of auctions again, buying gold and antique jewellery.'

'Blimey, you don't miss much about what goes on in Gosport and you ain't even living here at present. Bloody good luck to her, I say. She's got guts, that girl. Is that her little one over there?' Em peered across the hall to where a young red-haired girl was sitting on a stool next to a grey-haired woman who was laughing with a pretty young woman sitting at her side.

'She's growing up fast is that girl. And it's good

that Marlene's mother's back home after living in Littlehampton. The three of them are together at last.'

'He asked her to marry him, you know?'

'What, Mac asked Marlene?'

'Yes. But they're leaving it a bit. He wants her to move into his house when he's finished tarting it up, and she wants to make a success of her stall, independent madam that she is! And I say good luck to her, she's a grafter, that girl.'

'Who's that pretty young thing with Marlene's mother?'

'Aha! So you, Mrs Nosy-Parker Gladys Smith don't know everything! That's Judy.'

'Judy?'

Em thought Gladys looked like she was sucking a lemon. 'Judy is Mac's constable's wife.' She pointed out a young man holding a half pint of beer, beside him was a pushchair with a child sprawled out fast asleep. 'That's Ben Chambers, her husband, and their kiddie.'

Gladys nodded then said, 'I could do with a cuppa. Anyone not here who should be?'

'I invited Carla and Ruby. Not all the girls from Priddy's have arrived yet, either. Siddy's over there, talking to Ben.' She saw Gladys smile at the mention of Siddy.

'He came to the hospital to see me, you know," Gladys said. 'Think I'll chat to him in a minute.'

Em watched the crowded dance floor. The tempo had changed and a fast tune was being played, so some of the dancers had settled for sitting on chairs with their drinks.

She thought of the times they'd had in this hall. The parties for weddings, engagements and now a Christmas celebration combined with Janie's christening last Sunday, and Lizzie and Joel's marriage that was taking place in the New Year. Who knows, she thought, maybe the war would end soon and then they'd have the party to end all parties.

How lovely it was, now that the blackout had been lifted. The lights had gone on in London again. It was almost a new beginning.

The band was playing 'In the Mood'. It wasn't a new beginning for the bandleader Glenn Miller, she thought. He was missing in a plane accident over the Channel. Another sad loss.

Gladys was tapping her feet to the music and Em looked down lovingly at her. She was a good friend, the best Em had ever had. She'd never forget how Gladys had saved her life by endangering her own.

As though sensing Em was studying her, Gladys looked up and asked, 'Any news yet about that toerag Samuel Golden or whatever his poxy name is?'

'Mac told me that three women have come forward

after reading about him in the *Evening News*. Apparently he'd swindled them out of money as well. His trial's coming up at Winchester in the New Year, but he's going to be behind bars for a long, long time.'

'I still can't get my head round anyone who'd steal stuff from a house when it's just copped a bomb. I'd want to make sure there was no one in the ruins first and help them if I could.' Gladys was indignant. Then she looked up at Em with her tongue hanging comically out of her mouth as far as she could push it.

Em sighed. 'All right, let's go into the kitchen and I'll put the kettle on.' She pulled the heavy wheelchair around . . .

'Let me take that.' Joel seemed to emerge from nowhere. He moved her out of the way and took hold of the wheelchair's handles. 'Kitchen?'

Gladys said, 'I'm gasping.'

'I could see that!' Joel laughed at her. 'That's a long tongue you got.'

Lizzie, dressed in a green woollen dress that clung to her figure, was first in the small lean-to kitchen. She lit the gas and put the kettle over the flames.

'Where's Janie?' Em asked.

'She's with Marlene and her mum.'

Em nodded, that was all right, she was safe.

The kitchen at the back of the hall was an oasis of calm. Lizzie foraged in the high cupboards for cups and teapot and Joel said, 'We both need to talk to you.'

'If it's family talk and you need privacy, you can wheel me outside in the cold,' piped up Gladys.

'If you ain't family, I don't know what you are,' Em said. She pulled out a kitchen chair and sat down beside the table.

Lizzie said, 'I'll come straight out with it, Mum. I love Joel, he loves me. But it wasn't always like that.' She sighed. 'I left Gosport as soon as I knew I was pregnant. I figured you'd had enough worries on your plate and to have everyone pointing their fingers at you because I wasn't married was the last thing you needed.'

Joel stood beside her, his arm around her waist. His normally happy face was serious. 'Lizzie needed to be with you when Gloria came on the scene pretending to be Lily.' He paused. 'But she figured the shock of her pregnancy wasn't good for you. Anyway, I suggested we tell you that I was the father.' He paused. 'You know what happened next. I lied.' A blush had crept up from his neck and now covered his face. 'We said we couldn't get married because I had a wife who'd disappeared.'

Em narrowed her eyes and stared at Joel. He was speaking softly, like he didn't want to get the words out but knew he had to. She felt sorry for him. She knew him well enough now to see how ashamed he was of what they'd done.

'So you pretended to be the baby's father?'

He nodded. He leaned forward, took Em's hands in his and looked into her eyes. 'I am *so* sorry for deceiving you. I've hated myself for lying . . . And for allowing Lizzie to lie to her *mother*, of all people . . .'

'Stop it!'

Lizzie jumped at Em's harsh voice. 'You think I'm silly enough not to be able to work out dates? Then out comes a little one the image of her father! Not you with your blond locks, but hair as glossily dark as Blackie Bristow's?' Em paused. She stared down at Gladys who had her mouth open. 'I've known all along that kiddie isn't yours. But I've loved you all the more for taking Janie on as if she was.' Em turned away and looked at Lizzie.

'And you think I'd be angry because you wanted to spare my feelings?'

Lizzie opened her mouth to speak but her mother held up her hand. 'I'd have said something soon enough if you both hadn't come to your senses and made it up. Couldn't you see you were made for each other?'

Joel threw his arms around Em's body. 'That lie has been killing me,' he said.

'And so it should,' piped up Gladys. 'You can believe a thief but you can't believe a liar.'

Em shook herself free. She picked up Lizzie's hand and looked at her engagement ring. 'This ring is a promise between the two of you to love each other, and is a prelude to the wedding where a gold band will seal that love, for ever. I want that love to be shown in the way you both care for each other, like still holding hands when you are so old you can barely walk down the road. The past six months have been hell. Not just for you two, but for most of these people in this hall. We've buried people we loved and tried to keep loved ones safe during this awful war. Soon it will be 1945. The war MUST end soon, it must.'

She waved her hand towards the kitchen door and in the direction of the dancers on the floor. 'Look, life's too short for lies, unhappiness and not forgiving the people you love and who love you.' Em took hold of Joel's hand and enclosed it in Lizzie's fingers. 'Get on that dance floor and get cuddling each other.' She pushed them towards the hall and the band now playing 'String of Pearls'.

Lizzie smiled at Joel. 'I guess that's told us.'

'She can be a very forceful woman, your mother, when she wants to be,' Em heard Joel say.

Em looked down at Gladys, who was still staring up at her open-mouthed. Then she made her way towards the teapot.

'About time you and me had that cuppa, eh?'

Acknowledgements

Thank you, as always, to Juliet Burton, my patient agent, and to Jane Wood, editor par excellence, and to Alainna Hadjigeorgiou, Therese Keating, and the many lovely people of Quercus who have enabled this novel's seed to bear fruit.